CRA

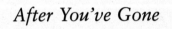

After You've Gone

After You've Gone

JOAN LINGARD

First published in Great Britain in 2007 by
Allison & Busby Limited
13 Charlotte Mews
London W1T 4EJ
www.allisonandbusby.com

10 9 8 7 6 5 4 3 2 1

ISBN 0 7490 8153 8
978-0-7490-8153-9

Typeset in 11/16 pt Sabon by
Terry Shannon

Printed and bound in Wales by
Creative Print and Design, Ebbw Vale

JOAN LINGARD is the acclaimed author of over 40 books for both children and adults. She was born in Edinburgh and brought up in Belfast, the inspiration for many of her novels, including the compelling *Across the Barricades*. She was awarded the MBE in 1998 for Services to Children's Literature.

Also available from
ALLISON & BUSBY

Encarnita's Journey
The Kiss

Also by Joan Lingard

Dreams of Love and Modest Glory
After Colette
The Second Flowering of Emily Mountjoy
Sisters by Rite

Acknowledgement

The letters in this novel are based on a journal kept by my father Henry James Lingard, who served on the HMS *Danae* with the British Special Service Squadron on a world cruise, November, 1923 to September, 1924.

In memory of my parents
Elizabeth and Henry Lingard

~ 1 ~

Freetown, Sierra Leone,
West Africa
11th December, 1923

Aboard the light cruiser HMS Danae, serving with
the British Special Service Squadron, under the
commands of Vice-Admiral Sir Frederick Laurence
Field and Rear-Admiral the Hon Sir Hubert Brand

HMS Danae
Captain FM Austin
Officers and men 470
Length 471 feet, 4,700 tons
Guns 6 – 6 ins, 2 – 3 ins
4 – 3 pounders   & 2 pompoms
1 machine gun, 12 torpedoes

Dear Willa,
     I am sure you will be glad to hear that we have
arrived safe and sound in Sierra Leone, having left
Chatham Dockyard on 23rd November and covered
the first 3,161 miles of our journey. We are
travelling in the following order: HMS Hood, Delhi,
Dauntless, Repulse, Danae, Dragon. The Dunedin,
the seventh ship, will join us later.
     Sierra Leone became a British Colony in 1808.

Why we bothered with it I am not sure – there are nicer places in the world. It has been known for years as the White Man's Grave, malaria being prevalent, due to the swamps where great swarms of mosquitos breed. There is a plentiful supply of rice, tapioca, peanuts, bananas, oranges, limes, mangoes and pineapples. We are enjoying the last two especially. They are most refreshing. The heat is intense and moist so that one perspires continually.

Willa shuffled her chair closer to the range seeking its warmth. The letter had been dated early December but here in Edinburgh they were into the first days of 1924. It was a cold new year at that. Squalls of wind and rain were rattling the window making it difficult to imagine this overheated alien place in the heart of Africa. That was what Tommy himself had called it. 'To start with,' he had said, 'we shall be going to the very heart of Africa', and shown her the pink blotch on the globe. He prided himself on his phrases, something she had noticed on the first night she had met him at the Palace Ballroom, at the foot of Leith Walk. 'Would you like to take a little turn around the floor with me?' he had asked, extending one hand to her, keeping the other tucked behind his back. She kept having a recurring dream in which he appeared, standing, with one hand visible, the other, not.

The globe was standing on the table in amongst the clutter of odds and ends, the salt and pepper shakers, shaped like gnomes, a scatter of kirby grips, a packet of Bismuth lozenges, their passbook for the Prudential Insurance company. Anything and everything was tossed onto the table. All the surfaces in the room were covered. When Willa had first moved in the mess had bothered her, but by now she had adjusted to it. She had had no option. This was the way her mother-in-law lived.

Tommy had bought the globe so that they could follow the progress of the squadron on its world tour. Willa pictured them steaming in line, advancing in stately fashion through the oceans of the world, leaving white ripples of foam behind them. They were to be away for almost a year.

She went back to the letter written by this man who was her husband but whom she was finding difficult to recognise in these carefully scripted lines. He had asked her to keep all his letters, as a record: that might explain it. Normally he talked in a rather fast jokey sort of way, but Willa realised that when people wrote letters they often changed their tone of voice. She had a feeling that he had not been thinking of her while he was writing.

A horse will not live in the heat of Sierra Leone so the transport is carried out by natives carrying goods on their heads. This gives the woman a fine upward straight figure with majestic carriage.

Trust Tommy to notice that. Would they be wearing clothes, these black women with the splendid figures? Willa pulled herself up out of her slump. Tommy's mother was forever telling her she should be wearing a corset, especially now, after the birth of the bairn, or else she'd never get her figure back. Willa had, in fact, lost the extra weight she'd put on, whereas her mother-in-law's stomach sagged like an overstuffed pillow, in spite of being encased daily in a pair of greying-pink stays. When she slackened the laces in the evening she'd groan with the relief of it and fall back in her chair. Willa hated the sight of the stays which made her think of body armour for some enormous female warrior. Their owner strung them up on the pulley to air overnight and didn't bring them down until after they'd breakfasted. They sat at the table eating their porridge with the suspenders dangling over their heads. Willa, while taking care not to look up, remained conscious of them throughout. She could smell the dried sweat and other body odours.

She heard the front door open and then the sound of her mother-in-law's heavy footsteps as she advanced along the hall. Ina Costello came into the kitchen, her shoulders weighted down by her shopping. She dropped the bags on the floor with a thud.

'Those stairs'll be the death of me yet,' she announced.

'I could have got the messages,' said Willa. She usually did and was glad to, to escape from the house for a bit.

'I got some tripe. You couldn't beat the price.' Ina knew Willa wasn't fond of tripe and onions cooked in milk. Then she noticed the letter. 'Is that from Tommy?' she asked accusingly. To Willa, at least, the voice sounded accusing, implying that she should have waited till her mother-in-law, *his* mother, was present for the ceremonial opening of the envelope even though it had been addressed to her. *Mrs Thomas Costello*. She found it difficult to believe that was actually *her*. He'd printed SWALK on the back flap.

'He's in Sierra Leone,' said Willa. 'Eating mangoes and fresh pineapples. Not tinned.' Such exotic fruits were never to be seen in their local greengrocer.

'He'll need to watch his stomach.' Tommy's mother dragged a chair up to the range and collapsed onto it. 'It's aye been delicate. What else is he sayin' then?'

In the year 1897 a house tax was levied and the following year the natives revolted, led by their chiefs who wanted the old days of slavery and heathenish practices back again. This was quelled though unfortunately many whites were murdered. Tranquillity reigns supreme now.

'Thank the Lord for that,' said his mother. 'I'm not sure about some of those places he's going to.'

Willa skipped over the detailed description of how the natives built their huts which she would read herself later. She would read the whole letter over again, when she was alone in her room, so that she could think about him in peace.

The natives are timid in remote places but they do like bright colours. Some remarkable sights are to be seen amongst the black ladies who will wear any old article of European apparel, notwithstanding that it does not suit or fit them. We saw one with an old felt hat perched on top of her short-haired head while the rest of her was naked except for a loin cloth. The men are usually totally naked except for their loin cloths though we did see one wearing a battered silk top hat. You can't help laughing at some of them. Sunday is the best day for this kind of sightseeing. It is all very amusing.

'I hope they dinna go too close to them,' said Ina.' You never know what they might catch.'

'I hope they weren't laughing out loud at the women,' said Willa.

'Why in the name not?'

'Well, it's not very nice making fun of them, just because their customs are different from ours. We wouldn't like it if they came over here and laughed their heads off at us, would we?'

Ina snorted. 'No much chance of that. People like them don't come over here.'

'How do you know?' Willa felt stubbornness coming up her back, which was how her mother used to describe it. She was aware of a stiffening in her shoulders and the back of her neck.

'Stands to reason, doesn't it? Where would they get the money, tell me that if you can!'

That round went to Tommy's mother. Willa returned to the letter.

We set sail for Cape Town on December 13th. One and all are wildly excited, for two reasons. Firstly, the crossing of the line ceremony. Secondly, Cape Town has promised us a roaring good time. Who would not look forward to a visit to South Africa? I trust this finds you all well, including wee Malkie.
I have a bit of a rash on my stomach, due, no doubt, to the heat. But don't worry as I expect it will go away.
   Give Mother my love.
   Yours most fondly,
   Tommy xxx

'Told you he should watch his stomach,' said his mother. 'Too much fruit doesn't do you any good.'

'The rash is on the outside,' said Willa abstractedly, for she was studying the last three lines. *Yours most fondly.* Her eye jumped back up a line to *Give Mother my love.* Did Tommy equate fondness with love? She found it difficult to decide. He had never said he was in love with her, unless it came into a song, like 'Let me call you sweetheart'. He had a habit of breaking into song when he wanted to avoid an issue. He had a nice voice so, to begin with, she had found it amusing as she wasn't accustomed to singing men. On his last leave though, there had been a couple of times when it had annoyed her.

Her friend Pauline said she didn't think many men came right out and used the word 'love', not in Scotland anyway. They might be frightened of being called Jessies. Perhaps Italian men would be different but, then, Tommy was only half Italian, on his father's side, even though he looked wholly Italian. But he had been brought up by his mother, who was one hundred per cent Scottish.

'I'm very fond of you, you know, Willa,' Tommy had said when he'd asked her to marry him. By then she'd been expecting Malcolm though he'd sworn he'd been going to ask her anyway. They had been going out together for some months, in between his spells at sea, of course. He was forever coming and going. A niggle of doubt had stayed with her. Would he or would he not have asked her? The most important thing was that he did marry her.

He had written his name with a flourish. He had a fine hand; you could only admire it. His mother said he'd always been top of the class for writing. His letters sloped to the right without threatening to topple over and his loops were beautifully formed, reminding Willa of sitting at her school desk, copying the perfectly formed sentence above into the space below, watching that she did not go over the lines, dipping her pen carefully into the inkwell, anxious that it would not plunge too far in and stain her fingers. She usually did stain them, up to the first knuckle.

'What line's he talking about?' asked his mother.

'The equator.'

'What's so special about that?'

'They dress up, I think. Fancy dress.'

'He was good at composition at the school. There was one of his teachers, a Mr Jackson, who took a liking to him. He said Tommy could be a writer. He'd a friend who worked on the *Evening News*, offered to put a word in for him if he'd like. Tommy might have been working for the paper now if he hadn't upped and joined the Navy at fourteen.'

It was one of the few decisions that Tommy appeared to have taken without his mother's consent. He had gone out and done it and come back and told her. She had found a little comfort in the fact that he'd joined the *Royal* Navy, not the Merchant. *I joined the Navy to see the world,* he liked to sing, as he shaved in front of the bathroom mirror. *And what did I see? I saw the sea.*

He was seeing more than the sea now.

Willa could understand why he hadn't wanted to work on the *Edinburgh Evening News* and report local events, such as weddings, funerals and council meetings, though she'd have jumped at it herself if she'd got the chance. It would have been more interesting than sitting on a high stool in the Co-op office totting up figures, and she'd been good at English, too, at school. But Tommy had itchy feet; he hated sitting still, liked to be on the go. Where Tommy was, there was life. That was what she'd felt about him from that first meeting when he'd asked her to dance the Charleston. It was his kind of dance though he'd taken her up for a slow waltz afterwards and held her close, disturbingly close. She'd kept thinking she ought to try to move back a bit but his arm round her waist had been strong and unyielding. He'd murmured into her hair, telling her it was the colour of beech leaves in autumn. Willa's friend Pauline had snorted when Willa reported that. 'Don't trust a man with fancy talk!'

They'd been in the cloakroom combing their hair and collecting their coats after the last dance.

Pauline had just had her hair bobbed and Willa had been considering it but now she was thinking that maybe she shouldn't after all. Tommy had also said a woman's hair was her crowning glory but she was not going to repeat that to Pauline who would only sniff. He had asked to take her home and she was thinking that maybe Pauline was miffed about that though they had always had an understanding that if one of them met a man the other would go home on her own.

'You can see him coming from a mile off!' declared Pauline, batting her nose with her powder puff, then wrinkling it to make a face at herself in the dim mirror. Several of the bulbs along the top were dead. Their faces looked ghostly in the pocked glass. 'He's only out for what he can get, with that flashy smile of his. Fancies himself as the second Rudolph Valentino! You watch yourself, Willa!'

Willa thought he did look a little like the film star. She and Pauline had gone to see Valentino in *The Sheik* three times and had come out after each showing entranced.

'If he's got his mac with him you'll know he's got other things in mind,' said Pauline.

'How do you mean?'

'For lying on, stupid!'

'I'll ask him if he'd mind if you walked up with us.'

'He wouldn't want me tagging along. I'd get in his way, wouldn't I? I'll get a tram.'

Tommy didn't propose a tram. 'Let's walk!' he said. The night was warm and dry but he did have his mackintosh with him. He carried it slung over one shoulder. Still, thought Willa, with Scottish weather being what it was, he might have decided to be on the safe side. She wasn't going to damn him for that one little thing.

He had already ascertained that she lived in digs in Bread Street, which was on his way home.

'It's a great night for walking,' he said. 'And it'll give us more chance to get acquainted.' He broke into song. 'Shine On Harvest Moon'. He slid his arm round her waist and from time to time he squeezed it, pulling her in towards him, saying to cuddle up and keep the cold out. They were walking so close they kept bumping hips but he just laughed and when they rounded the corner at the east end of Princes Street he eased her into the store's doorway and kissed her.

'We could go for a little stroll through the gardens,' he murmured, running his fingers over her face, feeling her cheekbones. His touch was light and made her tremble.

'Will the gates not be locked?'

'I'll lift you over the top. I'm sure you're light as a feather. It'll be nice in the gardens. Nice and quiet.' It was May-time and the flowers were opening.

For a moment she found herself almost about to give way, then she shook her head. 'No, I don't think so.'

'Right you are!' He did not insist and she respected him for that.

She thought then that he might not ask to see her again and maybe Pauline was right, that he did only want one thing from a girl and if he didn't get it he would lose interest. On the way along Princes Street and up Lothian Road they talked about their lives, finding that they had both been pupils at Tollcross Public School, though at different times. He was five years older than her. He told her that his father had died when he was a baby and he'd been brought up by his mother. She told him that her father had fallen at Ypres and her mother had died in 1918 after a long struggle with tuberculosis. Since then she'd been on her own, lodging with a neighbour and working as a clerk in the Co-op.

When they reached her stair door he kissed her again but that was all. He didn't try anything else on, not like some of them who seemed to think they were entitled to a reward just for seeing you to your door. Tommy said he was off to sea next day but he'd like to take her out when he came back. She didn't expect to see him again but she did, at the Palace, a few weeks later. Pauline nudged her and said, 'Don't look now! Your Rudolph Valentino's back in town.'

'He's not mine.' Willa looked the other way, trying to assume indifference.

But he came straight over to her, cutting across the floor,

weaving his way through the dancing couples.

'Remember what I've said!' hissed Pauline. 'You watch yourself!'

Tommy held out his hand to Willa, the way he'd done before. 'May I have the pleasure?' She rose without a word and he moved in close on her and she remembered the feel of his legs against hers from the last time and the way his knee kept nudging between her knees.

'I was hoping I'd see you here,' he said. 'I didn't forget you, you know.' She felt too shy to tell him that she hadn't forgotten him either but she sensed he knew. They left before the last waltz.

His energy drew her. It was invigorating to be with someone who liked to enjoy life. 'Let's go!' he cried, snapping his fingers. 'Let's be a little crazy!' He waltzed her along Princes Street singing 'If you were the only girl in the world' in her ear, making her giggle and her neck wriggle with pleasure.

He told her he'd fallen for her hook, line and sinker! She laughed and he laughed. He wooed her and she succumbed quickly and easily to his charms, surprising herself, offering little resistance as she lay on his mackintosh in a hollow of the gardens with the dark castle standing guard high above them. When that moment arrived she forgot Pauline's warning. Saying no did not even come into her head. Nothing did. He was the first man she had lain with but she was aware that she would not have been his first girl. She resolved not to ask. What she didn't know didn't hurt her. That was to be her motto, and it was what she said to Pauline later.

'It's all right *saying* that,' Pauline retorted.

* * *

An angry cry erupted from the bedroom at the front. The bairn had good lungs on him. Willa made to rise but Tommy's mother was already pushing herself up onto her feet and telling her, 'You stay where you are. I'll get him. You could put a bit more coal on the fire.'

Willa shovelled a shuttleful of coal noisily into the range. When she'd finished she could hear Tommy's mother's voice mumbling. She came back into the room with the baby cradled against her big bosom.

'You're just the spitting image of your daddy,' she was telling him. 'The spitting image. But you'll no join the Navy and run off and leave your granny, will you, Malkie?'

'Malkie' grated on Willa's ears though she had been trying not to let it. After protesting a couple of times she'd realised she might as well save herself the trouble. Tommy had said 'Malcolm' was too po-faced for a wee bairn but he'd given in because Willa had felt strongly about it. It had been her father's name.

She wanted to take the baby into her own arms but his grandmother was holding onto him and rocking him and cooing into his face and he was gurgling and she was saying, 'You know your granny, don't you, son? Yes, you do, you know your ould granny.' The 'son' irked Willa too but, again, she tried not to let it. She sometimes wondered if the woman did it to annoy her. She couldn't make up her mind if Ina Costello was a kindly person or not. At times she seemed to be; at others, not. Willa was supposed to call her 'Mother' but she couldn't get the word out.

Pauline said she should thank her lucky stars that Tommy's mother had become attached to the child. It would have been awkward if she hadn't. After all, she'd taken Willa in and given her a home and it wasn't as if Willa had a mother of her own to go to. When Willa had started going out with Tommy she'd been attracted by the idea of being part of a family again. She'd realised that he was fond of his mother, and that had pleased her. Any man who was fond of his mother must be a good man. It showed a sense of duty and the ability to love. So she had reasoned.

Malcolm's face had turned brick-red and his eyes were bulging.

'He's filling his nappy,' pronounced his grandmother with satisfaction. 'I'll away and change him in the bathroom. You might reach me a clean nappy down from the pulley.'

When they'd gone Willa picked up Tommy's letter again. He'd added a PS.

Hope you have a good New Year. We have been told we shall celebrate Christmas right royally. The boys are really looking forward to it, yours truly included.

Was he hers *truly*? Could she be sure? Oh shut up, Willa, she said to herself. What good did it do thinking this way?

Tommy knew that they didn't celebrate Christmas much at all, not the way they did south of the border, in England. The shops were open as usual, the trams ran and folk went to their work. New Year was the big celebration, and that, like Christmas, had been and gone. On Hogmanay they'd gone up to Tommy's Aunt Elma's, his mother's sister. She lived in a three-bedroom flat in Marchmont with her master butcher husband Gerry, whom she insisted on calling Gerald, to his annoyance. Elma hated the name Gerry, for it made her think of the Huns, but he said he'd been called that when he was a lad, long before he'd ever heard of them. He'd managed to stay out of the war, which was the way Ina Costello put it. He had a dodgy stomach, was forever sucking Bismuth lozenges, which he kept in a tin in his top jacket pocket. 'Whose stomach is perfect?' Ina wanted to know. Her Tommy's wasn't, yet look at him! He'd seen active service and been torpedoed in the North Sea, after which he'd been brought back to a convalescent hospital in Edinburgh, to her relief. 'See you don't make too quick a recovery,' she'd told him. 'It's nice and comfy in here. When they do put you out and the war's over we'll see if we can get ourselves a better place.'

The war had ended and the Costellos had stayed on in the same one-bedroom flat with the box room where Tommy had slept as a boy. His mother had surrendered her bedroom to the young couple on their marriage and made do now with a double bed-settee in the sitting room where she was comfortable enough. They seldom used the room so it didn't cause much inconvenience. Most folk who visited were taken through to the kitchen at the back where it was warmer, the only exception being the minister and, very occasionally, the doctor. The last time he'd been in the house was when Malcolm was born. Willa had been fortunate in having a relatively short labour and straightforward birth; as her mother-in-law had stressed for she herself had suffered greatly bringing Tommy into the world. But she had never held it against him, not for a single minute.

'When Tommy gets promoted we'll get a two-bedroom,'

she said. He was currently a Yeoman of Signals, hoping to be elevated soon to the rank of Chief Yeoman.

She envied her sister Elma her three-bedroom flat in Marchmont, a more select district than Tollcross.

For New Year Elma had spread her table with plentiful quantities of shortbread, Black Bun, Dundee Cake and Cloutie pudding. She'd laid them out on dainty, frilled doilies, which seemed out of keeping with the heaviness of the offerings. Elma took pride in being 'particular'. Gerry kept the whisky circulating. When one bottle was finished he reached for another and tossed the old one over his shoulder into the bin. 'For luck,' he said, ignoring his wife's baleful eye. He'd been in the pub earlier so that he was pretty well stotious by the time Willa and Ina arrived. As the hours went by Willa herself became a little tipsy and her mother-in-law warned her she'd better watch she didn't get her bairn drunk. The whisky would go through on the milk. But even she was looking flushed and laughing at Gerry's risqué jokes and she sang along with the neighbour who'd come in to first foot them with a lump of coal. If Tommy had been there he would have done it for he was darker than any man present. The darker the man, the better luck he would bring with him.

'I belong to Glasgow,' sang Tommy's mother, who had visited the city only once and returned to report that it was clarty and not a patch on Edinburgh.

Then Bunty, Ina's youngest sister, embarked on 'Knees Up Mother Brown', hiking her already short skirt up above her knees to show off her red satin garters, which caused her sister Elma to issue a rebuke. 'Honest, Bunty, at your age! It's time you grew up, so it is. You'd give anybody a red face.' When she went out to the kitchen Gerry snapped one of the garters against Bunty's leg and Bunty screamed in mock protest. Everyone laughed. Elma was the only one of the company to remain starkly sober. She'd allowed a trickle of sherry to pass her lips at midnight but nothing more. Even that had caused her to grimace, as if it were cough medicine she was swallowing.

Ina had to take Willa's arm on the road home. They walked back from Marchmont to Tollcross at three o'clock in the morning, Willa pushing the pram through a smattering of sleet, flanked by Tommy's mother and aunt. She enjoyed the walk, with the streetlamps glimmering in the white mist and lights blinking at windows. The city was still awake. There were folk on the street, merry for the most part and good-natured, on their way home from parties. As they passed they called out, 'A Happy New Year to one and all!' and they called back, 'And the same to you!'

They passed the King's Theatre, shuttered and dark, and Ina said they must go and see *Goody Two Shoes* before the show ended. Bunty said Florrie Ford had been great in *Cinderella* at the Empire. Her friend Mr Parkin had taken her.

'I think I'd prefer *Goody Two Shoes*,' said Ina. 'It's a bit different.'

'How is it?' demanded Bunty.

'Well, everyone's seen *Cinderella*, haven't they? I mean to say, it's quite common.'

Bunty let it drop. She wheeled off shortly to go to her own place.

'Mr Parkin seems to think he's the bee's knees,' commented Ina.

A drunk was loitering in the doorway of their stair.

'Excuse me,' said Ina and gave him a little push to the side. He made no move to resist. His eyes were glazed and his mouth slack.

Willa bumped the pram up the step and Ina closed the door behind them and put the latch down.

'He'd be in here relieving himself, given half a chance,' said Ina.

Willa parked the pram at the end of the lobby, by the door that opened into the communal back green, put on the cat net, and carried the baby up the stairs against her shoulder. Ina had to rest on both the first and second landings. The three flights were getting to be too much for her, especially with her bulk.

'Well, that's 1923 over and done with,' she declared, as they came into the flat. 'Now it's back to auld claes and parritch.'

'We had a good time, though,' said Willa.

'Aye, and the house has been redd up.'

They had toiled the whole of Hogmanay, blacking the range, washing windows and curtains, scrubbing floors and polishing furniture and brasses until the place shone. Ina Costello would not allow a speck of dirt to stain the beginning of a new year.

'Pity, though, Tommy wasne with us,' she added with a sigh. 'I missed him.'

Willa nodded. Even to think of him brought a lump into her throat.

~ 2 ~

Cape Town,
South Africa
27th December, 1923

Dear Willa,

She paused to study the address, needing to let her mind adjust to the shift of time and place. When Tommy had written the letter he had still been in the old year and here they were well on in January. She felt out of step with him in a way she had not been before and was going to be for the best part of a year. With just herself and the baby, and Tommy's mother. The latter was waiting expectantly.

This is a wonderful city to visit. Beautifully laid out, with Table Bay for a sea front and Table Mountain behind, it is truly a striking and picturesque spectacle. The suburbs are pretty, the lawns beautifully kept, with large, vividly coloured flowers growing in profusion. This would be a wonderful country to live in. Who knows? One of these days...

We have had a few dips in the sea at Camps Bay and also been enjoying the surf bathing. It is a fine pastime, and very refreshing, especially at this time of year. I took to it straightaway. I am sure you

would too. But I think our Scottish seas might be a
bit cold for it. Brrr.

Willa allowed herself a small sigh. Unlike Sierra Leone, with
its steaming heat and mosquito swamps, she could form a
picture of this place in her head. She could hear the pounding
of the surf and see the golden sand and brilliant flowers. The
seaside in South Africa would be nothing like what it was at
North Berwick, washed by the steel-grey North Sea. She'd
managed to go in as far as her ankles when she and Tommy
went there for their three-day honeymoon. His mother had
been nippy about them going, had said she was surprised they
were bothering with a honeymoon, under the circumstances,
and they might be better putting the money towards the
baby's layette. When she'd first heard that Willa was pregnant
she had been surprisingly accepting. 'Och well,' she'd said,
'these things happen. Better if they didn't, mind,' she'd added
with a touch of tartness in her voice.

Willa and Tommy had stayed in a bed and breakfast on the
front in North Berwick so they'd been able to hear the sea at
night. She'd liked that. It had been nothing of course to
Tommy, who was used to the sounds of several seas, bigger
and more boisterous than that edging the East Lothian shore.

They'd walked along the sands, arms entwined, and he'd
sung to her. 'Oh! I do like to be beside the seaside'…That had
made her laugh but 'After You've Gone' had sobered her.

After you've gone, and left me crying, after you've gone,
there's no denying, you'll feel blue…

It was he who was going to go away, not her. She couldn't ever
imagine leaving him. She'd said, 'Och, don't sing that, Tommy. I

don't want to think about you going away.' He'd laughed and said, 'It's only a song.' He loved singing. It meant that there were never any silences between them. He'd moved on to 'I wonder who's kissing her now', breaking off to stroke her cheek and say softly, 'I'd kill anyone I caught kissing you.' At the time it had given her a little thrill to think he cared so much.

'It's nice he's getting some sea bathing,' said his mother. 'It'll be a good tonic for him. And he's a braw swimmer. He's got all sorts of certificates.'

He'd learnt to swim at Warrender Baths in Marchmont, as had Willa herself, though at different times. When he'd told her how he used to go to the baths she remembered watching a young man with sleek black hair – a boy, really, only fourteen – standing on the edge of the top diving board, his toes curled over. She'd have been about nine at the time. She'd watched him, wondering if he would dive. After a couple of minutes he'd raised his arms very slowly above his head and still taking his time moved up onto his toes and plunged into the green water like a perfect arrow, his muscles taut. Emerging, he'd shaken his head and at that moment she'd caught his eye and he'd winked at her. Later, when she'd started going out with him, she had realised that it must have been him. After that time in the baths she hadn't seen him for years as he'd been about to go off and join the Navy. That had been his last dive before freedom, he'd joked.

His mother was looking at her. She resumed reading.

The Cape is wonderfully healthy with a very clear atmosphere. Fruit is plentiful and most houses in the suburbs have fruit trees in their gardens. The people look fit and are jolly fine sportsmen. They have the breezy colonial manner, which makes them easy to get on with. There are plenty of black people to do the heavier work.

The population is very enthusiastic about the squadron's visit and the hospitality is far beyond anything we expected. The list of entertainments we have been invited to partake in includes tennis, shooting, picnics, parties, motor driving and dances. It is not possible to accept every single invitation we receive. We have been snowed under with them. Everybody wants us!

'I'm sure Tommy would be popular wherever he went,' said his mother. 'He's got a good way with him.'

He had, Willa knew. His ready smile and friendly manner made people warm to him straightaway. He was a tactile person, too. He'd put his hand on a person's arm when speaking to them. She remembered his touch on her arm, on the nape of her neck...

'What are you waiting for?'

Willa's head came up.

'You were miles away,' said her mother-in-law.

We spent Christmas with various newly made friends in their lovely homes and they showered us with gifts. It made us realise how much our colonies value us. My mate Bill and myself were taken to a superb house out in the veldt where the family made us extremely welcome. They had a turquoise-blue

swimming pool (bit smarter than Warrender Baths!)
in their garden. We swam in the evening under the
stars and afterwards were served iced cocktails on
the verandah followed by a sumptuous meal
comprising various kinds of white fish, lobster,
prawns, chicken, different meats, salads, etc. We ate
till we were stuffed. My rash has gone, you will be
pleased to hear.

Give Mother my love. I hope her chilblains are
not bothering her too much.

I remain, as ever, your fond husband,
Tommy xxx

'What a rare life he's leading,' sighed his mother. 'Showered
with presents! That was nice of him asking after my
chilblains. He was always a thoughtful boy. When you write
back tell him they're no too bad yet. There's still a fair bit of
winter to come, mind.'

'Will I tell him about your corns?' asked Willa, feeling a
little wicked.

'I don't think you need to do that,' said Ina uncomfortably.
When Tommy was at home she went into the bathroom to
pare them.

Willa folded up the letter. No mention of the baby!
Malcolm had been only three weeks old when his father had
left Edinburgh so perhaps it was not surprising. Tommy
probably didn't think of him very often, not like her, with
him night and day. He was never out of her head. She'd
have to rib Tommy about it in her next letter, say something
like, 'Hope you haven't forgotten you've got a son!' She

wondered how often he thought even of her, with all those entertainments on offer. *Parties. Picnics. Dances. Cocktails on the verandah.* There would be girls at the dances, well, of course there would, young girls, pretty girls, carefree girls, with smooth tanned skin; and Tommy was not one to sit on the sidelines watching. He'd be up on the floor as soon as the band struck the first chord, holding out his hand.

Would you care to take a little turn with me?

She returned the letter to its envelope. He'd put SWALK on the back flap again but somehow it didn't seem to offer much comfort. She got up.

'I'm going to the library.'

'You're never away from the place.'

'I read fast.'

The library was her main source of pleasure, always had been, but especially now, with Tommy away – apart from the baby, though he, whilst she loved him dearly and intensely, was not an undiluted pleasure. At times, when he wouldn't settle and she was sitting nursing him in her room, looking out at the rain, she felt so frustrated she thought she could burst. She longed to go to the pictures or the dancing with Pauline, not that she'd ever think of doing that. Tommy wouldn't like her to go to the Palace or the Palais de Danse without him and his mother would be scandalised. There was only one name for married women who went to dancehalls without their husbands.

'You can leave Malkie if you like.'

'All right.' Willa nodded. When she took the pram she had to leave it at the library door and lift Malcolm out and then sometimes he'd wake up and girn or occasionally burp up a gobbet of sour milk and the librarian she didn't like would give her a look and she'd have to be quick and choose the first two books that came to hand.

'You could go to the fishmonger's on your way back. Get a couple of herring. Make sure they're fresh, mind! Don't let him palm you off on yesterday's.'

Willa went through to her room at the front where Malcolm lay asleep in his cot, tightly swaddled in his shawl. He needed to be well wrapped up for the room was high-ceilinged and warmed only by a small paraffin stove that took the chill off, but not much more. Willa leant over the cot, studying her child's face. She spent hours gazing at him. He was a bonny baby; others thought so, not just herself. His granny said he was the image of his daddy when he was a baby. He had strong features, a thatch of dark hair and very long dark eyelashes. Streetsweepers, his Great-aunt Bunty called them. And his eyes were large and darkening rapidly from the blue they'd been at birth. 'He'll break a few hearts, that one,' Bunty had said when she'd seen him the first time. 'Funny how you can tell straightaway.' Then she'd winked at Willa where she'd sat bolt upright against the pillows in her bed. Tommy's family seemed prone to winking, which disconcerted her. Not his mother, though. Tommy hadn't been home for the birth but he'd got leave and come a week later. He'd stayed five days before going back to rejoin his ship and prepare for their world cruise.

Willa straightened herself up and went to the window to check if it was still raining. It was. They'd had snow, too, recently. It was proving to be a hard winter and already there was a coal shortage. There was also talk of strikes. Unlike Tommy's mother, Willa liked living at Tollcross. From up here, she could look down on the intersection, the meeting of the ways, and the traffic coming from four directions. It was a hub, maybe not of the world, but of the city. She enjoyed seeing the motor cars going by and the horses clopping along in their cart-shafts and the trams as they came rattling round the clock, the overhead cables sparking as the pole clicked on a point. She didn't mind the banging of their wheels as they passed over the rail joints or the clanging of the warning bells as they slowed on approach to a stop. At times the trams might get stuck in a jam but they'd soon be on the move again, going somewhere, even if it was only down to Princes Street or Leith Walk or up to Morningside Station. She wasn't so keen on watching the men coming up from the underground toilet on the clock island, often still buttoning themselves up. But none of the noises of the street bothered her. At the rear of the house, in the kitchen, when Ina was out, it was dead quiet except for the tick of the big wall clock. You looked out, if you looked out at all, on the backs of other tenements and back greens where washing hung on sagging lines.

She'd brightened her room with yellow curtains and two brilliant-blue velvet cushions that glowed when the lamps were lit. She'd bought them with some of their wedding-present money. She hadn't been able to afford new wallpaper so must live with the autumn leaves. Ina had sniffed and said she didn't know why Willa was throwing good money away when there'd been perfectly good curtains at the windows already, chenille, colour of putty, colour that would go with anything, didn't show the dirt. Being on the main street, surrounded by chimneys spewing out dark smoke, there was no lack of that. All the rooms in the flat were decorated in shades of beige, brown and russet. Autumn colours were nice, said Ina. But these were dying autumnal colours, at the back end of November, when all life has gone out of them.

Willa took her library books from the bedside table, John Galsworthy's *A Man of Property* and *The Crimson Circle* by Edgar Wallace, and put them in her shopping bag. She'd enjoyed each in its own way. They'd taken her into different worlds, far removed from her own. They'd allowed her to dream a little. She lifted her mackintosh and umbrella and checked again on the baby before going into the hall and calling out, 'I'm away now. Malcolm's sleeping. I'll leave the door open so that you can hear him.' She knew his grandmother would have him up, whether he wakened or not, the minute she was out of the house.

As she tugged the flat door shut behind her, their neighbour across the landing came up the stairs. Mr MacNab was a printer but currently jobless. He'd been out of work for over a year and felt bitter about it for he'd fought in the war and been gassed, which had left him with a racking cough. Nobody seemed to care, he said. They were having to live on the 'parish', he and his family, for the national insurance had stopped after six weeks. They had been means-tested and given vouchers for essentials such as bread, margarine, cheese, tea and sugar. One day Willa had landed up in the Co-op when Mrs MacNab was at the counter paying for her few groceries with the vouchers. She'd looked embarrassed to be seen with them. Walking back up the road with Willa, she'd told her that a 'visitor' had called to see them and had poked into every corner of their flat, looking to see if they had any money stashed away or any valuable items they could have pawned. He had even looked under the lino!

Mr MacNab's shoulders were slumped and failure was written all over his face so Willa knew she needn't bother asking him if he'd managed to find any work. He'd gone on the hunger strike to London in December, 1922. The men, gathered in their hundreds in Princes Street at the bottom of the Mound, waiting to set off, had been quite a sight. Willa had cheered them on, along with many others. But, as Bunty said, what good did it all do?

'How're you doing?' asked Willa.

Mr MacNab shrugged. 'I went to see if there was anything going at the rubber factory over in Fountainbridge.'

'The North British?'

'Aye. I heard they were taking on men, but they only wanted half a dozen and there was a queue a mile long when I got there.'

'I'm sorry.'

That was another thing Pauline said Willa should thank her lucky stars for: Tommy's job was secure and she got money paid direct to her, and regularly. Willa suspected the MacNabs often couldn't buy enough food. They had five children to feed and their faces looked pinched. Sometimes Tommy's mother, if she'd been baking, would pass in a cake or a pie to them. That was the kind side of her mother-in-law; Willa acknowledged that.

'Oh well, better luck next time, Mr MacNab,' said Willa limply. The sight of him or his wife always deflated her. Mrs MacNab, in her mid-thirties, looked fifty. 'Be warned,' Pauline had said to Willa. 'You're not wanting five weans.

Though I suppose with Tommy away so much it limits the chances. If you fall again let me know. I heard of a woman in Morrison Street.'

Mr MacNab went into his house and Willa ran down the stairs, her mood lifting as she headed for the open air and freedom, even if it was only for an hour or two. She didn't even mind that it was raining. It was refreshing after the stuffiness of the kitchen.

She rounded the clock and went up Lauriston Place, passing George Heriot's school on her left and the Infirmary on her right, and turned into Forrest Road. As a child she used to run as she got near the library and her mother would say, 'Hold on a minute!' It was her mother who had taken her to the library in the first place. She'd been a great reader too. Once Willa reached George IV Bridge, she quickened her step, even now, in anticipation.

The inscription above the library door never failed to make her smile. LET THERE BE LIGHT. That's what she had always felt: that the library brought light into her life. Pauline couldn't understand her excitement, although she enjoyed a Marie Corelli from time to time and had loved Florence Barclay's *The Rosary,* in which a painter falls in love with an unbearably ugly woman, the dilemma being resolved by him going blind. 'A bit of luck that,' Pauline had commented. 'Depends on your point of view,' Willa had responded. 'There's often two ways of looking at things.' She'd been thinking of herself looking at Tommy out in the big wide world, whilst there he was looking back at them, cooped up in their small flat, with drying nappies over their heads and the smell of cat piss on the stair.

The cinema and the dancehall excited Pauline more than books, but the latter depended too much on chance, on who asked her up and if anyone offered to see her home. It was possible to come out of the dancing dejected, on a bad night. She said, too, that it wasn't the same without Willa. She went now with another girl from her work but she was a regular wallflower and that tended to spill over onto Pauline. Willa, like Pauline, enjoyed going to the pictures, but books meant even more to her, for with them she could curl up in her chair and lose herself completely, whereas picture houses were anything but peaceful. She wished the audience would shut up! They read out the captions, cheered and catcalled, hissed and jeered at the villain; and the women pretended to go into a swoon whenever Rudolph Valentino or Douglas Fairbanks made an appearance.

Willa preferred the quietness of the library's rooms, lined and smelling of books. Both readers and librarians moved around slowly; there was no click-clack of hurrying feet to disturb the peace and she understood why babies were not welcome.

She laid her books on the counter. The librarian she liked was on duty today.

'Did you enjoy those, Mrs Costello?'

Willa still found it odd to be addressed Mrs Costello. When she was, she instinctively wanted to look round to see if Tommy's mother was behind her.

'They were great.'

'Are you wanting to read the sequel to *The Man of Property*? I have it here.' The librarian reached underneath the desk and brought up *In Chancery*.

'Thanks a lot. I'd love to.' Willa took the book into her hands. She was about to ask if the woman could recommend anything about South Africa when she remembered that Tommy might not be there any more, he most likely would have moved on. There could be no keeping up with him.

'Your man still away?'

'He's touring the world.'

'Lucky him! Will he be going to America?'

'I think so. Eventually.'

'Here's a novel by an American called Sinclair Lewis. It's just been brought back, only been out the once. *Main Street*. You might find it interesting.'

Willa thanked her again. This librarian was helpful and often put new books her way. Willa moved off to have a wander round the shelves. All the possibilities were tempting but she thought she would just stick with these two. She took a copy of the *National Geographic Magazine* and went to find a seat at a table.

When she looked up, after she'd been reading for a bit, she saw that a young man was sitting at the other end of the table, also reading a copy of the *National Geographic*. He looked up at the same time and, nodding at her magazine, smiled at her. She gave him a little smile in return and went back to the dangers lurking in the jungles of Peru, which she hoped would not be on Tommy's list of entertainments when his ship reached the shores of South America, but she was no longer so absorbed now. The man had intruded into the cloak of privacy that she felt encircled her whenever she came into the library, out of the orbit of Tommy's family.

She heard the young man's chair move and saw his shadow

as he walked away. It was not unusual to find men sitting reading magazines and newspapers during the day. If they were out of work they had to do something to fill in the time, and the library was free, and warm. She read a little longer, then got up, put the magazine back in its rack and went to have her books stamped.

The rain had eased off. She shook the raindrops from her umbrella and fastened the strap round it. As she did, the door opened behind her and out came the young man who'd been reading the *National Geographic*.

'Rain stopped?' he said, holding out his hand. 'That's good.'

She began to walk; he fell into step beside her.

'We seem to be going the same way. I live in Lauriston Place.'

She didn't offer any information in return.

He said, 'I've seen you in the library before. You come a lot.'

She felt it would be churlish to maintain a silence. She said, 'I like reading.'

'So do I. I saw you were taking out *Main Street*. I'd just brought it back.'

'So it was you?' She half turned to him.

'I enjoyed it. It's about a small town in America.'

They began to talk about books they'd read and before Willa knew it they were approaching the foot of Lauriston Place and he was making no effort to detach himself. She was uncomfortable, worried that she might be seen by one of Tommy's family. Not that she was doing anything wrong, simply walking along the street talking to a man about books, but they might not see it like that.

'I'd better be on my way,' she said. 'I've to go to the fishmonger's. Cheerio then!'

'Oh righto!' he said. 'See you another time? You can tell me how you liked *Main Street*.'

In the fishmonger's, she bumped into Mrs Cant, Pauline's mother.

'Oh, hello there, Willa. Did I not see you coming down Lauriston Place a wee minute ago?'

'I'd been at the library.'

'Oh, is that where you were?'

'I was getting books.' Willa held up her shopping bag, not that she needed to offer proof to Mrs Cant.

The woman didn't ask any more questions but she'd no doubt tell Pauline that she'd seen Willa walking down the road with a strange man. She paid for her fish and left.

When Willa asked for herring she was told there was none left. It made a cheap meal and sold out quickly.

'You should have been in earlier, hen.'

'I'll take a haddie then. A fat one, enough for two.'

The fish was wrapped in newspaper and passed into Willa's hand. On her way home she passed Bunty's newsagent's and tobacconist's. When Bunty saw her through the window she came to the door. She had a cigarette in her hand.

'Mrs Cant was just in.'

'She was quick off her mark,' said Willa sharply.

'What have you been up to then, eh?'

'Nothing, Bunty. Absolutely nothing. I went to the library, that's all.'

'She said you were with a man?'

'I wasn't *with* him. He'd been in the library too and we just happened to be walking the same way.'

'It's difficult for a young woman like you, with her man away so much. It's no life.'

'It is not difficult at all. And I do not even know what the man's name is. He is a total stranger.'

'All right, keep your hair on!' Bunty took a long drag on her cigarette. 'But if you ever do get up to anything just be careful. I dinne think Tommy'd be the forgiving type.'

~ 3 ~

Durban, Natal,
South Africa
4th January, 1924

Dear Willa,
  Durban is a seaside resort with a fine wide beach
which is always thronged and another suitable for
surfing. You can surf even at night as the water is
illuminated by searchlights set on high poles. One is
tempted never to go to bed, the evenings are so
balmy and so beautiful.
You would find much to admire in this town, which
is well laid out and beautifully kept. The people we
have met all love their lives here! No complaints,
they say. I should think not! Some of them seem to
spend most of the day on the beach.
  Mother would like it too, for I know she is fond
of suburbs.

'That's true,' acknowledged Ina Costello. In late spring she
liked to ride out to Colinton on the tram so that she could see
the flowers blooming in the gardens. She sat on the top deck,
front seat, if she could get it. 'I used to take Tommy with me
when he was a wee lad. He'll mind that. We had rare times
together, the two of us.'

The suburbs, as in Cape Town, are most attractive, especially in the Claremont district, with their sloping green lawns, which require constant watering in this warm climate. The black servants in their white singlets and shorts, embroidered with a red edging, look very smart. They are well trained and exceedingly civil. The rickshaw boys, who appear to be a fine type of men, are picturesque in their native head-dress. The most notable entertainment has been an exhibition of war dances given by the Zulus.

'We could do with one of those servants to redd the place up for us,' said Tommy's mother. 'I wouldn't care what colour their shorts were. As long as they were clean,' she added as an afterthought. 'I wonder if they wash stairs. Seems it's our turn for it.' The notice had been hanging on their door handle when she'd opened the door to the postie. 'It was the MacNabs' shot last week. That means it'll be manky in the corners. She's got no more strength than a canary in those skinny wrists of hers.'

'I'll do it in a minute,' said Willa. She always did. She couldn't very well allow her mother-in-law to hump a bucket of water up and down the stairs and get down on her arthritic knees. They'd not long finished the clothes wash; it was Monday. The scrubbing board had left Willa's hands red and raw, her shoulders ached from turning the mangle and the kitchen was full of steam from the copper boiler. Over their heads, on the pulley, hung the heavy wet washing, giving off the odd drip. It had been too damp outside to take it down to the back green.

Their neighbour below, Mrs Begg, took hers to the steamie,

pushing it there in an old battered pram. Ina said the women who went to the steamie tended to be a lower type of person, and she was not excluding Mrs Begg, who was always cadging, popping up the stairs to borrow a cup of sugar or a wee drop of tea, as she'd run out and the shops were shut, and she'd pay you back, no bother. Believe that if you will!

Monday was Willa's least favourite day of the week, with Tuesday following close behind, for then the linen had to be starched and the ironing done. They wouldn't rest until everything was folded and put away. On days like that Willa wished she were back at her desk in the Co-op office. She missed the company, too.

At least the washing was over for one week. She was going to reward herself with a trip to the library.

'What else has Tommy got to say?' demanded Ina. 'Don't be keeping it all to yourself.'

Tomorrow we depart for Dar-es-Salaam and Zanzibar. As we set sail the bands will be playing and the steamers tooting their sirens and there will be cheers, which we shall heartily return. Our visit has been a great success. We were told it would never be forgotten. An event of a lifetime, one young lady called it.

A bundle of your letters arrived this morning and I was glad to hear that Malkie is doing well and putting on weight.

Give Mother my love,
Your very fond husband,
Tommy xxx

Malkie was sitting on his granny's knee sucking his thumb. He loved being picked up and cuddled against a warm body. Willa thought it wasn't good for him to be lifted every time he cried; it would make him too dependent, so she'd read in *The Woman's Book,* which claimed to contain everything a woman needed to know, from how to treat your servants and the care of household silver to keeping poultry. His granny disagreed. What did books know about babies? She said it hadn't done Tommy any harm, getting cuddled. 'Look at him, stravaiging about all over the world!' The book, which Willa consulted in the library every time the baby had a slight cough or felt a little too hot, also said that it was desirable to let the baby sleep out of doors during the day as much as possible. Not much was possible living in Tollcross. She wasn't going to put Malcolm out in his pram on his own in the back green and the air wasn't that fresh either. You could smell the rubber works most days and, if not, the brewery.

She laid the letter aside, took the bucket and mop from the cupboard, ran in some hot water and soap powder, added a dash of ammonia and went out to wash the stair, starting from the top. There was a strong smell of cat on the landing. Animals came in and out as they fancied with the bottom door left standing open most of the time and any amount of notices asking the other tenants to close it behind them got nowhere. She wondered if some of them could read. They might not. And one or two, like Mrs Begg, didn't do much on the cleaning front either. Willa had seen her standing on the top step chucking the water over the stairs to bounce and splash its way downward as it chose.

Willa supposed it would be nice to live in one of those new

bungalows they were building further out and have your own back yard and garden, especially with a well-watered, sloping green lawn where a small child could play and run about. *One of these days*...Maybe.

When she had reached the bottom lobby and thrown the dirty water out into the gutter, she saw the man with the Cumnock Creamery milk cart crossing the road. He came over from Morrison Street. Their milk and butter were always fresh and the milk was sold in sealed bottles. They had two dairies in their own street, but Willa liked to buy from the Cumnock now and then. She felt sorry for the man having to push the cart through the traffic and negotiate the tram tracks. She knew his wife was sick and they had half a dozen children.

She asked him to wait while she ran up to fetch some money and when she returned she bought two pints of milk and a pat of butter.

'How's business?'

He made a face. 'Money's tight. Thanks, lass.' He doffed his cap to her and gripping the cart handles, pushed it off up the hill.

On her way back, Willa stopped at the MacNabs' door on the landing and knocked. Inside, one of the children was crying, which was nothing new. After a moment or two Mrs MacNab opened the door two or three inches, enough to reveal that she had a swollen eye, which was beginning to turn a disturbing shade of purple. She covered it with her hand when she saw Willa's eyes go to it and muttered something about knocking it against the corner of the kitchen door.

Willa held out one of the milk bottles. 'I was just getting

some milk from the Cumnock. I was wondering if you could do with a pint?'

'I've no money for it.' The door opened a little wider.

'It's a present.' Willa thrust the bottle into Mrs MacNab's hand and left before she could start blurting out her thanks. She felt awkward, in the role of giving out charity, like Lady Muck, though Tommy's mother couldn't understand why. 'You're doing them a good turn. What have you to be embarrassed about? We're not that well off ourselves. They should be grateful to you.'

She was still sitting with the baby, shoogling him on her knee and singing 'Rock a bye baby on the tree top'.

'I'm going to the library,' said Willa, 'so I thought I'd take Malcolm with me. He could do with an airing. The steam in here's bad for his lungs.'

'I'll give him a hurl round the links. He'd prefer that. You don't want to go to a stuffy old library, do you, Malkie? The air on the links'll do him good. No, you go on, Willa. I don't mind taking him and you'll get a better chance to look at the books without him.'

Tommy's mother often seemed to have all the arguments on her side.

'I might take him up to Elma's afterwards so don't worry if we're not back for a bit.' Ina loved showing off her grandson. Willa supposed she could hardly grudge her that.

She went to fetch her library books.

As soon as she was heading up Lauriston Place her irritation lessened and by the time she went through the library portals she was in a good mood again. The sour librarian was on, though even that didn't dampen her spirits.

This woman never brought books up from under the counter but Willa was content to trawl along the shelves, taking books out and browsing a little. Her fingers swept over Marie Corelli and Ethel M Dell, whom she'd read when she was younger, but who seemed rather dull compared to those she was reading now. She picked out a book with the title *Anna of the Five Towns* by a writer called Arnold Bennett whom she did not know, and a voice behind her said,

'I think you might enjoy that.'

She jumped. Turning she saw the young man she'd walked up the street with and who had caused Pauline's mother's tongue to wag, not that she could actually blame *him* for that.

'Oh, thanks.'

'It's set in the Potteries. In England. How did you like *Main Street?*'

'*Shush,*' said a woman beside them, for which Willa was grateful. She was able to turn back to the shelf and the young man moved away. Out of the corner of her eye she watched him go over to a table and sit down.

He took a sheet of paper out of a folder, a fountain pen from his top pocket, unscrewed the cap and began to write, frowning a little, stopping to ponder from time to time and to push his thick fair hair back from his forehead. She wondered what he could be writing. He was quite young, perhaps a little younger than herself. He looked up and their eyes met. His were a deep, intense blue, so intense that they were startling. At least, she felt startled. He smiled. She blushed and looked away.

She decided to take *Anna of the Five Towns*. She liked the title. For her second book, she chose another Edgar Wallace,

The Green Archer. She rather enjoyed thrillers, especially in the evening when Malcolm was asleep and it was dark and quiet outside, except for the rumble of the occasional late-night tram.

The young man was still sitting at the table when she went to the counter to have her books stamped, although he had finished writing and had put the paper back in its folder and the fountain pen in his top pocket. He was neatly dressed and wore a tie with a gold pin in it.

For once, it was not raining. It was a sharp, frosty day, but the sun was out and the sky a brilliant blue, perhaps as brilliant as the sky in Durban, Natal. Willa loved this kind of Edinburgh winter day, when the air seemed to sparkle and everything stood out so clearly. She stood on the step for a moment taking it in before setting off homeward.

As she was nearing the end of George IV Bridge she heard footsteps behind her. She did not turn her head and when he caught up with her and said, 'Mind if I walk with you?' she was able to look surprised.

'Did you take *Anna*?'

She showed him that she had.

'What else do you read? Robert Louis Stevenson?'

'Oh yes!'

'Scott?'

'Not much. He's a bit, kind of—'

'Heavy?'

'Well, yes.'

'He just takes a bit of getting into.'

They began to talk about books again and he told her that he admired Stevenson greatly and wished he could write like him.

'Are you a writer then?'

'Well, I write. But I haven't published anything yet.'

'I saw you writing.'

'Oh, that! It was only a letter. A job application.' He was subdued now.

'What kind of job?'

'Clerk.' He shrugged. 'At Galloway's, the tool makers.'

'In Home Street? That's near me,' she said involuntarily.

She suddenly realised that they were almost at Tollcross. Up ahead was the clock, and the windows of their flat, glinting a little, touched by an oblique angle of sunshine.

'You've gone past your house,' she said.

'That's all right. I was enjoying talking to you.'

She began to feel anxious. 'I'll need to go, I'm afraid.'

'Cheerio then! I'll see you again?'

'Expect so. At the library.'

She swiftly crossed the road, dodging a motor car which blared its horn at her and then a bicycle, and went on up Home Street, passing her door, not wanting to let him see exactly where she lived. Her face burnt and she felt foolish. She should have told him she was married, slipped it into the conversation somehow. But how? There hadn't really been an opportunity. *My husband likes Stevenson too.* But in a way there had been no need to bring him into it. The young man hadn't been trying to chat her up. They'd just been having a friendly conversation about books. He was obviously the friendly type. He probably recommended books to half the people that came into the library, men or women, young or old. He might be lonely. He had a whole day to fill in. She was reading more into these casual encounters than was there.

She didn't feel like going home and Malcolm would still be out with his granny. She decided to call on Bunty.

Bunty was making a cup of tea in the back shop. She lived in a room and kitchen at the rear. It was enough space, she said, her being on her own. The only thing she wished she had was a bathroom. She had a privy out in the back yard and came round to Ina's for a bath. She had been on her own for a long time, since her husband had died, only six months after their marriage. He'd had an accident on his bicycle; he'd collided with a rag and bone cart – he'd been drunk, Ina claimed – and had sustained head injuries that had proved fatal. He'd left Bunty the shop and she'd also got £250 compensation from the council.

It was the mid-morning lull, after the early rush and the lunchtime custom.

'Business is down, of course,' said Bunty, as she poured Willa a cup of dark tea. 'Men can't afford as many fags as they'd like.' One smouldered in her ashtray. 'Never mind, we'll get through, one way or another. I had a win at Powderhall last night. I picked a couple of good dogs. Wasn't a fortune but enough for a new pair of shoes. Nigger-brown suede. I'll show you them after.'

She'd gone with her man friend, Mr Parkin, who was just a friend, you understand, for she always spoke of him as such. He took her to the pictures or to *The Gaities* in the Music Hall in George Street. A bit of company, she called him, though she never brought him to family gatherings. Elma would have a blue fit if she did. He was talking of taking Bunty on a winter cruise.

'Tommy might not be the only member of the family to go

sailing on the high seas! I might be able to wave to him in passing.' Bunty folded *The Scotsman* over to show Willa an advertisement urging its readers to avoid the winter and have sunshine and health.

'*Avoid the winter*,' Willa read aloud. '*Have sunshine and health. Nelson liners to the Canary Islands. Return fare £25. 1st class.*'

'I fancy avoiding the winter,' said Bunty. 'Even a couple of weeks would do me. You could mind the shop for me.'

'That'd be fifty pounds for the two of you.' Quite a few weeks' wages, but Willa thought Mr Parkin probably earned more than that, to judge from what he spent. He seemed to have a senior position in some kind of finance company. Bunty was vague about it when questioned. 'Do you think he will? Take you?'

Bunty shrugged. 'It'd be nice, wouldn't it?'

'It would. Very nice. I expect the passengers would be pretty posh. I read somewhere that film stars like going on cruises.'

'What if Rudolph was to be on board! I could ask him up for the ladies' choice.'

They had a laugh.

Willa enjoyed a chat with Bunty. She was relaxing company and seldom down. She laughed a lot and when she did her earrings swung from side to side. Willa lingered, reluctant to go back to the flat – Tommy's mother's flat – and got up only when the shop door pinged, announcing the arrival of a customer.

'Better see who it is,' said Bunty, stubbing out her cigarette. 'Might be a millionaire wanting to buy the shop. Then we could all go to the Canary Islands.'

Willa followed Bunty through to the front. Standing on the other side of the counter was her young man. Not *her* young man. Her acquaintance from the library. She took a step back and bumped into a box of pencils, knocking them off their precarious perch. The shop was small, and storage space scarce. The lid flew off the box and pencils scattered in all directions.

'Can I help?' asked the young man, making a move to come round the back of the counter.

'No, it's all right,' muttered Willa, down on her hands and knees, hiding her hot face.

'You canne swing a cat in here.' said Bunty cheerfully. 'Dinne fash yersel, hen. I'll pick the rest up later. No harm done.'

Willa was forced to surface.

'Hello, there,' the young man said to Willa. 'We meet again!'

'Are you no going to introduce us then, Willa?' asked Bunty, parking a hand on her hip and looking from one to the other. Her earrings were birling madly.

'I'm Richard Fitzwilliam,' he said, thrusting out his hand. Bunty took it and shook it warmly.

'Pleased to meet you, I'm sure. I'm Bunty McGregor, sole proprietor of this establishment! And Willa's aunt.'

'Bunty's my husband's aunt,' Willa added quickly.

'Oh, I see.' His eyes dropped to her left hand where she wore a thin gold band on her fourth finger. It had been her mother's wedding ring.

'Do you live round here, Mr Fitzwilliam?' enquired Bunty.

'Lauriston Place.'

'I thought you'd not been in before.'

'No, I don't normally come this way.' His face was pink now. 'But I just happened to be passing and thought I'd buy *The Scotsman*, if you'd happen to have a copy?'

'I do indeed.' Bunty laid it on the counter. 'That'll be two pence if you please.' He fished in his trouser pocket, produced a sixpence, and she gave him his change.

The transaction completed, he hovered uncertainly for a moment before saying, 'Well, I'll be off. I'll say goodbye then.' He had no hat to lift to them though he looked as if he wished he had.

'Cheerio!' responded Bunty. 'Come again, Mr Fitzwilliam.' Willa said nothing.

The door jangled again as he went out.

'Well-spoken young man,' said Bunty. 'You could tell he would buy *The Scotsman* and not the *Daily Mail*. Twice the price for a start. And more class. He must come from a good family?'

'Bunty, I know nothing about his family, or him. We bump into each other in the library and talk about books.'

'I thought you weren't allowed to talk in the library?'

'We talk *outside*. We walk up the street together, that's all. We happen to go in the same direction. I didn't even know his name until he introduced himself.'

'Rather nice looking,' mused Bunty. 'In a different way from our Tommy, of course.'

~ 4 ~

Dar-es-Salaam,
East Africa
16th January, 1924

Dear Willa,
 Dar-es-Salaam is the chief seaport of Tanganyika Territory and the terminus of a caravan route which trades in ivory and rubber. Perhaps some of the rubber ends up in Dundee Street, Edinburgh? Who knows! They say it's a small world.

To his readers, it appeared enormous. Although they could follow his progress on the globe he seemed a million miles away. He'd gone down one side of Africa, round the bottom, and was now up the other side. And Africa was not small. Scotland, in comparison, looked tiny. When Ina studied the globe she frowned, unable to quite follow it.

In 1884 the territory was declared a German Protectorate and in the following year a bitter struggle ensued between natives and Germans lasting 18 months, in which 20,000 natives died. Lucky for the people, we captured it in 1916 after a heavy naval bombardment in which a wireless station and a floating dock were destroyed.

'They'll be a sight better off with us than the Jerries,' said Bunty, who had dropped in.

'An awful lot of people died, though,' said Willa. 'Twenty thousand.'

'I don't suppose they live long in those parts anyway,' said Tommy's mother. 'I'm glad Tommy's only there for a few days.'

'Talking about living long,' said Bunty, 'did you see in the paper the other day, somebody to do with Sanitary Engineers – I think it was the president – he was saying that the death rate was too low?'

'You're haverin',' said Ina. 'How can the death rate be too low? Is he wanting us to kick the bucket early?'

'He said it was because the more intelligent classes were getting smaller in comparison with the less intelligent and that would not be good for society.'

'That's horrible,' said Willa.

Ina was frowning. 'Who was he meaning by the less intelligent?'

'Work it out for yourself, Ina,' said Bunty.

'He's only a stupid old sanitary engineer,' said Willa and returned to the delights of the tropics.

> The beautifully coloured butterflies are very large and the white coral under the water is very pretty. I watched some native women catching fish this morning. They wade breast-deep into the sea and stretch out a dark sheet under the surface of the water. They then throw bait into the sheet and when the fish swim for it they lift the sheet with them trapped inside.

'I bet the sani man would say those women are less intelligent, but isn't that clever of them?' said Bunty.

'I don't suppose they can read, though,' said Ina.

Willa was thinking that the women's breasts would likely be bare. Would they be wearing anything at all, even down below? She imagined the sailors – well, one, Tommy – gawking, eyes out on stalks. The idea of it bothered her more than she thought it should though why she didn't know. It was not as if Tommy was going to run off with any of them. However, she did like to hear about the women's lives in those far-off places. For her, they were the most interesting parts of the letters.

'He has a rare turn of phrase, does Tommy,' said his mother. 'He really should have joined the *Evening News*. He's wasted his chances.'

'I don't know,' said her sister. 'He's having a great time, gadding about, seeing things we'll never see.'

'Leading a fine old life certainly.' Ina sniffed.

'You wouldn't want him to be leading a nasty old one, would you, Ina?'

'Of course not. But what are they meant to be doing out there?'

'Showing the flag. Isn't that what Tommy said.'

'What's that supposed to mean? I ken Tommy's in Signals but he doesn't stand on the deck all day waving flags, does he?'

'Of course not,' put in Willa. 'He sends signals to other ships. Well, something like that,' she tailed off.

'They're out there to remind them that Britain's in charge and they're not to forget it,' said Bunty, breaking into song and conducting with an imaginary baton. '*Rule Britannia, Britannia rules the waves. Britons never never never shall be slaves!* You can't argue with that, can you?'

'I wasn't arguing about anything.'

Willa had noticed that the sisters often did argue when they got together, in a niggly way, about all sorts of things that they didn't really care about. She had not had brothers and sisters herself so Tommy's family had been an eye-opener for her. Her parents had not been arguers and she'd not had siblings to quarrel with.

'Want to hear some more?' she asked.

'Read on, MacDuff!' said Bunty.

Our stay here is proving extremely pleasant and peaceful. The water is beautifully clear and buoyant and we have had some excellent bathing. On the shore, at low tide, there are all manner of different coloured shells to be seen and gathered. I shall bring some home for Malkie.

'Malkie will like that, won't you, son?' said his grandmother. He was sitting on her knee chewing the handle of a rattle. Willa had refused to let him have a dummy-tit. Ina couldn't see what was wrong with it but Willa had been adamant. She hated the sight of dummies stuffed into babies' mouths to shut them up and she said it stopped them talking. Ina had gone ahead anyway and bought one. Willa had been furious and thrown it into the bucket. It was one battle that she had won. 'It's nice that your daddy's thinking about you, isn't it, Malkie?' his granny went on.

'Well, once in a while,' said Willa.

It was only with the arrival of Tommy's letters that she'd come to realise what it would mean for Malcolm having a sailor for a father. *The Woman's Book* said great care must be taken in the choice of a nurse for the little ones, but it didn't say anything about taking care to pick the right father. Her child would have a father who would seldom be here, who would appear at intervals, like a hero, bringing excitement into the boy's life for short spells of time, would kick a football round the Meadows with him, take him to the fun fair at Portobello, then go. Leaving her to pick up the pieces. You should have thought of that before, she could hear her Aunt Lily saying in her ear, saying triumphantly, but she hadn't thought, had she, she'd allowed herself to be swept away by his handsome looks, the movement of his body against hers as he'd guided her round the dance floor and, of course, his winning smile. A smile that must have conquered other hearts before hers. And perhaps was still doing so.

> *Yesterday a number of us sailed with some new friends out to a small island off shore. We picnicked and swam and stayed to watch the sunset, which was comprised of the most amazing colours. I have never seen one like it. It was quite hypnotic and made one feel that one could stay there for ever. This could be an ideal place for a quiet and interesting holiday.*

'Tommy makes friends easily,' said his mother, reflecting what Willa herself was thinking. Very easily. Perhaps it was easier on warm tropical beaches washed by green water. Here, folk kept their coats buttoned up to the neck and hurried on by, muttering a few words of greeting, anxious to get out of the wind.

'What's he going on about?' demanded Bunty. 'When did he ever want to go anywhere quiet? He likes the bright lights.'

'He went to North Berwick,' Willa reminded her.

'True enough. But he'd other things on his mind, didn't he?' Bunty winked.

Yes, he had, thought Willa with a pang. Those three days were the longest stretch of time they'd ever had on their own together. Apart from that, they had been living with his mother. Even in bed Willa had been conscious of the woman across the landing. She never shut her door properly, always left it slightly ajar. For air, she said. They could hear snoring.

'Well, you wouldn't catch me going to a place like yon,' said Ina, nodding at the letter. 'You'd never know what you'd catch.' She laughed, as if she'd made a joke. Nobody else joined in.

'I'd go,' said Willa. Anywhere. Like a shot. She folded the letter, omitting to read out that Tommy sent his mother his love.

'Not a hope in hell of that, though, is there?' said Bunty.

'No, I don't suppose there is. Women don't get many chances to do things, do they? I can't join the Navy. I don't even get the vote yet. Not until I'm thirty, another seven years.'

'What's up with you?' Bunty looked at Willa. 'You need to get out a bit more, hen. Why don't you come to the flicks with me? I'm going to see Douglas Fairbanks in *Robin Hood*. It's on at the New Picture House. Ina'll mind Malkie, won't you?'

'That's all right by me.'

Willa felt she should turn down the offer; she was worried that she was leaving the baby too often with his grandmother. On the other hand, as she argued to herself, she was with him all evening and all night. He was asleep for most of it of course but she did take him out during the day and she spent time with him alone, feeding him. In *The Woman's Book* there was no concern expressed about leaving your child with other people. It was constantly talking about what the baby's nurse should do and not do, which left you with the impression that the parents didn't see an awful lot of him.

'He might need feeding before I get back,' said Willa, still hesitating, still tempted. It had been weeks since she'd been at the pictures.

'I can give him a bottle,' said Tommy's mother. 'Can't I, Malkie son?'

Willa gave in and went to get her coat. Bunty said she should put on a hat as it was frosty out and they'd probably have to queue, but Willa didn't like covering her head. She said she had her hair to keep her warm. She had still not had it bobbed even though Pauline told her she was looking old-fashioned every time she saw her. Bunty kept hers shingled. She had bought herself a new cloche hat in Jenners' sale that fitted snugly round her ears while leaving her earrings free to dangle. She liked to be in the fashion as much as possible though she drew the line when it came to binding her chest with bandages to flatten it. It would take some doing to flatten her chest! To complete her outfit, she slung her fox tippet around her neck. Willa hated the sight of the fox's beady eye. She felt it was glaring at her.

'Let's go!' cried Bunty, taking Willa's arm. She needed

support in those shoes she was wearing. The heels were too high, making her tilt forward, and the straps were biting into the fronts of her plump ankles. Fashion would always take precedence over comfort as far as Bunty was concerned. Time enough for that when you're dead, she said.

They took the tram down to Princes Street. A queue had already formed outside the cinema by the time they arrived. Queuing was part of the outing. They joined on the end. The commissionaire, smart in his gold-buttoned uniform, walked up and down the line, looking important and keeping order. There were occasions when he had to clip a young lad round the ear. Bunty greeted him with a 'How're you doin' the day, Jocky?', which did not please him. He liked to maintain his dignity and he didn't want any of the others in the queue to start calling him by his first name and being cheeky. Bunty knew him well; he bought his cigarettes from her and she sometimes allowed him to have them on tick.

'Hey, there's your young man, Willa?' Bunty leant out from the queue to get a better view. 'He's four or five ahead of us.'

'He's not my young man,' said Willa in a low voice. 'How many times do I have to tell you?'

She had seen him twice again in the library. The first time, she had managed to slip away while he was writing at a desk; the second, he'd come out with her and they had walked down the road, as before, and talked about books and parted in Lauriston Place. She had supposed, since he was still coming to the library during the day, that he had not got the job he'd been applying for, but she had not asked. She thought it must be depressing when people kept asking.

He appeared to have heard Bunty for he turned and looked

round and, being taller than anyone near him, he saw them. Bunty stood up on her toes to wave, he waved back and detached himself from the queue, giving up his place, and came to join them. Bunty shifted over and made room for him.

'Thought I recognised you! It's Mr Fitzwilliam, isn't it?'

'Richard, please.'

'Do you never get Dick or Dickie?'

'No, not really.'

'Richard is nicer. It's more manly, isn't it, Willa?'

Willa did not reply.

The queue shuffled forward. Bunty chatted to Richard about pictures she'd seen. She thought Charlie Chaplin a great laugh and, as for Valentino, well, he was every woman's idea of a good lover, wasn't he? Mind you, Douglas Fairbanks was all right too. She wouldn't say no to a night with him. Willa squirmed and Richard murmured politely. He appeared to have seen most of the films that Bunty had. She went to the pictures at least twice a week. Willa didn't speak.

They only had to queue for forty minutes before it was their turn to be waved by Jocky into the shining interior.

'We're going to the Balcony,' said Bunty, laying out two and sixpence for herself and Willa. It had been agreed beforehand. 'I had a wee win on the dogs last night. Ever go down to Powderhall, Richard?'

He shook his head.

'Is that all right?' asked Willa, meaning going to the dearer seats. 'Of course,' he replied, though she wondered if he might not have meant to go to the stalls if he'd been by himself. The downtown cinemas were dearer than the local ones like La Scala, commonly known as the Scabby Lala.

Richard ended up in the middle, between the two women. Bunty said with one man and two women it made sense.

They'd come in in the middle of the film so that they had to stay and see it right round again. Throughout, Willa was conscious of Richard sitting next to her and once or twice when she moved her leg, or he his, they brushed against each other's and both simultaneously apologised. Apart from that, they did not communicate. Along with the rest of the audience, Bunty cheered on Robin Hood and his merry men shouting out, 'Come on, Dougie, you can do it!' and she laughed heartily at the cartoons, digging Richard in the side every now and then, saying, 'Isn't that a scream!'

When they finally emerged, warm and flushed, Bunty proposed going up to the café for an ice cream.

'It's on me.'

'I really should get back for Malcolm,' said Willa.

'Ina'll give him a bottle. She'll be in her element.'

Richard turned to Willa. 'Have you got a baby?'

'He's four months old.'

'Bright as a button,' said Bunty, but refrained from adding, 'Just like his dad,' which Willa suspected had been on the tip of her tongue. Perhaps it would have been better if she had come out with it for then the fact that she had a husband would be clearly established.

'Well, shall we go?' Bunty took an arm of each of them and propelled them up the stairs.

Willa said she would have to go to the ladies first and Bunty joined her. While they were waiting in the queue, Willa said,

'You shouldn't encourage him, Bunty.'

'Encourage him, to do what? I just thought it would be nice for us to have a bit of different company. What's the harm in that? Relax, love. You've got me as your chaperone!'

He was waiting outside the door for them. They had to queue again for the café but, finally, they were taken to a table and Bunty ordered three vanilla ices with raspberry sauce.

'That'll cool us down a bit.' Her face was flushed. She lit a cigarette and leant back in her chair. 'So tell us about yourself, Richard.'

'Not much to tell,' he started, but Bunty interrupted saying she didn't believe him and gave him one of her winks. 'I grew up in Edinburgh,' he went on after a moment, looking flushed himself now.

'And where did you go to school?'

'Heriot's.'

'Heriot's, Willa! I told you he came from a good family.'

Willa was uncomfortable, on two accounts: Bunty's determination to give Richard the third degree, and a certain dampness she was beginning to feel in her chest area. She was leaking milk, in spite of the fact that she'd tucked a piece of flannel inside her brassiere before coming out. She tried to keep her arms across her breasts and prayed that they would be served quickly. About Bunty she could do nothing, for once she'd got the bit between her teeth there was no holding her back.

'So, what does your father do, if I might be so bold as to ask, Richard?'

Richard was embarrassed. Perhaps his father was dead or he'd never had one.

'I hope they won't take long,' said Willa, glancing round to see if she could pick out their waitress. 'They seem to be awfully slow here.'

Bunty was looking expectantly at Richard.

'Well,' he said, 'he used to have an accountancy business.'

'An accountant, eh? They do all right.'

'He went bankrupt,' Richard continued hurriedly. 'He made one or two unwise investments.'

'What a shame,' said Bunty.

'So we had to move out of our house in the Grange to a flat in Lauriston. And I had to leave university.'

'What were you studying?' asked Willa.

'English literature.'

'That explains it. How you know so much about books.'

He smiled and for the first time that evening so did she.

'Did you read *Pride and Prejudice*?' He'd recommended it when he'd seen her last.

'Oh, I did. I liked it a lot. I'm going to read it again.'

'That's a mark of a good book. So my mother says,' he added awkwardly.

Bunty did not like this turn in the conversation. She hadn't finished with her questioning. 'What do you plan to do with your life now then, Richard?'

'He'd like to be a writer.' Willa answered for him. 'Well, he *is* a writer. He writes.' They smiled at each other again.

'What kind of a writer?' asked Bunty.

'A novelist.'

'That Edgar Wallace makes a mint, so I've heard.'

'I don't know that I'll be writing like him.'

'You could do worse,' pronounced Bunty. 'Much worse. Take it from me.'

'He's got to write about what inspires him,' said Willa.

'You're right, Willa.' He nodded. 'You understand.'

'You can't live off fresh air, mind,' said Bunty.

Willa was pleased to see their waitress coming towards them bearing a tray set with three little silver dishes. By this time the milk was trickling down her front and she was worried that they might be able to smell it or see the damp patches on her blouse. She ate her ice cream quickly and reached for her coat.

'I really *must* go. I don't like leaving Malcolm too long.'

'Hang on!' cried Bunty. 'You've no' got a train to catch. Wait for us!'

'Are you walking?' asked Richard, once they were out in the street.

'If you are, we are,' cried Bunty gaily.

They walked three abreast, with Richard in the middle. Bunty took his arm. 'You don't mind, do you, Richard? It's these pavements, the council should do something about them.' Willa walked on her own, keeping close to the shop windows, pretending to take an interest in them. They reached the west end of Princes Street and turned up Lothian Road, Bunty chatting all the way.

They parted at the clock at Tollcross.

'It's been a nice evening,' said Richard. 'Thank you for the ice cream, Mrs McGregor.'

'Please call me Bunty! Everybody does.'

'Good night, Willa,' he said.

'See you again, Richard!' Bunty called after him. 'Pop into the shop any time you're passing and I'll make you a wee cup of tea. What a lovely young man,' she said to Willa while he was still in earshot. 'I could have fallen for himself myself if I'd been thirty years younger. Or even twenty! What a pity his dad lost all his money.'

When Willa went in she found Malcolm fast asleep in his cot.

'I've settled him for the night,' said his granny, who was ready for bed with her curlers in and her stays up on the pulley. 'I gave him a feed about an hour ago. Lapped it up so he did.'

He looked as if he had been overfed. His cheeks were puffed out and there was a spill of regurgitated milk on his sheet.

Willa went into the bathroom and expressed her milk into the sink.

~ 5 ~

Trinconmali, Ceylon
30th January, 1924

'Isn't that where the tea comes from?' said Ina.

'Some of it,' said Willa and began to read.

> *Dear Willa,*
>
> *We arrived here in a very heavy tropical rainstorm. You cannot imagine it! You never see rain like it in Edinburgh. It just buckets down relentlessly, flattening all the vegetation. It's amazing how the flowers perk up afterwards. En route we joined up with the* Dunedin *and that completes our squadron. She had mail for us, including several of your letters. I was glad to hear that a good New Year was had by one and all and that Malkie is putting on weight. He sounds a great wee lad.*

'You are, aren't you, son?' said his granny, bouncing him on her knee. 'Just a great wee lad, like your daddy says.'

'Watch he doesn't bring his feed up,' said Willa. He'd guzzled at the breast until she'd had to force his mouth off her nipple and then he'd roared with rage. He wasn't easily satisfied. A bit like his daddy there, too. Tommy would always want the world. Nothing less would do. And now he had it.

'You fuss too much over the bairn,' said his granny.
Willa took a deep breath and carried on reading.

> The Dunedin *reported that she had lost a man in the*
> *Red Sea. He fell overboard and quick as a flash a*
> *shark nabbed him. A boat was lowered but just as it*
> *was about to reach him he disappeared in a pool of*
> *blood.*

'Oh, dear God, think of his poor mother,' said Ina. Willa
thought of his poor wife, the ring at the door, the yellow
telegram being handed in, the lurch in her heart as she
stretches out a reluctant hand to receive it. 'There's times
when I wish Tommy had never joined the Navy,' Ina
continued, 'no matter what Bunty says about it being a great
life. I asked him not to do it but by then it was too late. He'd
already signed on and he said they'd sue him if he broke his
contract or clap him in jail.'

'Tommy would never fall overboard,' said Willa, who was
birling the globe round, looking for Ceylon. Ah, there it was,
sitting tucked under India. They must have sailed straight
across the Indian Ocean.

> Ceylon, *after a chequered history, became British in*
> *1802 and has since remained so. It supplies a*
> *quarter of all the world's graphite so you never*
> *know the lead in your pencil might have come from*
> *right here! Also to be obtained are tea, rubber,*
> *coconut, rice, ebony, satinwood, sapphires and*
> *rubies. Moonstones are dirt cheap.*

'Sapphires and rubies!' exclaimed Ina. 'I wonder if he'll bring any home. I've always fancied a ruby.'

'I doubt if he can just pick them up.'

'How do you know? He might find them in rocks.'

'It doesn't sound very likely.'

'Not to you, maybe.'

Willa desisted from retaliating. She mustn't fall into the arguing habit, the way Bunty did with her sister. It could be only too easy.

'Well, moonstones, then,' insisted Ina.

Willa had a vague idea that moonstones were unlucky.

> *Two parties from the squadron went to Kandu by motor but I was not with them, fortunately for me, as one of the motors overturned taking a hairpin bend. Some of the roads leave something to be desire – this is not GB. Several men sustained injuries and a Petty Officer from the* Repulse *was killed, sad to report.*

'If it's not one thing it's the other!' Ina shook her head. 'The men are going down like ninepins.'

'There's quite a few to go, though. Didn't Tommy say 470 on each ship? That's over 3,000 in all.'

'Must be quite a sight, the lot of them going ashore in their whites.'

'A bit like an invasion.'

'It's not *war* they're waging.'

'I never said—' Willa stopped.

*The harbour is too dangerous for bathing. The
natives have to be careful when they're paddling
their canoes. One false move and they'd provide a
tasty meal for the sharks.*

'I don't think it was very nice to say *tasty*,' said Willa,
shuddering at the image it conjured up.

His mother ignored that. 'Are they all black in the countries
he's going to?'

'Not in Australia, as far as I know. Or New Zealand. He'll
be going to both countries.'

'Elma's neighbour, Mr Gilchrist, had a cousin who came
over from Australia and he was white.'

'I imagine he would be,' said Willa. 'After all, Mr Gilchrist
is white.'

*Must sign off now. Work to do. Must get everything
shipshape! We are about to set sail for the Malay
Straits.*
> *Give Mother my love.*
> *Yours fondly, as ever*
> *Tommy xxx*
> *P.S. And a kiss for Malkie too. He'll be a big boy
by the time I get back.*

'He will,' said Willa, tucking the letter back into its envelope.
Tommy wanted the envelopes kept as well, and their stamps.
He had a stamp album that he'd started when he'd joined the
Navy. She enjoyed browsing through it herself. The stamps
looked so exotic, from places like the Gilbert and Solomon

Islands, compared to their dull ones of the king's head. 'I think I'll go to the library.'

'I'll take Malkie for a walk up to Marchmont to see how Elma's getting on for tonight.'

It had become accepted now that when Willa went to the library Malcolm's grandmother would look after him.

'You're remembering we're going to Elma's for our tea, aren't you?' asked Ina. It was Elma's birthday, her sixtieth.

'I'd better get her a present.'

'Nothing too dear, mind. You should be able to find something for a shilling. She won't expect much. You could try Parker's Stores. Oh, and while you're there you might get me some new laces for my stays. The old ones are wearing through.'

Willa escorted her mother-in-law and her child down the stairs, then she headed for George IV Bridge. Every time she passed George Heriot's school and saw the boys out in their navy-blue uniforms she thought of Richard. The building looked a bit like a castle and had nice grounds. It must have been a pleasant place to go to school, a lot less dingy than Tollcross Public.

Richard was already in the library. She no longer made a pretence of not seeing him; that would seem daft after having sat together in the pictures, along with Bunty, of course, and gone to the café afterwards. After all, they were just friends who liked to talk about books. They had nothing to hide. He looked up from the exercise book he'd been writing in and waved and she waved back.

When she went into a bay to look for books, he got up and followed her.

'Do you want me to recommend something?'

He pulled out *Chrome Yellow*, by Aldous Huxley. 'He's quite new. I've just read this myself. It's a satire, set in a country house, quite cynical. I'm not sure what you'll make of it.'

'I'll try it. How many books do you read in a day?'

'Just one,' he said, a bit embarrassed. 'Unless they're short,' he added. He was still having no luck with his job-hunting.

For her second book, Willa chose Dorothy L. Sayers' *Whose Body*.

'Did you like *Emma* as much as *Pride and Prejudice*?' asked Richard.

'Perhaps not just quite as much. But I did like it. A great deal. I could have kicked Emma, though, she seemed so annoying, and Mr Knightley seemed so nice.'

The sour librarian came by with a bundle of books that she was stacking in the shelves. 'If you want to talk you'd best go outside,' she said.

'Shall we?' said Richard.

Outside, they stood on the steps, in the shelter of the doorway. The rain had come on again, not heavy like it would be in the tropics, lashing down and drenching everything, but enough to wet your head and shoulders in a few minutes. They could not stand there all morning for people were coming and going and they kept having to move out of the way.

'Would you like to go for a cup of tea?' offered Richard.

Willa thought for a moment before answering. 'All right. Where could we go?'

'There's a wee place in the High Street, not far.'

Their hair was dripping wet by the time they arrived there,

even though they'd run most of the way. They laughed and shook their heads free of the worst of the water and chose a table in the corner away from the steamed-up window. Willa led the way. The window might be fogged up but if it were to clear she would not want to be sitting in full view of the street. Not that she was doing anything wrong, she reasoned within herself yet again, but a married woman taking tea with a young man might be misread by some, by women like Mrs Cant who had needle-sharp eyes and snapped up any titbit she could find to gossip about. Mrs Cant was not a nasty woman – she could be kind and had been to Willa when her mother died – but she couldn't pass up the chance of gathering material for a good blether.

They ordered two cups of tea and Richard insisted on paying. No, said Willa, she didn't want anything to eat, she wasn't hungry, though, in fact, she could have eaten one of the home-baked scones. They looked and smelt tempting but she knew Richard had little money to spare. It must be wonderful to be away on a ship for a year and know that you needn't think about money or where the next meal was coming from.

They warmed their hands round their cups and Willa noticed that hers were looking chapped and red. She withdrew them and put them on her lap out of sight. She must buy some hand cream at the chemist's on the way back.

'It's great to have someone to discuss books with,' she said. 'I used to, with my mother, until she died.'

'I'm sorry.'

'It's a while ago.'

He fiddled with his teaspoon. 'What about your husband? Does he not read?'

'Oh, he does, but adventure stuff mostly. *Bulldog Drummond*. Not the kind of thing you could talk about much. At least, I wouldn't think so.' Tommy wouldn't have any time for Jane Austen. There wouldn't be enough action in her novels for him, apart from the fact that his patience would soon run out with the goings-on of women like Mrs Bennet. Willa added, 'He's in the Navy so he's away a lot.'

She went on to tell Richard about the world cruise of the Special Service Squadron and how Tommy was writing from each port of call describing the place and the people.

'I'd love to see the world,' said Richard. 'Wouldn't you?'

'I suppose, but I've got a baby to think of.'

'His letters sound interesting. Where has he been so far?'

Willa began to talk about the places the fleet had visited, relating as much as she could remember of the contents of the letters. Richard prompted her and asked questions. She stayed longer than she had intended.

'I must go!' She felt it was her perpetual cry. She jumped up. She was going to take the tram – she could get a 27 or a 23 from George IV Bridge – as it would be quicker and would save her from getting wet again. He walked her to the stop.

'See you soon,' he said, as he handed her up onto the step. He waited on the pavement until the tram took off. She was glad that there was no one she knew on the tram. As she took a seat she reminded herself yet again that she had nothing to feel guilty about.

They had gone only two stops when she remembered Elma's birthday present. She hopped off at the Infirmary and cut through George Square to Parker's Triangle on the corner of Crichton Street. She had to run all the way. She found a crêpe de Chine silk scarf for eleven pence and hoped the shade would not be too bright for Elma.

She was out of breath by the time she got home.

'Where on earth have you been?' demanded Tommy's mother. 'Does it take that long to pick two books? The dinner's near dried up.'

'I got Elma a scarf.' Willa took it out of its bag.

'Elma never wears green. She says it's unlucky. Gerry's aunt was wearing a green coat when she got knocked down by a motor cycle.'

'That doesn't prove anything. Anyway, she was ninety-two and blind.'

Ina sniffed. 'I hope you remembered the laces for my stays?'

Willa had not.

They walked up to Marchmont at six o'clock for the birthday tea. Malcolm was wide awake in his pram, propped up on his pillows, fascinated by the streetlamps. The nights were beginning to lighten a little, Willa noted gratefully. She had had enough of long dark evenings shut up in the flat. On a light evening she'd be able to push the pram down to Princes Street and have a walk in the gardens.

They presented Elma with a tin of lavender talcum powder that Tommy had given Willa for her birthday and which she'd never opened. She wore the green scarf herself.

'That colour suits you, Willa.' Bunty nodded her approval. 'It sets off your hair.'

'Wouldn't catch me dead in green,' said Elma.

They drank her health in sherry. She had her usual sip; the rest had refills.

'Any excuse,' she said, shaking her head. 'It doesn't take much to set the lot of you off. I knew this would happen.'

'Ah, come on, Elma,' said Gerry. 'Let your hair down! You're only sixty once in your life.'

'Thank goodness for that.'

The sisters' cousin Betty had also been invited to the party. Betty's attitude to alcohol was the same as Elma's except that she was totally teetotal and would not permit her lips even to graze it. She belonged to a Temperance Society and went round public houses with leaflets. Gerry said it was a wonder she didn't emerge from some of the rougher ones with a black eye. She even did the pubs down Leith Walk. Somebody had spat at her once but that was the worst she'd had to endure apart from verbal abuse and she hadn't let that deter her. She was powered by the Lord and convinced that if everyone in the world stopped drinking alcohol there would be no more broken homes and no more wars.

'Can't tempt you, Betty?' asked Gerry, waving the bottle at her.

'I can enjoy myself without, thank you very much, Gerald. I don't need it.'

For tea, they had an excellent steak and kidney pie with rich brown gravy, made in Gerry's own shop, and for pudding, sherry trifle, with another wee glass of sherry on the side to help it down, as Gerry put it. He had opened a second bottle.

'I like your idea of *wee*,' said his wife.

At the end of the meal, Ina announced that she thought she would burst.

'For God's sake don't do it here!' cried Gerry. 'It'd make an awful mess of Elma's best cloth.'

'Away and loosen your stays,' advised Bunty.

Ina looked offended, but a few minutes later she went without a word to the bathroom and seemed somewhat relieved on her return.

Gerry cranked up the gramophone and put on 'Limehouse Blues'.

'Who's for a wee jig? Willa? You love dancing, don't you, hen, and your man's away?' He held out his arms to her.

Willa got up to partner him. She liked Gerry though she wasn't totally sure about him. Sometimes she thought he liked to run his hands up her back too much but maybe that didn't mean anything other than that he liked to have physical contact with people. When he was addressing Bunty or Ina he often put his hand on their arm. She noticed that he never touched his wife, not in public, anyway. Bunty said it didn't surprise her that they'd never had children. Elma was reputed to dress and undress underneath her nightgown.

After watching Gerry and Willa for a few minutes Bunty couldn't sit still. She jumped up.

'Come on, Ina! You used to like dancing.' It was in a dancehall that Ina had met Roberto Costello, the father of Tommy.

Ina, while protesting, allowed herself to be pulled up. For a heavy woman, she was light on her feet. It wasn't long before they were all laughing; the dancers, at least.

Elma and Betty decided to go to the kitchen and wash the dishes. They closed the door firmly behind them.

'Turn up the music!' cried Bunty.

It was late by the time they took the road for home.

'Nothing like a bit of family fun, eh, Willa?' said Bunty,

who was walking on one side of her, a hand on the pram. Ina
had a hand on the other side, while Willa was in the middle.
'I can't imagine how Gerry came to marry our Elma.'

'You can never understand why anybody marries anybody,'
said Ina.

Penang, Malay States
7th February, 1924

Dear Willa,
    I enclose a Menu for a dinner given to us by the
Chinese Community. (Please keep safely.)

It was a big bulky envelope this time, with a rash of brightly coloured stamps strewn across the top. She was always careful when opening the envelope not to tear the stamps.

The menu was printed on a cream-coloured folded card, measuring about six by four inches, with the crossed flags of the Union Jack and the Red Ensign at the top of the front page.

'Come and look at this,' she said to Ina and Bunty. They read over her shoulder.

DINNER GIVEN BY THE CHINESE COMMUNITY OF TAIPING
In honour of the Officers and Men of His
Majesty's Light Cruisers' Squadron
on 6th February 1924,
at the Kwong Toong Wooi Koon, Taiping

Inside, the menu was written in Chinese on the left-hand side, and English on the right-hand.

1. Chicken Soup
2. Sharks' Fins
3. Malayan Fish
4. A' La Suckling Taiping
5. Broiled Chicken
6. Fancy Rolls
7. A' La Fukien Mee
8. Duck and Lotus Seeds
9. Lichee Jelly
10. Tropical Fruits
GOD SAVE THE KING

'I wonder if the Chinese knew the words of "God Save the King",' said Bunty.

'God save Tommy's stomach,' said his mother, 'if he ate through all that lot. It never took much to make him throw up when he was wee.'

'He's a big lad now though,' said his wife.

'A' La Fukien Mee!' said Bunty. 'What on earth can that be?'

'Enough to turn anybody's stomach, I should think,' said Ina. 'The chicken might have been all right. At least it was only broiled.'

'And the duck,' added Willa.

'But lotus seeds! What in the name would they be like?'

No one had any idea.

'Still,' said Bunty, 'they were obviously wanting to do the

boys proud. That was real nice of the Chinese community.'

'Ah well, it'll be herrin' in oatmeal for us the night,' said Ina.

Willa was reading on down the letter. 'He says he burnt his mouth on some spiced meat and couldn't get the burning feeling to go even though he ate bread and drank water.'

'I knew it wouldn't do him any good, all that funny stuff,' said his mother. 'I hope he's all right.'

'He must be, mustn't he?' said Bunty. 'Otherwise he couldn't have written the letter.'

An ordinary English lunch would have been more to our liking but it was a novelty and an experience for most of the party.

'Something's dropped out of the envelope,' said Ina.

Willa picked it off the floor. It was a postcard on the back of which Tommy had written: *Burmese Girl Singing a Song on Stage*. Willa turned it over. The girl was not so much singing as writhing in a very tight, ankle-length skirt with her wrists splayed out at a funny angle. In the fingers of one hand she held a fan. Her mouth was closed.

'He seems to be having a very interesting time right enough,' said Bunty.

The classical dances are very stately but others more lively in which the performers caper and twirl and twist about. Burmese girls for walking wear a long skirt with a slit up one side but for dancing the skirt is wrapped tightly round their

legs and sewn together. This produces an effect of
amazing slimness and enables her to use the skirt
as a support while dancing, their knees being
pressed against the sides. In the posturing dances
the head and hands may be said to dance. There is
little movement of the feet but skilful use of the
hands.

'Looks like they use more than their hands?' Bunty winked.
'He's watched closely right enough.'

'Give me Scottish country dancing any day,' said Ina.

'Aye, you can't beat the "Dashing White Sergeant".' For once Bunty was in agreement with her sister. 'I'm quite fond of the "Gay Gordons" and all.'

Tommy had written screeds about the Malay Straits. Willa jumped over some of it, picking out the parts that might interest his mother and aunt.

The entertainment committee had everything well
planned for our stay and must have felt great
satisfaction when they saw the enthusiastic manner
in which the sailors accepted and enjoyed every
outing. There were trips to the Snake Temple, a run
up the Penang hills, concerts, dances, games, picnics,
swimming parties, as well as an excursion to Alor
Star, Ipoh and Taiping.

'I hope he didn't go too near the snakes,' said his mother.

'I expect he wrapped one round his neck,' said Bunty. 'A cobra, for choice. What do you say, Willa?'

'Or maybe an anaconda. I've a feeling it's even longer.'

'Might get it wrapped round twice then,' said Bunty.

Ina gave her a sour look.

I went to Taiping. We left at 6 a.m. on a ferry for Prai and were then taken by train through forty miles of plantations. The natives working in the fields were just as curious about us as we were of them. Arriving in Taiping (11 a.m.) we were met by motors that took us to the King Edward School, which had rigged up accommodation for us. We were given refreshments and everyone felt jolly and happy in the sunshine. The following day we were driven to the outskirts of the jungle and were met by a party of elephants. Half of us mounted, the others walked alongside.

'Are elephants not meant to be dangerous?' asked his mother.

'I don't know if they're *meant* to be,' said Bunty, 'but I believe they sometimes trample folk to death. They've got muckle big feet. But they wouldn't walk over our Tommy. He'd be too tough for them.'

'What do you mean by tough?'

'Nothing, Ina.'

'He says they had to watch that their legs didn't crash against the tree trunks as they went by,' said Willa. 'Or they might have got torn off.'

'God Almighty!' exclaimed his mother, placing her hand over her heart.

'I expect he's just trying to wind you up,' said Bunty. 'He likes his bit of drama, does Tommy.'

We also saw a tiger trap. It is similar to our mousetrap, the difference being that when the tiger steps on the platform to eat the bait it is shot by a rifle mounted on the trap. We weren't lucky enough to see one for ourselves.

'Tigers as well,' said Ina.

'No lions?' said Bunty. 'There must be some prowling around.'

The concert commenced at 10 p.m., after we had dined with the Burmese community (rather weird food again, but we managed to eat it, though give me good old fish and chips with salt and brown sauce any day of the week!) and continued until half-past midnight. During the singing and dancing all kinds of cigars and cigarettes, as well as drinks, were freely passed around. They were most generous.

'Want to keep in with the British, that's what it is,' said Ina, nodding her head. 'They'll know which side their bread's buttered on.'

'If they eat butter,' said Bunty.

The true Malay comes from the island of Sumatra, separated from the peninsula by the Malacca Straits. Most people probably do not know that the expression 'to run amok' is a term used when a Malay suddenly dashes down the street with a 'Kris', a large native knife, in his hand until he himself is killed.

'Oh my God,' said Ina.

'You didn't know that, did you, Ina?' said Bunty.

'Did you?' demanded Ina.

'But you'll be pleased to hear that this undesirable trait is no longer so common as Malays have not carried knives in the street since 1890,' said Willa.

'The Lord must be looking after your lad, Ina,' said Bunty. 'He must hear your cries in the night.'

Ina ignored that remark. She said, 'When all's said and done, there's nowhere like Scotland. It's bonny. And we've no snakes or tigers lurking round corners waiting to pounce on you.'

'That's more or less it,' said Willa, putting the letter back in the envelope. She thought she might take it up to the library and read it to Richard. He would be interested in the descriptions of the native villages and the flora and fauna of the jungle, which clearly Tommy's mother and aunt were not, or, at least, only marginally. They never gave her peace to read a letter right through, they had to keep interrupting.

'Fancy chumming me up to Bruntsfield, Ina?' asked Bunty. 'I've to get a fitting for my new skirt.'

'Aye, I'll do that. We could take the wee one with us.'

Willa saw them off and headed in the opposite direction.

Richard was very interested in Tommy's letter and listened attentively while Willa read it to him. She omitted only the ending about Malkie and giving mother his love and your fond husband and the kisses. They were the only customers in the café and the waitress had gone through to the back so Willa was able to read aloud without anyone listening. Not that it would have mattered if they had been; there was nothing private or intimate in it to reveal.

'He writes very well,' said Richard. 'Especially—' He stopped for Willa had given him a sharp look. He cleared his throat and went on awkwardly. 'I was only going to say, especially since he left school at fourteen, didn't you tell me?'

'So did I,' said Willa, 'leave school at fourteen. We'd no chance to do anything else.'

'I didn't mean to imply anything.'

'No, I'm sure you didn't.'

To hide his embarrassment Richard bent down and lifting up his briefcase he took out *The Scotsman*.

'There's something in here that might interest you.' The newspaper was folded back. 'The new franchise bill to give women the vote had its second reading at the House of Commons yesterday and was passed by a majority of 216.'

'That's great!' said Willa.

'Well, maybe. But it goes on to say that even its Socialist authors were doubtful about its chances of going any further as some of the MPs thought it smacked too much of the extreme feminism of the suffragettes. It was a private member's bill. My mother supports the suffragette cause,' he added.

'So do I,' said Willa. 'But how are we ever to get the vote?'

'My mother believes that you will, one day.'

'One day,' sighed Willa. One day the moon might turn blue or she might go to Penang and eat duck and lotus seeds.

'My mother says it's only a matter of time and keeping up the pressure. She says the tide turned for women with the war.'

'She sounds a strong person, your mother?'

'Oh, she is. She never gives up if she thinks something is worth fighting for.' Richard spoke with pride. 'She went out on a demonstration to support the miners. I went with her. Their conditions are deplorable. Did you know that one in six is involved in an accident *every* year? It's absolutely disgraceful, isn't it?'

'It is,' agreed Willa, feeling that she, like Richard's mother, should be doing something about it.

She picked up the menu to put it in her bag.

'It makes you think it might be worth joining the Navy,' said Richard, pointing at the menu.

'To get a Chinese meal?'

They laughed.

'You're not really considering the Navy, are you?' said Willa, though if Richard were to join he would probably start off as a commissioned officer, not as an able seaman, the way Tommy had. She would miss her chats with him if he were to go away. She'd come to depend upon him being in the library when she went in. A friendly face. A ready wave. Someone to suggest a new book. Someone to talk to, really talk to. She'd often save something up to tell Richard, something that had happened, or had crossed her mind, or she'd read in the paper and wondered what he'd think about it too. You couldn't call her exchanges with Ina and Bunty really talking. There was no point in asking either of them what they thought about Ramsay MacDonald or what the Labour

Party, now that it was in power, was going to do about unemployment.

'I don't think I'd be any use as a sailor.' He made a wry face. 'I got seasick going over to the Bass rock from North Berwick.'

She laughed. 'Anyway, you might not get to go to all those exotic places and be treated to all those banquets. This is something unusual that Tommy is on with the Special Service Squadron. A once-in-a-lifetime trip, he called it.'

'I'll have to do something. I had an interview yesterday. Junior clerk in a lawyer's office.' Richard shrugged. 'The man who got it had four children. He needed it more than I did.'

'That's generous of you, thinking that way.' Willa liked the idea that he had principles. She supposed his mother had encouraged that. She was obviously an admirable, highly principled woman, giving so much of her time to good causes; and it was nice that her son appreciated her.

'My father's managed to get a job, down in Leith, looking after a wheelwright's books. Doesn't pay much but it's better than nothing.'

'Not enough to let you go back to university?'

'Nowhere near. I've got to be self-supporting.' Richard had got some work tutoring a Heriot boy in English and Latin a couple of evenings a week but the money from that wouldn't go far. 'Still, never mind, something will turn up, as our friend Mr Micawber used to say!'

They were back on happier ground, talking about books again. Willa was keeping an eye on her watch, however, mindful of the fact that she couldn't be late every time she went to the library. Ina might start to be suspicious.

She paid for the tea today; she insisted.

'I'll do it next time then,' he said.

It was pleasing to think there'd be a next time. She put the letter and menu back in her bag and he picked up his folder from the table. He'd been writing when she arrived at the library.

'At least you're getting some time for your writing,' she said.

He nodded. 'I've started a novel.'

'You have! That's fantastic! What's it about? Or do you not want to talk about it?' Willa had read somewhere that writers often didn't like to talk about their work in progress. They felt it might make their ideas evaporate into thin air before they gelled.

'I'd rather not. I'm not sure if it's going to work out or not.'

She didn't press him.

They accompanied each other along the road though Willa kept a bit of space between them so that if they were seen they wouldn't appear to be actually *together.* He seemed to understand and didn't try to reduce the gap. They always parted halfway down Lauriston Place now; he didn't offer to escort her as far as the clock.

'See you soon!'

Willa walked on down the hill and met Bunty coming out of the Clydesdale Bank on the corner. She didn't actually see her until she'd almost bumped into her.

'Hey,' said Bunty, 'you nearly walked right into me! And me with a new pair of shoes on. Just bought them at Baird's up the street. Grey suede. What do you think?' She held up one foot and put a hand on Willa's arm to steady herself.

'They're lovely.' Willa fingered them. She often wondered how Bunty could afford so many new clothes. Ina had hinted that Mr Parkin had deep pockets. What he did to fill them was still mysterious. Bunty had said when questioned that it was something to do with money and Ina had said tartly that that was obvious, wasn't it?

'Where have you been?' said Bunty. 'You looked as if you were away in a dwam coming down the road there!'

'I was just up at the library.'

'Amazing the effect books seem to have on you, Willa!'

~ 7 ~

Singapore, Malay States
16th February, 1924

Dear Willa,
   Singapore, the chief town of the straits, situated at the tip of the Malay Peninsula, has a population of about 350,000, 7,000 of whom are European. The island was acquired for Britain in 1819 by treaty from the ruler of Jahore.

'Britain seems to have been able to snap up any country it fancied,' said Ina.

'I don't know why they did fancy it,' said Willa, her eyes travelling further down the page. 'Tommy says much of the land is low lying and swampy, which means mosquitoes, and the climate's not great. Pretty hot and steamy.'

It was certainly not that here in Edinburgh. Her bedroom was like an ice box. There was a skein of white on the window panes in the morning. The only room that was warm enough was the kitchen where they hugged the range from morning till night. There'd been heavy frost and snow all over the country and roads had been blocked. A man in Aberdeen had been found frozen to death by the roadside. In the midst of so much cold, Willa found it difficult to imagine steamy heat.

'I hope he's not got another of those heat rashes,' said Ina.
Willa read on before her mother-in-law could start
worrying about mosquitoes as well.

> It is a regular port of call for liners and a host of
> smaller craft collect the produce of the east and store
> it here. A great argument is in force as to whether it
> should become a great naval base with the view of
> protection of our colonies as Singapore is in a good
> position to guard Australia in particular.

'What would they be wanting to protect Australia for?' asked
Ina.
'They must think it could be invaded.'
'Who by?'
Willa shrugged.

> Personally I hope it does not for climactic reasons. I
> would not like to be stationed here. It has rained
> continuously since our arrival. Crocodiles lurk in the
> swamps. After killing their prey, whether man or
> beast, they do not eat the meat fresh but hide it away
> until it has gone rotten. You can buy stuffed
> crocodiles but I doubt if Mother would like one in
> her kitchen grinning at her.

'The very idea!' Ina shook her head. 'Well, I don't know – first,
sharks, now, crocodiles. They'd be safer staying on the ship.'
'But think of the fun they'd miss,' said Willa.

There is a famous hotel here called 'Raffles',
favoured by those travelling in the East. Bill and I
went in but as soon as we saw the prices we
skedaddled. We went on an interesting motor run
round the island. Some of the Jap and Chink houses
were very nice with beautifully carved furniture but
others were filthy beyond description. All kinds of
races live here, the yellow predominating. There are
many curios for sale, such as Chinese brass gods and
tea sets. After much haggling I bought a bamboo
and ivory mah-jong set. Lovely stuff, ivory. Nice to
handle.

'What in the name could that be?' asked Ina. 'Ma, whatever it
is?'

'We're going to find out,' said Willa.

'How long now till he'll be home?'

'Seven or eight months.'

His mother sighed.

Willa cocked her head. 'What's that noise? Is it Malcolm?'
She was on her feet straightaway. He was asleep in the
bedroom. But the noise was too loud for a baby to have made.

'It's Mrs MacNab,' said Ina, shaking her head. 'He's at it
again, God help her.'

'Maybe we should go and see.'

'Now listen, Willa, you stay out of this. You can't interfere
between man and wife.'

'What if he's knocking her about?'

'But even the polis don't like to butt in. Not when it's a
marital dispute.'

'So we're just supposed to sit here and not lift a hand?'

'He might lift his hand to you too, that's the trouble.'

'I wish Tommy was here. He'd go through.'

'Aye, he probably would. He's got a hot temper on him when he gets his dander up and he wouldn't stand for a woman being harmed.'

Willa went out into the lobby to listen. When the screams grew louder she opened the door and went across the landing. Ina came and stood in their doorway, cautioning her, telling her to mind herself.

Suddenly the MacNabs' door flew open and out came Lecky, the oldest boy. 'He's going to kill my ma,' he shouted.

Willa went straight in. Mrs MacNab was in the bedroom cowering against the wall, her body buckled. Blood was running down her face. Her husband was facing her, his puny right hand balled into a fist. He's mad, thought Willa, stark raving.

'Leave her alone!' she cried.

'You bloody well leave us alone! Bitch!' He swung round towards her and she ducked and ran out of the room.

The other children were bunched up in the kitchen. Their eyes looked glazed.

'Go next door!' she told them, taking two of them by the shoulders and propelling them. The others followed as if in a trance. 'Go and see Granny Costello. She'll look after you. Take them in, Ina,' she said, once she'd got them as far as the landing, 'and don't open the door. I'm going for the police.'

She ran then, as fast as she could, down the stairs and out into the street, hoping desperately she might find a policeman on the beat instead of having to go to the station. They patrolled the area regularly. As she rounded the clock she saw one standing on the opposite corner chatting to the postie.

She yelled across to him and he came hurrying over.

'What's up, hen?"

He began to run when she yelled out that a man was murdering a woman on her stair. He went ahead of her, taking two stairs at a time, his boots clumping on the steps. At the top they paused to listen. There was no noise now coming from the MacNabs' flat and their door was shut.

The constable pulled the bell hard, then rapped with his knuckles.

'Go away and bloody well leave us alone!' Mr MacNab's voice came from the back of the door. 'I don't want to have to tell you again, you interfering bitch, or I'll give you what for too.'

Willa marvelled, for normally the man had such a quiet, almost feeble voice.

This time the constable banged on the door with the flat of his hand, and roared, 'Open up in the name of the law!'

Nothing happened.

'I'm warning you. This is the police here. I'll break your bloody door down if necessary.'

The door opened and Willa saw, standing there, the pathetic little man that she was accustomed to passing on the stairs. He didn't seem capable of swatting a fly. He didn't look at her.

'May we come in, sir?' asked the constable, pushing past without waiting for answer. 'I would like to interview your wife.'

'She's in the bedroom,' said Willa.

Mrs MacNab had slid down against the wall and was

sitting with her back to it looking like a broken doll.

'I'll call an ambulance,' said the policeman. 'And, you, sir, will please go into the kitchen and remain there and not attempt to leave.'

Mr MacNab meekly went.

When the ambulance arrived Willa said she would go with it to keep Mrs MacNab company. She went through first to tell her mother-in-law what was happening.

'And am I supposed to look after all this lot?' demanded Ina. 'Help my kilt! I've only got one pair of hands.'

She had Malcolm in her arms who, today, as luck would have it, was not in such a happy mood as usual. He was teething and one cheek was bright red, and he kept arching his back, which was making life even more difficult for his grandmother. She was having a struggle to control him. He was strong for his age. Like a wee bull, his Great-aunt Bunty had once remarked. The five MacNab children were sitting round the kitchen table with the air of startled rabbits caught in the headlamps of a motor car.

'I'm afraid so. Can you manage?'

'I'll have to, won't I? Maybe Elma'll look in. She said she might after she'd done her Saturday shopping.'

The ambulance bore Mrs MacNab and Willa the short distance up the street to the Infirmary while the constable led Mr MacNab off to the police station.

Willa sat on a hard bench in an overheated corridor that smelt of disinfectant, listening to the various hospital noises around her, the clink of instruments, the running of water, the tap-tap of the nurses' white-shod feet as they moved up and down, the murmur of voices talking of life and death, or so she imagined, but perhaps they were only asking a patient if he needed a bedpan.

She wished she'd brought her book with her but she'd been in too big a rush to think of it. She was reading *Sense and Sensibility*. She sat thinking about the Dashwood sisters and their troubles. It seemed such a gentle world that they inhabited. A man might have a nasty side to him like the calculating Willoughby who broke girls' hearts without any feeling of remorse but there was no actual violence involved. None of the women got beaten up and given black eyes or had miscarriages. But then who knows what had gone on underneath the surface of those genteel lives?

She was lost in the early nineteenth-century world of Jane Austen, where large houses stood in parkland and mothers wrung their hands in anguish over their daughters' failure to make good marriages and thus be assured of financial security for the rest of their lives, when she became aware that a nurse was standing in front her. A sister, to judge from the starched hat and the starchy manner. Willa got to her feet.

'Are you a relative of Mrs MacNab's?'

'No, just a neighbour.'

'Does she have any relatives?'

'I'm afraid I don't know. Well, apart from her husband and children of course. Is she all right?'

'Depends what you mean by "all right". She'll live. She's got a broken nose and three broken ribs.'

'Can I see her? Would she like to see me?' Willa had no idea if she would. They had never exchanged more than a few words in passing, often about the weather.

'She's asleep. We've given her a sedative to quieten her. She was very agitated. Worried about her children. Five, I believe?'

'Yes, five.'

'We may have to arrange for them to be taken into care until she is fit enough to look after them. Where are they now?'

'With my mother-in-law.'

'Would it be possible for you to keep them overnight until arrangements are made?'

'I suppose so. Well, I mean we don't have much room. But, yes, that would be all right.' Willa thought she'd like to feel someone would look after Malcolm if she were ever to be in a similar situation, though she couldn't imagine Tommy raising his hand to her. Not that they'd lived all that long together of course. He'd said that was the good thing about his coming and going: it was like being on honeymoon every time. There'd be no chance of their marriage getting stale. 'Look at Aunt Elma and Gerry!' he'd said. 'Married nearly forty years and never a day apart! It wouldn't do me.'

Willa had been a little hurt that he had linked the two of them to Elma and Gerry. Also, it would have been nice to think that he'd hated parting from her as much as she had him. Of course he'd been excited about his round-the-world trip. Pauline thought men were different from women in that way. They could switch on and off more easily. 'Out of sight, out of mind.' 'Or else,' Willa had countered, 'absence makes the heart grow fonder.' Did she believe it?

Walking home down Lauriston Place from the hospital she thought of Richard, wondering if he would be in the library writing. She had hoped to go herself today but there would be no chance of that now.

Elma was in the house. She had been given Malcolm to hold

while Ina made lentil soup to feed the children. She had a towel over her shoulder and she was holding the baby as if he were a stick of dynamite.

'Thank goodness, Willa!' she said, thrusting her charge into his mother's arms. 'I could scarce keep hold of him, he's that strong. Like a wee right bullock, as Bunty says.'

One of the little girls had wet herself, Willa saw. There was a puddle under the table. She gave Malcolm to his grandmother and took the child into the bathroom and asked if she'd have any clean knickers in her house. Mary shook her head. She didne know, she said. The policeman had given Willa a set of keys to the MacNabs' flat he'd found lying on the kitchen table so Willa went through to look. She was appalled at the poorness and shabbiness of the children's clothing. In the end she put a pair of her own knickers on Mary and pinned them at the waist.

When Ina and Elma heard that the children were to stay the night they almost threw a fit and Willa had to hush them and say, 'The *children*!' Elma said she was terribly sorry she couldn't stay and help but she had to get back for Gerry's lunch.

'I thought you said he was playing golf?' said Ina.

'I'm not sure when he finishes, though.'

Elma departed.

After they'd eaten the soup, Willa suggested a walk across the Meadows, thinking that a blow of fresh air would be good for the children. They were still looking stunned by what had gone on, too stunned to ask where their mother and father were. Willa told them that their mummy was in hospital but she was getting on fine and would be home in a day or two. She did not mention their daddy.

She took the two-year-old on the end of Malcolm's pram and the others trailed along behind, the two youngest clinging to Ina's hands. They were calling her Granny. Malcolm was not pleased at having to share his carriage with another and girned all the way. And he kept pulling his mitts off so that he could get at his cheeks with his nails. He'd drawn blood in a couple of places.

'Keep your pawkies on, Malcolm!' Willa snapped at him, her patience beginning to frizzle out.

He paid no attention.

'We must look as if we're on an outing from an orphanage,' said Ina. The MacNab children's coats were missing buttons, their socks full of holes, and their shoes held together with string. 'I hope we don't meet anybody we know.'

They called in briefly on Bunty who, as they had hoped, gave each of the children a lollipop, except for Malcolm, which gave him something else to complain about.

'I'll have one though,' said Ina. 'I could do with a wee sweetener.'

'You've got your hands full there,' commented Bunty, as she stood in the shop doorway watching them set off again.

Going up Middle Meadow Walk, they met Richard.

For a moment he stood, stock-still, on the path, his eyes goggling, as he took in two small children in a pram and four others with granny behind, all sucking lollipops. Willa did not speak. Neither did he. He stood to the side to allow them to pass.

'Thanks, son,' said Ina, taking out her lollipop. Her tongue had turned green. 'Nice manners,' she commented in a loud voice, as they continued on their way.

Willa did not look round.

So, one way and another, they managed to put in the day. By early evening the children were exhausted, even Malcolm. The MacNabs were bathed and put to sleep, head to toe, in Ina's bed-settee, which had first had a rubber sheet spread over its mattress. Ina was to sleep with Willa.

The dishes cleared away, the two women settled down by the kitchen range. Willa took up her book, Ina, the *Edinburgh Evening News*.

'We must ask Tommy to buy us a wireless when he gets back,' said his mother. 'Elma says there's some great programmes on it.' Gerry had recently bought a set. 'She heard Dame Nellie Melba singing the other day.'

Within minutes, Ina was fast asleep and snoring, the newspaper in danger of sliding off her knee.

They went to bed early and the next morning were relieved, yet a little sad, when a policeman arrived with a lady in a grey serge coat to take the MacNabs away. The children cried and tried to hang on to Willa and Ina. But, as Willa was forced to say, it was out of the question for them to keep them. By the time the children's cries had died away down the stairs she felt wrung out.

She went through to Ina's room and stripped the wet sheets from the bed. Then she put on the copper boiler, in spite of it being Sunday. Ina wasn't as bothered as her sister Elma would have been about working on the Sabbath. They agreed that they would give church a miss that morning. To push the pram down the hill to St Cuthbert's seemed rather daunting. They were both tired.

They'd got married in St Cuthbert's, Willa and Tommy, she

in a navy-blue suit and a little navy hat with a half-veil both of which she'd bought in Patrick Thomson's on North Bridge, he in his naval uniform; and they had promised the minister that they'd bring up any children of their union to be God-fearing and adherents of the Church of Scotland. He hadn't known there was one on the way already; there had been no need to disclose that. Pauline had been their bridesmaid, Gerry the best man. A photograph of the four of them stood on the dresser. It had been a quiet affair, with the half-dozen of Tommy's family and only two from Willa's, her Aunt Lily and Uncle Alec, who lived on the Clyde coast in Ardrossan. Uncle Alec had given her away. Aunt Lily had had a few words with her the day before.

'I hope you're going to be able to make this marriage work. He's too handsome for a husband, if you want to know what I think.' Willa had not, of course, but was hearing anyway, with as much patience as she could muster. 'I feel I can speak plainly to you, with your poor mother having passed away. She'd have wanted me to speak to you. He's too flash. You'll never have a minute's peace. Of course I can understand you falling for him. He certainly knows how to turn on the charm!'

'It's too late now, Aunt Lily,' Willa had said with a little smile. She had not told her, though, that she was pregnant.

Mrs MacNab refused to press charges against her husband so he was to be released and allowed home. The policeman said there was nothing they could do if she didn't charge him. They'd given him a stern warning and had to hope that might have an effect. But interfering in marital disputes was tricky.

Well, you never knew exactly what was going on, did you? Often it was not as one-sided as it seemed. Willa looked at him.

'You're not suggesting that it might be Mrs MacNab who starts the fights, are you?'

'Keep the heid, dear! I'm not suggesting anything. It's just that some women seem to provoke their men as if they want him to—'

'Break their nose?'

He held up his hands. 'I'm not saying it's right.'

'Good.'

'If there's any more trouble let us know.'

They didn't hear Mr MacNab returning. He must have come stealthily, during the night. In the morning, they heard his hacking cough.

Mrs MacNab was allowed home from hospital after a week, with two blackened eyes and a large plaster covering her nose, and the next day the children were ushered back up the stairs by the lady in the grey serge coat. Willa watched them go inside and the door close behind them. For better or worse, the MacNabs were reunited.

~ 8 ~

Fremantle, Western Australia
8th March, 1924

Dear Willa,
*   The squadron was met on arrival by several small*
pleasure steamers, one of which displayed a notice
saying 'Coo-ee City of Perth entertainments. Goat
races nightly.' We were much amused. By the way,
you are probably unaware that coo-ee is a long
drawn out call used in the bush and can be heard a
great distance away, which would be very handy
should one get lost.

'It sounds like the back-of-beyond.' said Elma, who had popped in to see how they were getting on and if there had been any more dramas at the MacNabs'. There had not, or none that they knew about. All seemed quiet on that front, for the moment. Uneerily quiet. They couldn't even hear the children when they listened at the door and Ina had begun to wonder if he might not have murdered the lot of them. But they'd surely have heard that?

Elma had been at the hairdresser's up the road having a perm. Her hair was screwed into tight curls against her head and when she'd asked them what they thought Ina had said that she looked like a flattened golliwog, which hadn't pleased her. She still smelt of the perm solution.

'Goat races!' said Elma. 'I mean to say!'

'We have dog races,' Willa pointed out. Elma disapproved of Bunty frequenting them so that subject was allowed to drop.

'I hope Tommy's not planning on going into the bush,' said Ina. 'You wouldn't like your daddy to do that, would you, Malkie? No, you would not.' She was dandling him on her knee as usual.

'I don't suppose he will and if he did I'm sure he wouldn't get lost.' Willa wondered if her mother-in-law knew what the bush was. She had read an article about it in a geographical magazine, which reminded her that she must go to the library today. She'd finished her books and she couldn't bear not to have a book on the go.

'Gerry got lost in a maze once,' said Elma. 'He had to shout his head off before anyone heard him.'

'I've often wondered what happened to his head,' said Ina. 'Pity he didn't know how to shout coo-ee.'

Tommy's mother was in fine fettle this afternoon. Willa resumed reading before Elma could retaliate.

> *The people of Perth and Fremantle are being very good to us lads and making us feel welcome by putting on all manner of entertainments. There is a dance laid on for the squadron at the Town Hall every night of our stay. They're making sure we won't be bored!*

'Every night?' echoed Elma.

'There's a lot of them, about 3,000,' Willa told her. 'Maybe they can't all go the same night.'

'They'd be tramping on each other's feet,' put in Ina.

'Where do they get their partners from?' asked Elma. 'It's only men on the boats, isn't it?'

'Well, what do you think, Elma!' said Ina. 'You ken fine there's no women in the Navy. The men won't be dancing together! They'll get their partners in the *town*. They won't come out of the bush shouting coo-ee.'

'How was I to know? You said Tommy was always writing about black women.'

'They won't invite *black* women to their dances. For goodness' sake, woman, have a bit of wit!'

> *One is ill-advised to venture too far into the Australian bush on one's own. Many have perished for their foolishness.*

'Tommy's no fool,' said his mother.

Elma looked as if she might be going to comment so Willa read on.

> *A trip up the Swan River from Fremantle took us through picturesque scenery, past many resorts given over to yachting and other aquatic sports, to the city of Perth. It is a fine city with electric trams and many attractive buildings and shops as well as zoological gardens.*

'There's nothing wrong with our zoo,' said Elma.

'Nobody said there was,' said Ina. 'Could we just hear what Tommy's got to say, if it's all the same to you?'

'He says the foundation stone of the city was laid by

Captain Stirling on 12th August 1829,' said Willa.

'So the British didn't have to capture it in a battle this time?' said Ina.

'It must have belonged to somebody before 1829,' said Willa. 'Probably the aborigines.'

'Who were they when they were at home?' asked Elma.

'Natives,' I suppose' said Ina.

> *Beautiful weather has prevailed throughout our stay. The climate would appear to be agreeable all year round, somewhat kinder than our windy city. One can enjoy more outdoor life. I think this would be a great place to live and bring up children. Either here, or South Africa.*

'I hope he's joking,' said his mother.

'I expect he is,' said Willa. 'Anyway, he's in the Navy, isn't he? He doesn't actually *live* anywhere.'

'This is his home,' said his mother, miffed. 'And it's not windy all the time in Edinburgh. You're not going to go away and live in some foreign country with black men, are you, Malkie? No, you are not. Your granny wouldn't let you. This is where you belong.'

'You've got that child spoiled rotten, Ina,' said her sister.

'What do you know about bringing up children, Elma?'

'That's it,' said Willa, 'except for the usual at the end. Can I get you a cup of tea, Aunt Elma?' Elma liked to be given the title, whereas Bunty did not.

'No, thanks, I'll need to be on my way.' Elma was annoyed; Ina's last remark had needled her. She addressed herself to

Willa. 'I thought I'd bake some flies' cemeteries for Gerry. They're his favourite. He likes home-made.'

When she'd gone, Ina said, 'Elma can be awfully thick so she can. The questions she asks! And she likes to put on that pan-drop accent of hers. As if being married to a master butcher was the be-all and end-all! Of course she never was very bright at the school, not a patch on Bunty or me, though I say so myself. We always got prizes.'

The three sisters each had different accents, which interested Willa. Elma's was on the plummy side, consciously put on; Bunty's was the most Scottish in that she liked to say 'didne' and 'wouldne' and 'dinne ken'; and Ina's the most straightforward. They'd been brought up by a mother who had wanted them to speak as pure English as possible and had frowned on playground speech being brought into her house. She'd sent them to elocution lessons. Bunty said she'd have been better off using the money to put more food in their mouths. Ina referred to her mother as having been 'ladylike'. She had put great emphasis on holding your knife and fork correctly and putting your pinkie out to the side when you drank a cup of tea. (None of them did that now, though.) They'd lived up at Bruntsfield in a two-bedroom flat and their father had been a brewery foreman. Their mother had died before Ina married, which Elma said was probably just as well. She would not have approved of Ina's choice of Roberto Costello, who sold ice cream for a living. He'd worked in his uncle's shop in Leith Walk.

'I came down in the world when I married, there's no denying it,' Ina had told Willa and when Willa had said that she must have been in love she had looked uncomfortable.

'Aye, Elma can get up my back at times,' sighed Ina.

'I thought I'd go to the library,' said Willa.

'Malkie and I might chum you, for the walk. It's quite a nice day. The sun was out earlier.'

'It's a bit of a push uphill.'

'But you can push the pram going up, can't you? And I'll take it coming down.'

'Well, are you sure? You might rather go across the Meadows. We couldn't take the pram into the library.'

'We'll wait outside. You won't be long, will you? You've only to change two books. And we can walk across the Meadows on the way back.'

They fetched their coats and Malcolm was fed into his knitted woollen pram suit, trousers, coat, bonnet, mittens. He was less pliant these days and he hated being dressed. He struggled throughout as Willa forced his legs down the trouser legs, his arms into the sleeves, and his hands into the pawkies. She was red hot and bothered by the time she'd finished.

'He's getting to be quite a lad,' said his granny.

He didn't like being strapped into the pram, either.

'Reminds me of his daddy,' said his granny. 'Doesn't give in easily.'

They were struggling with the pram straps outside on the pavement when Mr MacNab came along. He was walking with his head down and would have gone by without acknowledging them had Ina allowed it.

'Good afternoon, Mr MacNab,' she said in a voice loud enough to carry across the street. 'And how is Mrs MacNab the day? We haven't seen her for a while.'

He muttered something and made to go round them into the stair but Ina was not ready to move out of the way yet. She was standing in front of the open stair door.

'I hope her nose is coming on?'

He nodded.

'Tell her if there's anything she needs just to tap on our door. We'll be there right away.'

This time he did not so much nod as jerk his head and Ina let him pass. Willa wasn't sure that speaking to him like that would help, except that it might let him know that they had their eye on him. Ina had given up the idea that they shouldn't interfere between man and wife. She told Willa that she was lucky she had a man who would never lift his hand to her and Willa had said she'd hit him back if he did, while knowing that if it ever came to that she'd lose out. Tommy was a lot stronger than she was. Ina had laughed.

Finally, with Malcolm restrained, they set off up the hill, Willa hoping that Ina might change her mind halfway up and turn back. Her mother-in-law plodded stolidly on and Willa resigned herself to the fact that she was going to stand guard outside the library. Not that Ina would think she was actually standing *guard*. And not that Willa was going to be up to anything in the library. But she had been looking forward to a chat with Richard. She hadn't seen him since that day in Middle Meadow Walk and she wanted to explain about the gaggle of children. He surely wouldn't have thought they were all hers, would he? Did it matter if he did? It was nothing to him, one way or the other. Nevertheless, she wished to explain.

They reached the library.

'Are you sure you want to hang about?' asked Willa. 'There's a bit of a breeze.'

'I've got my hat and gloves on, and so has Malkie, good boy, haven't you?' He'd kept his pawkies on today.

He grinned, showing his solitary tooth.

'You mustn't forget to tell Tommy about his tooth when you write,' said Ina.

'I won't,' promised Willa. 'I might be a few minutes. I like to take my time choosing.'

'That's all right. We can walk up and down if we feel the cold. You go on in and don't worry about us.'

Willa went in and as she was returning the books she glanced around and saw Richard at a table, with his exercise book in front of him, a fountain pen in his hand. He waved. She lifted her hand just a couple of inches, in case she'd been followed in, though she had not, for she was keeping a watchful eye over her shoulder.

She went into an empty bay. A couple of minutes later, he joined her.

'Hello, Willa, nice to see you. It's a while since I have.'

'I know. That day on the Meadows—'

'Oh yes?'

'Those weren't all my children. Only the baby.'

'I didn't think they could be.'

She told him about the MacNabs. A woman was giving them cold looks. They retreated further into the bay and dropped their voices.

'Have you heard from your husband again?'

'I got a letter this morning.'

'Where's he got to now on his journey?'

'Australia. I'll tell you about it another time. I can't go for a cup of tea today, I'm afraid.'

'I was hoping—'

'My mother-in-law's out there with the baby.'

Willa realised, even as she was saying this, that she was letting Richard know that her meetings with him were clandestine. But he must have guessed that already. For she was a married woman, after all. But if he had guessed, what did he think about her reasons for meeting him secretly? She said.

'Can you recommend me something? I haven't got much time.'

'Let me think.'

Willa was glancing from her watch to the door.

'There's a new woman writer I've found, or rather my mother has. She's very well read, my mother. It would be nice if you could meet her sometime.'

Willa made a murmuring sound. She could not conceive of ever being introduced to Richard's mother.

'So this new writer?' she said, wanting to urge him on. He enjoyed telling her about books and giving his advice and he liked to take his time, which she appreciated, but he would not be able to appreciate how limited her time was, reduced to stolen fragments, away from family ties, two of which were waiting outside on the pavement at this very moment.

'Well, she's not exactly new,' Richard went on, 'just to us, mother and me. She's from New Zealand, or was. She died last year, quite young, only mid-thirties. TB.'

'I'm sorry,' said Willa, thinking of her own mother.

'Her name's Katherine Mansfield. She wrote short stories. Would you be interested?'

Willa nodded.

'Let's see if we can find anything in of hers. M. We'll need to go back a bit.'

She followed him round the bays. They passed the unsympathetic librarian, who stared at her. Willa felt that she was attracting too much attention by being seen so often with Richard. She would have to take more care in future. Formerly, she'd enjoyed the privacy and anonymity of the library. It was fortunate, though, that this was territory where Tommy's family did not venture. Bunty liked to read, cheap paperback romances mostly, and magazines which she stocked in her own shop. Elma read *Woman's Weekly* and the church magazine.

'Here we are!' said Richard. 'Mansfield! Katherine. *Bliss*! Nice title, isn't it?' He took it from the shelf and gave it to her. 'Does it appeal to you?'

'I'll take it.'

'Good. How about Rebecca West?'

Willa had not heard of her.

'She's not Scottish but she lived in Edinburgh. Her book *The Judge* is set here.'

There were so many writers, so many books waiting to be read that Willa felt dizzy at the thought. Would there be enough time in life?

They went back round the bays, re-passing the librarian she did not like. They were standing perusing the spines looking for 'West' when Willa heard a familiar voice behind her saying her name.

She spun round to see Pauline's mother.

'Your baby's been sick all over his pram cover, made a right mess he has,' said Mrs Cant, her eyes going past Willa to rest on Richard. 'Tommy's mother sent me in to fetch you.'

~ 9 ~

Adelaide,
South Australia
14th March, 1924

Dear Willa,
   We anchored for four days in Albany on the way
here, during which time all the ships were freshly
painted. Do we look smart now? We certainly do!
On our arrival there, each ship was presented with
a kangaroo as a pet! Ours has been named Tommy
though, as you can imagine, I am not over the
moon about that. But there are a few Tommies on
board amongst the 470 men so I cannot take it
personally.

'Still,' said Ina, 'it wasn't very nice of them. Calling a kangaroo Tommy!'

'How in the name can you keep a kangaroo on board a ship?' Bunty wanted to know. 'Some of the things those sailors get up to are beyond me.'

Willa said she thought the poor animal would probably prefer to be on dry land.

'I expect it's a laugh for the sailors having a kangaroo hopping about the deck,' said Bunty, getting up to demonstrate.

'Bunty!' said Ina, shaking her head.

We plunged into the Great Australian Bight on leaving Albany, a crossing that has an evil reputation. We certainly rolled a bit due to the heavy swell but it was not too bad and I came to the conclusion that seas have their good times as well as their bad.

'Like folk,' said Bunty.

'I hope the kangaroo wasn't seasick,' said Ina.

So now we are in Adelaide, a beautiful city, well laid out on modern lines with the streets running at right angles. It is surrounded by parks and has a fine race course, zoological and botanical gardens.

A piece of paper drifted down to the floor.

'You've dropped something,' said Ina, picking it up.

'It seems to be a cutting from an Adelaide newspaper,' said Willa, taking it from her.

AMONG THE BLUEJACKETS
Dance at the Palais
PRETTY GIRLS AND CHARMING FROCKS

Scores of petty officers and blue jackets from the ships of the British Special Service Squadron had their first experience of how Adelaide girls can dance, at the Palais Royal, North Terrace, last night. The party was arranged by a committee of forty-one hostesses, who had gone to endless trouble to make

sure their guests had a good time. If 'Jack's the boy
for work' he's also 'the boy for play' and he – every
single one of them – dances as to the manner born.

'They're not telling us anything we didn't know!' said Bunty.
'Jack can play all right! And to the manner born. Our Jack the
lad has never needed any lessons.'

Ina ignored that, saying, 'Imagine, forty-one hostesses!
What could they all be doing?'

'Looking after the boys. Making sure they have a good
time. Finding nice partners for them.' Bunty rolled her eyes
and when Ina glared at her she said, 'Well, you canne dance
on your own, can you?'

The Palais was a festive scene with its myriad of
coloured lanterns and balloons, and the floor was
thronged every time Mr Val Royal and his orchestra
struck up the latest dance tune. Huge punkahs
swayed to and fro above the heads of the dancers,
and coloured lights gave a kaleidoscopic effect and
changed the frocks of the girls to all the hues of the
rainbow in turn. Wherever the lads in blue may go,
they will nowhere see a prettier array of girls than
those with whom they danced in Adelaide. There
were some charming frocks worn and dozens of
bobbed and shingled heads were to be seen.

'I'm sure our girls at the Palais could give them a run for their
money,' said Bunty.

Willa doubted it. The girls in Adelaide sounded as if they

could be in pictures. She put her hand up to her hair and again wondered if she should get it bobbed, but then she remembered how Tommy had loved to run his hands through it.

'He'll have been getting up to a few high jinks there no doubt,' remarked Bunty.

'What on earth's a punkah?' asked Ina.

Nobody gave her an answer.

> *Variety was lent to the party by the clever turn at the piano of Mr Sherman, from the Majestic Theatre, who imitated a grand organ, a musical box and a Russian pianist playing a well-known ditty concerning bananas. Mr John Fisher sang 'Shipmate o' mine' and was encored.*

'Yes, *we've got no bananas*,' sang Ina, surprising them.

'Bravo!' cried Bunty. 'What's the brave boy himself got to say about all that dancing?'

Willa went back to the letter.

> *Nine hundred girls were present by special invitation and I should think they were carefully selected – a real bevy of beauty, by any standards, adorned with gorgeous dresses of all colours and styles. An excellent supper was served.*

'Too bad if you're plain,' said Willa. 'You get left out.'

'That's the way of the world,' said Bunty.

'I'm glad they fed them,' said his mother. 'Tommy can't go without his food.'

'No, he can't, can he?' said Willa. He liked to be fed on demand, as his son did.

'He doesn't feel well if he doesn't eat,' said his mother.

'Oh, and would you believe it, two nights later they went to yet another dance!' said Willa.

'God help us,' said Bunty, 'it's a wonder their feet weren't wore out!'

'Tommy's got good feet,' said his mother.

> *The next night's dance was held at Port Adelaide, halfway between Semaphore Anchorage and Adelaide. There were about 4,000 on the floor. A buffet was set out on the quay alongside the ships for those who were on duty on board. A dance band was in attendance and before long there was dancing in progress on the quay as well as in the hall. You may easily guess that there weren't many left aboard! A fantastic evening was had by one and all.*

Bunty began to sing 'All the nice girls love a sailor'.

'I want to hear what Tommy has to say.' Ina glowered at her.

'One thing, you don't have to worry about your boy being eaten by crocodiles in Adelaide,' said Bunty. 'He's obviously having a whale of a time instead! Get it?' Neither Willa nor Ina laughed. 'He'll be coming back with a swelled head. As long as no other parts of him get swelled up.'

'At times, Bunty, I think you need your mouth washed out with carbolic,' said Ina. 'That wasn't a very nice thing to say in front of Willa. Or me, either,' she added on reflection.

Willa had got up and put the letter on the table and turned her back on it. There were further screeds about the charms of Adelaide but she couldn't care less about Adelaide. It could vanish into the bottom of the Pacific Ocean as far as she was concerned, taking its shingle-headed girls and punkahs with it. A quick spin of the globe showed her that it should be the Indian Ocean. Well, Indian Ocean, then. Either would do. There would be sharks hunting around in both, with wide open jaws and large teeth, ready to snap up tasty morsels. The globe showed her that Tommy was on the other side of the world now, as far away from her as he could possibly get.

'Och, dinne take on, Willa hen,' said Bunty. 'He'll just be having a wee bit of fun. You canne grudge him that, can you? What would you expect, with all that temptation lined up in front of him?'

Willa shrugged. She knew Tommy wouldn't be lying in his berth reading a book while the others were out frolicking.

'Any road,' Bunty went on, 'they'll be on to the next place by now and have left the girls in Adelaide behind. He's not going to be bringing one of them home.'

Willa knew that to be true but just the thought of him in the arms of a girl in a charming frock with sleek bobbed hair disturbed her. While he was dancing he would have forgotten her; and maybe even after he'd left the dance floor. She saw him dancing with a girl in a wispy-thin dress along the quay, leading her into the shadows, the strains of the band following them. She saw his hands moving down the girl's back, his mouth closing in on her ear as he sang to her. *I will be your sweetheart*...She saw the girl arch her long slender neck and her carmine-red lips part...

Ina had been creaking about on her chair. Her stays were obviously bothering her. 'I'm sure Tommy will remember he's a married man.'

Bunty snorted.

'Are you trying to say he wouldn't?' demanded his mother.

'I'm not saying anything. I just ken men. Especially when they're on the loose.'

'I don't know what's got into you today, Bunty. You're in a right funny mood and you're being very annoying. I'm sure Willa thinks so and all, don't you, Willa?'

'I'm going to the library,' Willa said. 'Malcolm's asleep. Can I leave him, Ina?'

'Any time, dear, you know that. Don't need to ask.'

'I'll chum you part way along the road, Willa,' said Bunty. 'I'm going up to the Infirmary to visit old Mrs McKinley. They've taken her in at last. She's been waiting ages. They say there's fifteen hundred on the waiting list.'

'That's a scandal,' said Ina. 'What's she in for?'

'She's had her insides out so I said I'd visit her. She's one of my regulars and she's got nobody else.'

'I wondered who the daffodils were for,' said Ina. Bunty had left a bunch on the dresser. 'I didn't think they'd be for us.'

Bunty lifted the flowers.

Walking up the road she said to Willa, 'I'm sorry if I annoyed you, love.'

'It's all right. I know what Tommy's like. A girl in every port, isn't that what they say?' It was what her Aunt Lily had said the night before the wedding. 'There'll be temptation waiting for him every time they dock,' Aunt Lily had added. She was a religious woman who liked to speak of sin and redemption. 'He'll come back to you, though,' said Bunty.

'I suppose.'

'Of course he will!'

'He's got to come back to his mother, hasn't he?'

'I have riled you.'

'It was the letter. Why does he send me a cutting like that?'

'He doesn't think, that's why. He's kind of naive. He's having a good time so he's going to let the world know. Men!'

Willa looked at Bunty. 'You do seem to be in a funny mood today?'

'I quarrelled with Harold last night.'

'Mr Parkin?'

'He wants me to marry him.'

'But you don't want to?'

'No, and when I told him so off he went in the huff. Why can't he just let things be? We're doing fine as we are. Three months living together and I wouldn't be able to stick the sight of him.'

'I expect he'll come back.'

Bunty sighed. 'Anyway, talking of men, what about your Richard?'

'He's not *mine*.'

'Mrs Cant said she'd seen you with him in the library.'

'That means nothing.'

'Not to Mrs Cant it doesn't.'

'I hope she doesn't say anything to Ina.'

'I warned her not to. I told her she'd just make trouble for nothing. It is nothing, is it?'

'Of course it is. I've never done anything but talk about books with Richard, I swear I haven't.'

'I believe you so don't get steamed up. But I think he's fallen for you. Seriously. He came in to the shop the other day to buy a paper so I took him through to the back for a wee cup of tea. He couldn't stop talking about you. He's a right nice lad.'

'Bunty, you know I'm married.'

'Aye, I reminded him of that and he went away looking sorry for himself.'

'He needs a job. He's got nothing to do except read books.'

'Of course I would understand if you were wanting a bit of excitement, with your man away so long. After all, you're young and you've got feelings.'

They'd reached the Infirmary gate.

'Give my best wishes to Mrs McKinley,' said Willa.

Her steps began to quicken as she turned into George IV Bridge. Before going into the library she glanced around in case Mrs Cant might be loitering and would follow her in.

She saw him straightaway, at his usual table, with his exercise book open in front of him and his fountain pen in his hand. The sight reassured her. She smiled and he waved to her. She returned her borrowed books and went to the start of the shelves, hoping to find *Persuasion*. It was there. She was holding it in her hands when he joined her.

'So it's in today. How did you like *Bliss*?'

'We could go for a cup of tea if you like and I'll tell you then?' She was looking forward to discussing it with him.

He said that he would like to. 'Will we go and see if that Rebecca West book is in?'

They went right round to 'W' and found *The Judge*. Willa was spending less time browsing these days but she accepted that there wasn't time for everything.

The nice librarian was on the check-out counter. 'Is that your husband home on leave?'

Willa found it an odd question. The woman must have recognised Richard, with him being almost a daily visitor to the library. Maybe the woman was just curious and wanted to draw her out. She blushed, anyway, and was annoyed with herself. 'No, he's still away. Richard's a friend, a friend of the family.'

Richard was waiting for her outside on the pavement. They would have to stop doing this or else start being more careful. But how could she say that to Richard? It would imply that she was reading more into their meetings than existed. She was glad when they reached the café and were tucked away inside. She was sure Mrs Cant wouldn't waste her money in cafés.

'What did you think of Katherine Mansfield then?'

'Oh, I liked her stories. They're quite different, aren't they.' She often found it difficult to say exactly how she felt about a book.

'Bliss is an interesting word, don't you agree?' he said. 'I was discussing it with my mother.'

Willa looked at him with surprise. She couldn't imagine Tommy discussing bliss with anybody! And certainly not with his mother.

'And what did you think?' she asked.

'We decided it meant something even more than being happy. It's like a state of complete and utter contentment.'

Willa was thinking that she'd had blissful moments with Tommy after he'd made love to her, but only after they were married. Before that, although she'd been carried away by his lovemaking, an edge of anxiety had hovered to trouble her. A worry that he might make her pregnant even though she was trying to take elementary precautions. A worry that he might get bored with her or think her cheap because she'd given in to him and dump her.

'We agreed that our cat is in a state of bliss after he's been fed and he's sitting in front of the fire purring like a steam engine!'

Willa smiled at the image. Perhaps they should get a cat for Malcolm. It would be good for a boy to have an animal and a dog would be impossible in their cramped flat. She didn't think Ina would agree, though.

'By the way,' said Richard, 'my mother thinks you might like Willa Cather.'

'You've told your mother about me?' said Willa, alarmed.

'You don't mind, do you? I just said I'd met this nice girl in the library and we talk about books. My mother understands, since she likes to do that herself.'

'You seem close to your mother?'

'Oh, I am. I'm closer to her than to my father, I'm afraid. I've never been able to talk to him in the same way. He didn't like it when I chose to do English Literature at university – he blamed my mother's influence. He wanted me to go for law or medicine. Good old Edinburgh traditional professions!'

'Are you the only son?'

He nodded. He told her he had an older sister who was married to a doctor and living in London. 'She's more conventional, like my father.'

'Your mother's not?'

'Well, I told you – she's a suffragette, a campaigner. Against all kinds of injustice.'

Willa murmured, to show approval, and wished she were more bold herself on that front. But her life didn't seem to leave room for it.

'She was at a meeting in the Central Halls last night about the pitiful conditions of the native people in some of our colonies.'

That made Willa feel slightly uncomfortable, though why it should she was not sure, for she had nothing to do with the natives in foreign lands herself. Perhaps it was because Tommy often made fun of the them. He didn't ever refer to their conditions. His letters seemed to suggest that they were as happy as larks at being visited by the British Navy.

'My mother says education is the answer.'

'Your father doesn't like her campaigning?'

'Well, he's not for injustice,' said Richard awkwardly. 'Don't misunderstand me. But he hates her going on marches. She went to a big one in London and got herself locked up for the night. They had a huge row over that.'

'Your mother can obviously stand up for herself though?'

'Oh yes! She was wondering if you'd be interested in the movement? She says there's still a lot to do until women under thirty get the vote.'

'It's difficult for me with the baby.' She wondered what else Richard might have told his mother about his friend in the library. 'So this writer?' she prompted.

'Willa Cather. She's American.' Richard opened his satchel and brought out a book. '*My Antonia*. My mother said you could borrow it.'

'That's kind of her,' said Willa hesitantly.

She opened it and saw that his mother had written her

name on the fly leaf. *Arabella Fitzwilliam*. She had a very fine flowing hand. It suggested confidence.

'*My Antonia* is the story of a girl from Bohemia who goes to live in America. In the state of Nebraska.'

'Sounds interesting.' Willa had only ever read one novel set in America, and that had been *Main Street*, which Richard had recommended. 'I'll be sure to return it.'

'Keep it as long as you like.'

'I read quite quickly.'

'I know that.'

He smiled and then he reached across the table and put his hand over hers. She felt a quick thrill at his touch. 'You realise I've become very fond of you, don't you, Willa?'

'I'm married, Richard,' she said in a low voice.

'I know that. But we can be friends, can't we? Good friends?'

'We already are,' she said and then, because the moment was seeming to become too intense, too difficult to hold, added, 'Would you like to hear about Adelaide? I got another letter from my husband this morning.'

He removed his hand and she took the letter out of her bag. She had left the newspaper cutting with its description of dancing girls in gauzy dresses behind. She began to read.

On arrival at Semaphore Anchorage, all ships went alongside except for the Baltic cruisers and the Danae. The reason we were not able to go alongside was that a merchant ship was occupying our billet...

~ 10 ~

Melbourne, Victoria,
Australia
23rd March, 1924

Dear Willa,
We arrived in style, after proceeding up the Yarra
River, escorted by aeroplanes soaring over our
heads. People were not allowed on the pier while the
ships were being secured but thousands were
waiting outside the gates full of excitement at our
coming. An Air Force guard of honour marched up
to the pier and halted abreast the Hood, looking
very smart in their blue uniforms. Admirals Field
and Brand then landed and inspected the guard of
honour. The weather was glorious.

The weather always seemed glorious in those far-off places.
Everywhere but Edinburgh. Or so it seemed to Willa. Would
one not tire of so much sun after a while? Maybe not. It was
April but she was still wearing her winter coat buttoned up to
the neck. A snell wind was coming in from the east blowing
the rubbish up the gutters, overspill from the buckets. Some
people – lazy lumps, Ina called them – would put them out
before going to bed instead of getting up in the morning and
then the cats were on them. You could hear them scrabbling
about. Ina would never tolerate putting your rubbish out at

night. They were up at seven, or, rather, she, Willa, was, for how could she let her mother-in-law do it? She humped the buckets down the stairs twice a week, hoping the lid wouldn't spill off the top of the ash can.

She skipped quickly over the detailed descriptions of the streets and public buildings of Melbourne, wondering where Tommy got all his information from. There were masses of details such as that the streets were one mile long and a hundred feet wide. He couldn't have gone out and measured them. They must be handed out pamphlets on arrival. Then her eye lit on the word 'pleasure' and that arrested her attention.

'Is that a letter from Tommy?' asked Ina, coming in with Malcolm in her arms.

Willa waited until her mother-in-law had removed her coat and hat and they'd put Malcolm into his chair and given him a rusk to chew on. Ina had to lift a book from the chair before she sat down. She squinted at the spine, holding the book out from her body.

'*My Antonia*. Doesn't look like a library book.' She turned it over.

'A friend lent it to me.' Willa put out her hand for it.

'Pauline? Didn't know she read much.'

'No, it was someone else.'

'You don't see a lot of Pauline these days?'

'She's out half the time,' said Willa. 'Going to the pictures. And the dancing.' Every Saturday night. The way she herself used to be. Sometimes on a Saturday evening she'd stand at her bedroom window and look down on the couples in the street below, walking hand-in-hand, making their way to the

Palais. And envy them. Yes, she had to admit that she did. She felt she'd lost something she could never get back. That carefree walking, the anticipation, the sound of the big band striking up…

'She always was a gadabout, Pauline,' said Ina. 'I'm sure her mother's dying for her to get married and settle down. If she doesn't watch it she'll end up on the shelf.'

'She's only my age.'

'Still. Your time can go past quick enough. And there's fewer men round now, the war saw to that. She might find she's missed the boat.'

Ina had opened the book and was frowning at the flyleaf. 'Arabella Fitzwilliam. Fancy-sounding name. Where did you meet her?'

'The library.' Willa was sweating a little.

'You'd like to spend your life there!'

Finally, Ina surrendered the book and Willa kept it on her knee, cursing herself for having been so stupid as to bring it into the kitchen.

Ina sat down and Willa went back to Tommy's letter.

St Kilda is the pleasure ground of Melbourne. It has a very fine beach, and three excellent dancing halls, the 'Carlyous', the 'Palais de Danse' and the 'Wattle Path', all beautifully decorated (the Palace at the bottom of Leith Walk has nothing on them!), with excellent floors and first-class bands. The wattle, you might be interested to know, is a little yellow flower and looked upon as a national flower. Also to be found here is Luna Park, which is full of amusements. All places of entertainment have been thrown open to the squadron and are being well used. At night St Kilda is a blaze of light. Millions of brilliant lights illuminate the scene. Thousands enjoy themselves nightly.

Including Tommy. Well, of course including Tommy. He wasn't going to lie in his bunk and stare at the ceiling, was he? She didn't care what the thousands were up to. Let them get on with it. Let their wives and sweethearts worry about them. She could only see her husband, his feet stepping deftly in and out between his partner's slender feet in their soft leather, ankle-strapped, high-heeled shoes, his hand positioned on the small of her back, holding her, guiding her, turning her, whirling her, spinning her to right and to left, round and round, round and round, until he is laughing and she is laughing, her cheeks flushed, her eyes locked with his. And then he starts to sing. *Let me be your sweetheart...*

She must stop this! It wasn't doing her any good, all this imagining, torturing herself. What had happened to her motto: what you don't know doesn't hurt you? There would be no holding Tommy back when it came to dancing; she had to live with that. According to Bunty, he'd got it from his father, who'd also had a way with girls on the dance floor. 'Twinkle Toes', they used to call him, or at least Bunty had. Twinkling toes and twinkling eyes, she said. Ina hadn't cared for his nickname. What Willa found difficult was trying to conjure up an image of Ina as his dancing partner. There were no photographs either of him or the two of them around the flat, not even of their wedding. She'd asked her once if she had any and Ina had said dismissively that she'd put them away when he died. 'No point in harking back,' she'd said. If it weren't for Tommy, Willa would have questioned the existence of Roberto Costello.

'Is that all?' asked Ina, nodding at the letter.

'No, there's plenty more.'

Everything has been thrown open free to the fleet: trams, theatres, dancing, cinemas. We can have anything we want! Talk about being spoiled!

'Anything they want,' echoed Ina. 'Wouldn't that be nice, even for a day?'

They were quiet, thinking about it.

The hospitality of the people is beyond praise. They all seem well-to-do, as they were in South Africa, with lovely homes and well-kept gardens. The difficulty for us is in accepting all the kind invitations that come pouring in, for motor runs, picnics, parties, lunches, dinners. We can take our pick of the picnics! Motor cars arrive daily at the pier offering to take us into the countryside.

The men would be at work during the day, Willa presumed, in order to pay for the lovely homes and gardens, so it must be wives and unmarried women who drove down to the pier with offers of lunch and runs into the country. Did they vie for the most handsome of the men? Did they vie for Tommy?

He'd be high up on their list. Perhaps, if the women were so well off, they would have chauffeurs and then they could sit in the back seat with the sailors.

'I don't really know about all this,' said Ina, shaking her head. 'They never seem to be doing any work.'

'They must, in between times.' In between their various pleasures. 'Scrub the decks and so forth.'

'Tommy wouldn't be doing that! Not as a yeoman of signals.'

Willa was often puzzled as to what he did do. He couldn't be sending signals to ships all day long. She knew that it had been a hard life for him in the beginning, as a fourteen-year-old able seaman. Conditions had been harsh, discipline severe, and he'd been maltreated by some of the older men. Once he'd got into Signals it had become a bit easier, except, of course, during the war. She hadn't known Tommy in those days but Ina said it had been a terrible time for her, she'd been half off her head with worry, and relieved when he'd been torpedoed and brought back to a nursing home in Edinburgh to convalesce. She had been one of the lucky mothers. So many young men had died in that dreadful war! Look at Mrs Bain in the next stair. Both of her boys were gone. And for what? Still, one thing, it had been so awful that there'd never be another. They'd been told there wouldn't. And if they hadn't fought the last war they might be living under occupation now and having to speak German.

A route march was given by the squadron through the streets of Melbourne which were packed with people. The scene was one of wildest joy, with

everyone cheering and waving. Employers gave their
employees time off to witness the march. Many did
not return to their work afterwards.

'It must cost a pretty penny trailing them all round the world like that, mind,' said Ina.

'You're right. They could spend some of it feeding kids like the MacNabs.'

They no longer handed in food across the landing. The last time Willa had gone to the door Mr MacNab had answered and he'd taken the bottle of milk from her and flung it against the wall, telling her that they didn't want her charity and she could stick it up her backside. Ina, who'd been standing in their doorway with the baby in her arms, had gasped at his audacity. He had then slammed the door in Willa's face. She had had to clean the mess up, collect the shards of glass and wash the walls and the steps, for he wasn't going to do it. Even then, she thought she smelt sour milk on the stair for days afterwards and she kept seeing little glittering splinters tucked away in corners.

'Anything else?' asked Ina.

'Regattas are held at Henley on the river and there is a fine racecourse at Flemington where the race for the Melbourne Cup is held.'

They had a racecourse just outside Edinburgh, at Musselburgh, that neither of them had ever visited. Gerry had gone once and bought himself a pair of opera glasses for the occasion, which had annoyed Elma. She'd been proved right: he'd never go to the races again, nor to the opera, either, so they'd ended up being a waste of money. They suspected

Gerry had lost a lot of money at Musselburgh. He'd been very quiet about it, whereas, if he'd won or come out even, he'd have talked.

They were recalling Gerry at the races when the bell rang and who was at the door but the man himself, with a blood-stained parcel in his hand.

'We were talking about you there,' said Willa, taking him in.

'No wonder my ears were burning coming up the stairs.'

'We were remembering how you lost the family fortune at Musselburgh,' said Ina, who had lifted Malcolm out of his chair and had him on her knee. 'He was getting restless,' she said to Willa.

'I've brought you some round steak, a tasty bit of liver – your favourite, Ina – and some potted head.' Gerry passed the parcel over to Willa.

He turned his attention to Malcolm. 'You're getting to be a right wee lad now, aren't you?' He held out his arms. 'Coming to Uncle Gerry?' He squatted down and put his face close to the baby's. His nose was very red, from either the cold or the drink, perhaps both, and there were bristles on his chin, which probably meant that he had left the house before his wife was up. If she had been she'd have nagged him to shave before appearing in public. She had her standards, as they were continually reminded.

Malcolm let out a wail and his face crumpled. Then he swivelled round on his granny's knee so that he could hide in her pillowy bosom. His little hands clung to her shoulders.

'There, there, Malkie son,' said his grandmother, rocking him and stroking his silky dark head. 'Granny's not going to give you away to any big bad man.'

'Turn him round, Ina,' said Willa, restraining herself from seizing her child from his grandmother's arms, 'so that he can see Gerry properly and get to know him.'

'And find out I'm no monster,' laughed Gerry, though Willa saw he looked hurt.

'He's just at that stage,' she said apologetically.

'He's not used to men,' said Ina.

'No, he's not,' said Willa, 'with his father on the other side of the world. Down under.'

'It's not Tommy's fault,' said his mother. 'He has to go where he's told.'

Willa pushed up the window and put the meat in the outside wall safe, then ran her hands under the hot tap to remove the blood stains. She turned back to Ina.

'Malcolm needs a nap. He's overtired. I'm going to put him down in his cot.'

'He can have a wee snooze here with me.'

'He'll get a better sleep in his cot.'

Willa reached out for him and Tommy's mother reluctantly surrendered the child. He didn't come without a protest; he tried to cling to his granny and he flailed with his legs, landing a few blows to his mother's stomach.

'You see,' she said, 'he's beyond himself.'

She carried him, still struggling, through to her room and closed the door. She was seething and wanted to let it out in a scream but she had to calm down as that wouldn't do the baby any good. She took the chair by the window and opened her blouse. He subsided once he'd got the nipple in his mouth and after a few sucks his eyelids closed and his mouth parted releasing her breast. She sat for a few minutes rocking him and crooning softly. *Golden slumbers close your eyes*...She longed to be able to take him away, to live in a little place of their own, just the two of them, until his daddy came back and made them three. But how could she afford that?

It was April. Tommy wouldn't be home until October. How was she going to get through all those months? And then what? He'd be home for three or four weeks before he was off again, to see the world.

She lifted Malcolm into his cot and tucked the covers gently round him. He'd sleep for an hour or more. She'd have time for a quick visit to the library.

'He's asleep,' she told Ina, 'so don't be lifting him unless he wakens.'

Ina did not respond. She rose from the table and started to wash the few dishes that lay in the sink, splashing water up over the bunker. She was in the huff. Well, let her be.

Gerry was finishing a cup of tea. He set the cup in the saucer and got up, saying he'd give Willa a hurl up to the library.

His van was sitting outside, smelling meaty from the parcels in the back. He didn't usually do deliveries himself but his man was off sick. 'Somebody's got to do it. Business is business, eh?'

There was a log jam of trams round the clock. A cable had broken and the repair men were on the job. In addition, a brewer's cart had spilled some barrels across the road. They would have to wait until the mess cleared.

'It can't be easy for you,' said Gerry, 'living with Ina.'

'No,' agreed Willa.

'She means well. You've got to stand up to her. But I'm sure you'll not let her walk over you. You're too strong-minded a lass, Willa.'

The trams were gradually beginning to shunt forward again. Gerry let in the clutch and as he did so his hand brushed against Willa's leg. She moved it away and looked out of the window and made a comment about the traffic jam. It had probably been accidental; she hoped that it was for she liked Gerry and thought he was a decent man and she wanted it to stay that way.

He pulled up outside the library door.

'If you ever need any help, Willa, you know you can come to me. Money, anything. Anything at all.'

'Thanks, Gerry.' She had her hand on the door handle. 'And thanks for the lift.'

'Don't forget!'

She slammed the door and waved to him as he drove away. It was a relief to walk under the sign saying LET THERE BE LIGHT and enter a peaceful, book-lined room. She was looking forward to a cup of tea and a chat with Richard about *Persuasion*.

He was not at his usual table. As soon as she had returned her books she took a quick tour round the bays. She couldn't see him! There had been two or three times before when he'd not been in. She couldn't expect him to coincide with her every single time. But today of all days! Her disappointment was acute and she was surprised by that. She went round all the departments: to make sure: music, art, reference. She returned to fiction and picked two books off the shelves: *The Garden Party,* stories by Katherine Mansfield, and, feeling like something lightweight, an Edgar Wallace thriller, *The*

Four Just Men. She chose them quickly, unable to concentrate today.

She took them to his table and began reading one of the Mansfield stories but she couldn't quite get into it in the way that she normally did when she opened a book. Every time the door opened she looked up.

After a few minutes she decided to abandon it. She had her books stamped and set off back along George IV Bridge, thinking that she might meet him on the road. If she did she could give him his mother's copy of *My Antonia,* which she had brought in her message bag, wrapped in brown paper. She'd been terrified of staining the cover.

She was waiting on the corner of Forrest Road, about to cross, when she saw him coming up Middle Meadow Walk. He was with a woman, an older woman in a long dark-blue coat and a wide-brimmed hat. She must be his mother. She was tall, almost as tall as her son, and stately. She held herself well. She would be a formidable campaigner. She would command attention. Willa had a vision of her standing full square, facing a police horse, refusing to give way.

Richard had his arm linked through his mother's, and they were talking, heads slightly inclined, engrossed in their conversation. It looked like intelligent talk. She was obviously not asking him if he'd fancy a haddie for his tea. Willa stepped back into a doorway.

As they reached the top of the walk they paused but continued to talk earnestly and, on Richard's part, avidly. Even from across the street Willa could see that his mother had what Bunty and Ina would call 'class'.

Richard and his mother were not of her class: that was

what Willa thought as she stood furtively watching them. She felt shabby in her old winter coat and scuffed shoes. Even if she were single she could not imagine Mrs Fitzwilliam finding her a suitable companion for her son.

She waited until they had set off again. They had not seen her on the other side of the road; they had been too absorbed in each other. Once the way was clear Willa walked slowly home, resolved to end her friendship with Richard.

~ 11 ~

Sydney, New South Wales,
Australia
11th April, 1924

Dear Willa,
We received an absolutely wonderful welcome
here. They'd been waiting on the shore and on the
hillsides while others were packed into boats. They
cheered at the tops of their voices. It is heart-
warming to know that His Majesty and his fleet are
held in such high esteem. The Hood *and the* Repulse
looked majestic as they made the short twists and
turns that this beautiful harbour is noted for.

Well, of course, they would get a wonderful welcome,
wouldn't they? What if one time people were to start hissing
and booing as they came sailing into harbour? Or pelt them
with rotten eggs, all over their nice clean white uniforms?
That would be a big surprise for His Majesty's Special Service
Squadron. But they hadn't done it, not there, in Sydney,
Australia. Australia, according to Tommy, was one of Britain's
most loyal colonies.

'It's amazing how many places in the world do belong to
us,' said Ina. 'Makes you feel proud.'

'Does it?' asked Bunty.

'Does it what?'

'Really make you feel proud to be British?'

'Well, why not?'

'You've never been to London. You've never been out of Scotland, woman! You're a Scot.'

Willa had never been across the border either. Bunty had gone to Blackpool once with Mr Parkin and had had a great time, had come back and said the lights were out of this world. Their relationship was going on as before, now that he had got over his disappointment at her turning down his offer of matrimony. Elma had strongly disapproved of her sister Bunty going off for an illicit weekend with a man she wasn't married to, though Bunty swore they'd had separate rooms at the bed and breakfast. 'Believe that if you will,' was what Ina had said, arms folded underneath her bosom.

'Carry on, Willa,' she said now, giving Bunty a frosty look.

Sydney was founded in 1788 and named after Viscount Sydney, who suggested colonising it when it became a British possession. The population is about a million today. It has beautiful buildings, two cathedrals, art galleries, an observatory, zoological gardens and extensive parks for strolling in. The shore around Port Jackson abounds with delightful coves, wooded bays and surf beaches, ideal places for picnics. They put on a wonderful spread for us wherever we go. Cold meats, chicken, fish, salmon (fresh, not tinned), crabs, lobster, stuffed eggs, fruits, sumptuous desserts. It makes your mouth water just to see it all laid out.

They fell silent at the prospect. Ina found her voice first.

'I suppose it'll taste much the same, in and out the tin, salmon.'

'Amazing how fond they are of picnics,' said Bunty. 'I've never cared for them myself.'

'Me, either.' For once the sisters were in agreement. 'You can get sand on your sandwiches!'

Ina laughed but Bunty did not. Willa managed a weak smile.

'All that sitting on the ground freezes your bum off,' said Bunty.

It would be warm sitting on the beach at Port Jackson. And then there were the coves, full of delight, tucked away out of sight...

Willa went back to the letter.

> *The flora is wonderful and varied, which fact led Captain Cook to name the adjoining bay Botany Bay.*

'I've heard of that,' said Ina. 'Botany Bay. Didn't a lot of convicts get sent there?'

'Don't suppose Tommy'll have met any,' said Bunty with a wink at Willa. 'So you'll not need to lie awake fretting on that score.'

Willa read on.

> *The resources of Australia are rich and numerous with plenty of room for new people who want to get on and are prepared to work hard. They have no*

time for slackers. Their policy, which, I think, is the
correct one, is to have the country populated with
white working people instead of having black
workers with white masters, as in South Africa, for
instance. To this end immigration is invited and
carefully scrutinised whilst coloured races are
excluded by a number of street laws. This is a
wonderful country with wonderful people.

'Must be wonderful to live in a wonderful country with
wonderful people!' said Bunty, the edge of sarcasm in her
voice missed by Ina, who demanded to know what was wrong
with Scotland?

'Nothing. Not a thing. Maybe you and Tommy should
think of setting yourselves up out in Australia, Willa. Nice
climate, good opportunities. Picnics galore. They wouldn't
want Ina and me, we're too old.'

'Tommy wouldn't want to live there,' said his mother.

'I've told you before he doesn't want to live anywhere,' said
Willa. 'He likes the life on the ocean wave.'

'Oh well.' Bunty sighed. 'I suppose I'd better get back to the
grind.' She'd closed the shop for an hour and put up a sign
saying 'Back in ten minutes.' She got up and stretched herself,
yawning. It was hot in the room. 'No rest for the wicked.'

'Well, it's you that's said it,' said Ina.

'He sends his love and all that,' said Willa and put the letter
back in its envelope. She looked forward to Tommy's letters
and was excited when the postie handed them in, but by the
time she'd finished reading she felt low and irritable. She was
going to go to the library.

She hadn't been for a while; she'd been avoiding the place. She'd been rereading all her old childhood favourites that her mother had bought her for birthdays and Christmas. She had them on the shelf in her bedroom. *Little Women. Good Wives.* She'd pondered on what being a good wife meant and come to the conclusion that it depended on your circumstances, whether your husband was away most of the time sending you letters about the pleasures to be found in foreign lands or coming home nightly at half-past five for his tea. She'd also reread the LM Montgomery books, *Anne of Green Gables, Emily of Lantern Hill, Rilla of Ingleside.* She loved the titles. They set her dreaming. She had a dozen or so of the Canadian woman's novels. If she were to have the chance of going anywhere abroad she would choose Prince Edward Island with its pretty apple orchards and wooden-framed houses.

But now she was desperate for something new to read.

'Can you look after Malcolm for an hour?' she asked her mother-in-law.

'I'll take him up to Elma's. I haven't seen her for a bit.'

'Lucky you,' said Bunty, stifling another yawn. 'I'll chum you down the road a wee way, Willa.'

Willa put on her lighter coat, a pale grey, and knotted the green scarf she'd bought for Elma's birthday at her throat. She was glad to have thrown off her shabby winter serge. It was a bright, slightly windy day, with puffy white clouds scudding across the sky.

'Spring's here,' she said as she and Bunty stepped out into the street.

'At last!' said Bunty. 'By the way, your friend Richard was in the shop the other day.'

'I've told you—'

'Oh, I know! He's quite love-sick about you.'

'Don't be silly!'

'Hey, watch!' Bunty pulled Willa back. 'Do you want to get run over by a motor? It'd be awful messy.'

'I haven't seen him for ages.'

'That's why he was in seeing me. I took him through the back and gave him a cup of tea.'

'You didn't have to.'

'He was worried about you. Real down-in-the-dumps he was. Thought you might not be well. Said it wasn't like you not to go to the library.'

'I had other things to read.'

'Any road, I told him you were in love with your husband. You are, aren't you?'

'Of course!'

'I thought it was better he didn't hold out any hope. I'll leave you here then, Willa. See and pick some nice books!'

Bunty turned off and Willa strode on up the hill. She couldn't stay away from the library for ever, could she? She would give Richard a friendly wave if he were there but if he suggested a cup of tea she would tell him she had to get home for the baby.

He was there, writing at his usual table. Willa wondered why he chose to write in the library and not at home but perhaps he wouldn't want his mother peering over his shoulder and asking what he was writing. Having seen her, Willa thought that possible. She looked like the kind of woman who would want to know everything. And, in an odd way, which Willa understood, the library was more private, in spite of all the other people around.

As soon as she came in the door he lifted his head. It always amazed her how he seemed to sense her entrance. His eyes lit up and his face broke into a wide smile, making him look very boyish. He waved and she raised her hand a few inches in return. Then, she too, smiled, although she had not intended to.

'Your friend's in,' said the librarian, the pleasant one. 'He was asking me just yesterday if you'd been in recently and I said no, I hadn't seen you. Have you been keeping all right?'

'Yes, fine, thanks.'

Willa moved away from the counter into a bay where two other women were already browsing, thinking that there might be safety in numbers.

Almost immediately, he was beside her.

'I've been wondering where you were.'

'I've been busy.'

'I'm pleased to see you, though.'

She concentrated on the book spines, or tried to, but she couldn't seem to focus.

'What do you feel like reading?' he asked.

'Jane Austen.'

Her world was neat and ordered; in the end, people were happy, or happy enough.

'Let's go and look,' he said.

She followed him round the shelves.

Northanger Abbey, which she had not read, was sitting on the shelf. He lifted it down and placed it in her hand like a gift.

'Now what?' He hummed softly while he pondered.

'Katherine Mansfield?' she suggested.

They went in search and found *The Dove's Nest*.

'Published only last year,' said Richard. 'After her death. My mother was reading it last week.'

Willa wished he had not told her that though why it should bother her so much she did not know. She had taken against his mother from what he had told her and after seeing the woman only once, and from the opposite side of the street! How stupid she was being. She went to the counter with her chosen books. Richard came too.

Without any discussion, they walked to the café in the High Street, *their* café, and found their usual table in the corner. Richard ordered a pot of tea for two and scones with butter and jam.

'I've missed you,' he said.

She said, 'I got a letter from Tommy this morning,' and took it out of her bag. 'He's in Sydney, Australia. It seems to be a wonderful city, with lovely parks and a zoo and cathedrals, two cathedrals. Shall I read it to you?'

'If you like.'

She felt his eyes watching her all the time she was reading. When she'd finished he said, 'You've got a lovely soft voice. I could listen to it for hours.'

She blushed.

The tea came and he said, smiling and turning the handle of the teapot in her direction, 'You can be mother!'

They drank their tea and he ate his scone but she could eat only half of hers. 'I'm not very hungry,' she said apologetically and he said that he would finish it if she didn't mind. His hand brushed hers as he took it from the plate.

The scone eaten and the bill paid, they left the café. He suggested a walk since it was such a nice day.

'Seems a shame to be inside when the sun's shining.'

They walked down the High Street and crossed North Bridge into the Canongate.

'Have you ever seen the secret garden in Dunbar's Close?' he asked.

She shook her head. 'I've read *The Secret Garden*.' It had been another favourite childhood book.

As it had been for him. They agreed that the idea of secret gardens was very appealing.

'Come on, I'll show you this one! Not many people know it's there.'

They turned into Dunbar's Close and there, behind it, lay the hidden-away garden, set out in formal beds, bordered with low hedges. It was very quiet, away from the hum of traffic and the call of voices. There was no one else in the garden but themselves.

'Willa,' he said and she felt her limbs begin to tremble. He took her into his arms and very gently kissed her. She did not draw away but after a moment she turned her head and rested the side of her face against his shoulder. He held her tightly.

'This is madness,' she said in a low voice.

'I know but I love you.'

'You can't.'

'But I do.'

They stayed, holding each other, not speaking, not moving, until Willa, with a sigh, lifted her head and took a step back. He released her.

'I must go.'

'Of course.'

They retraced their steps, back up the Royal Mile, towards George IV Bridge. To begin with, Willa struggled to make conversation about *Sense and Sensibility*, but after a while they both fell silent.

As they were approaching the library, Willa saw Pauline on the opposite side of the street.

'There's a friend of mine!'

Richard quickly said that he would go back into the library. 'I'll see you soon?'

Willa did not answer for Pauline had her in her sights and was waving frantically. Richard disappeared under the library portal and Willa crossed the road, without registering that a motor car was approaching. The driver sounded his horn and glared at her through the windscreen but she did not notice that either. She was out of breath when she reached Pauline.

'What are you doing here?' she asked, anxious to get the first word in. 'Shouldn't you be at work?'

Pauline had been at the dentist and had had a tooth out so was taking the rest of the day off. She was damned if she was going to sit on a high stool totting up numbers in a ledger with a swollen jaw. She had a Black Watch scarf wound round her face that a soldier had given her one winter. 'What have you been doing?'

'I was at the library.'

'You and your library! It's a wonder you're not cross-eyed with all that reading. Are you on your way home?'

The girls set off to walk back together. As well as suffering from a visit to the dentist, Pauline had another problem. A man. She'd met him six weeks ago at the Palais.

'He's a wonderful dancer. Almost as good as your Tommy at the tango. You know, real South American-like. He's got all the moves.'

'What's wrong this time?' asked Willa. There was always something wrong with the men Pauline met. She attracted a certain type. Wolfish, Bunty called them. Pauline didn't seem to see it herself. They tended to have sideburns, heavily Brylcreemed hair, small moustaches that they kept touching with nicotine-stained forefingers, small, watchful eyes.

'He's married.'

'Oh,' sighed Willa. 'That is a problem.'

'Thing is I'm in love with him and he's in love with me.'

'What age is he?'

'Getting on for forty. But young-looking. You'd never guess. He didn't try to lie to me about his age.'

Willa thought that probably meant he was pushing fifty.

'Children?'

'Four.'

'*Four?*'

'My mother had six.'

'That's not the point.'

'No, it isn't, is it?' said Pauline gloomily.

'He's not going to leave a wife and four children.'

'He says he would, if it weren't for the children. He's not in love with her any more. He's a really nice man, honestly he is, and genuine. You don't believe me, do you?'

'I don't know him.'

'You'd like him, I know you would.'

Willa remembered another man Pauline had fallen in love with and had discovered he was married only after she had been going out with him for six months. He'd also spoken of marriage. Then Pauline had bumped into him in Princes Street Gardens walking beside a woman pushing a baby in a pram, with a slightly older child sitting balanced on the end.

'I've never felt like this about anyone before,' said Pauline. 'He says it's the same for him. I haven't, I tell you! Don't look at me like that. This is different. I knew it from the minute he took me up on the floor. You fell for Tommy that first night at the Palace, didn't you? You said he made you feel weak at the knees.'

'At least he wasn't married with four children.'

'I didn't know Ernest was when I met him. But by the time he told me I was head-over-heels. There was nothing I could do about it.'

'What was he doing out dancing if he was married?'

'You said Tommy was dancing his way round the world. He's a married man, isn't he?'

That silenced Willa.

'I wasn't meaning to rub it in or anything,' said Pauline. 'I'm sorry, Willa.'

'That's all right.'

They stopped on the corner at Tollcross. Pauline wasn't ready yet to finish the conversation; she'd been bottled up too long.

'I can't stop seeing him, Willa, I just can't. I decide to, and then he comes and meets me out of work and that's it again! He wants me to go to Pitlochry with him for the night next Friday.'

'How can he manage to get away?'

It transpired that Ernest was a commercial traveller in

ladies' hosiery and so was able to control his own time. His wife was in no position to question him. As for Pauline, she was prepared to risk taking Saturday morning off work and claiming sickness. If she were to be found out, she'd be sacked.

'What about your mother?'

'I could tell her I've got Saturday off and I'm going to visit my cousin Madge in Aberdeen.'

'But she might find out you never got there.'

'We don't see Madge from one year's end to the next.'

'Well, I don't know,' said Willa. She looked over at the clock. It was later than she'd thought. It always was. 'I'd better go.'

'Hey!' Pauline called after her. 'Who was that fella you were with outside the library? Is that the one Mum keeps seeing you with?'

'He's nobody in particular.' Willa turned back to look at Pauline. 'Are you going to go to Pitlochry?'

'I haven't made up my mind.'

But she would go, Willa knew. She wouldn't be able to resist it.

Brisbane, Queensland,
Australia
20th April, 1924

Dear Willa,
   Our stay here is proving very enjoyable, as usual,
with various entertainments arranged for our
benefit. Picnics, boating on the river et cetera. The
people are extremely sociable and hospitable. In
return we held an open day and the quays were
thronged with people who couldn't wait to come
aboard. We had 20,000 visitors on the Danae. *It got*
a bit crowded at times but it was good fun!

'I'll bet,' said Bunty.

'It was nice of them, inviting them,' said Ina, her tone
defensive.

'Least they could do in return for all those picnics,' said
Bunty. 'Never mind the et ceteras!'

Ina gave her a look.

We have spent many happy afternoons on the beach
in Sandgate, a seaside resort about twelve miles
from Brisbane by train. We are finding the climate
pretty warm. You won't recognise me when I get
back, I'm burnt so brown!

'Well, I'm glad he's having happy afternoons,' said Bunty, passing round the jammy doughnuts she'd bought at the baker's on the way over.

'Let's hope we will know him!' said Ina. 'We don't want a black man for a daddy, do we, Malkie?' She bounced the baby on her knee and he chortled and tried to hit her on the nose with his rattle. She pulled back her head and laughed. 'You're getting to be a right wee Tuareg, aren't you?'

'You're going to turn that boy into a right wee Jessie if you're not careful,' said Bunty, licking the jam from her finger.

We can only swim close to shore as sharks regularly come up river attracted by the meat factories near the entrance. A man from the Dauntless *fell overboard and drowned and his body was recovered early the next morning, which was surprising. We thought the sharks would have eaten him.*

'Another one,' said Ina. 'God save us! You'd think the men would take more care.'

'Too much rum,' said Bunty. 'Well, I mean, how else would the man fall over? They must have a decent rail along the side. Otherwise they'd all be in the drink, inside and outside!' She laughed but Ina did not.

The doorbell jangled.

'Who can that be?' said Ina. 'I hope it's not Mrs Begg. The second post's been. And the coal came the morn.'

The coalman had brought up five bags and Willa, as instructed, had stood in the lobby and checked the bags as he'd heaved them over his shoulder into the coal-hole. Ina didn't trust them. She said they were up to all sorts of tricks, like not emptying the bag fully or putting four sacks in instead of five and charging you for the latter. She maintained they had their heads screwed on.

'She's a bit of a dragon, your ma-in-law,' the coalman had said to Willa, as he shifted his cap to the back of his head revealing a line of white skin between his hairline and his sooty face. 'She'll no let you off wi' nothing.'

The bell jangled again, and again. Somebody was giving it a hard pull.

'I'll go,' said Willa.

The bell went again before she reached the door. 'I'm coming,' she shouted, as she tugged it open.

On the mat stood Elma, her face stained an angry red.

'Are you all deaf in there?'

She pushed past Willa and preceded her into the kitchen.

'You're here,' she said to Bunty. 'I thought you would be when I saw your note on the door.'

'Aye, I'm here,' said Bunty, who had her mouth full of doughnut. She swallowed it. 'At least I think I am. I'm no a ghost. Pinch me and see!'

Elma glared at her sister. Her chest was heaving as if she were trying to get her breath.

'Willa was just reading a letter of Tommy's to us,' said Ina. 'A man from another boat fell overboard and got eaten by a shark.'

'The sea's swarming with them,' said Bunty. 'In Australia, that is. No here, fortunately. Sit yourself down, Elma, and take the weight off your feet. There's a spare doughnut in the bag you can have.'

But Elma was not interested in Tommy's letter, or jammy doughnuts. She was glaring at Bunty. She seemed too wound up almost to speak. Malkie gave the intruder a searching look and, sensing trouble, began to cry.

'There, there, your granny's got you safe,' said the woman herself, patting his back and turning his face away from Elma.

'Why don't you sit down, Elma, and tell us what's got up your back?' suggested Bunty. 'You look in a right old tizzy.'

'You know!'

'Do I?'

'Don't come the innocent with me!'

'I don't know what the blazes you're on about. I'm no a mind-reader.'

Willa pulled up a kitchen chair and Elma plopped down on it.

'You encouraged him!'

'Who?'

'Gerald, of course!'

'Encouraged him to do what?'

'That woman!'

'Oh, that,' said Bunty. 'I had nothing to do with it.'

'She's a friend of yours.'

'She's a customer. She comes in every afternoon for her *Evening News*, never misses. She likes to keep up with things.'

For once Ina did not chip in to say that it was a pity Tommy had passed up his chances to become a reporter on the paper.

'You give her tea through the back,' said Elma.

'I give tea to a few folk. She's a widow woman, in need of company.'

'And she got it with my Gerald!'

'Who are you talking about?' asked Ina.

'Do you want a cup of tea, Aunt Elma?' asked Willa.

Elma ignored them both. She was on fire. Willa wondered if steam might issue out of her nostrils at any moment.

'You introduced them!'

'She was having a wee cup of tea with me when Gerry came in. It would have been rude of me if I hadn't introduced them.'

'Well, you certainly started something.'

'Has he run off with her?' asked Ina. 'Whoever she is.'

'Of course not! Gerald wouldn't do that to me. He's not going to see her again. I've put a stop to that!'

'I'd better get back and open up the shop.' Bunty stood up.

'I would ask you not to serve that woman again, Bunty. You are my sister and families have to stick by each other.'

Bunty stared at her. 'You must be kidding. I'm not turning away a good customer. She buys cigarettes and chocolates as well.'

'I thought she was the type.' Elma sat back, looking satisfied. 'A smoker.'

'And a chocolate-eater,' said Willa softly.

'She's done nothing to me,' said Bunty, 'so you can put that in your pipe and smoke it.' Then she left.

'She's heartless, that one,' said Elma. 'And a cheeky besom.'

'Aye, she can be,' agreed Ina.

'You understand how I feel, don't you, Ina?'

'What's her name, this woman that Gerry's gone off with?'

'He's not gone *off* with her. And he's not going to!'

'Whatever.'

'I believe she's a Mrs Mooney.' Elma almost choked over the saying of it. Normally pallid, her face had taken on a purplish hue.

'Must be Irish.' Ina nodded. 'Did you see them together or what?'

'Mrs Cant saw them going into the Hermitage.'

'What was Mrs Cant doing up at the Hermitage?'

'What does it matter what she was doing? She was there, wasn't she? And she saw them. Hand-in-hand. A right harlot she is. And a papist to boot!'

'A papist,' repeated Ina. 'I suppose she would be with a name like Mooney. I must say I'm surprised at Gerry associating with one. And him an elder in the kirk, and a Mason.'

'It's as well it's been stopped before the minister caught on to it,' said Elma. 'Or that'd be Gerald out on his ear.'

'Would they excommunicate him?' asked Willa, about to add, 'Just for that,' but thought better of it.

'Put him out the church? It wouldn't come to that but they wouldn't let him go on being an elder. He's meant to be an example.'

'I didn't know that was what an elder was for,' said Ina. 'I thought it was to take up the collection.'

'They have different roles to play.' Elma smoothed back a strand of hair – it was seldom that any were out of place, which showed how shaken up she was. 'It's not often we see you in the church these days, is it, Ina? You either, Willa. It's up to you to set an example to your boy, you know. You're not wanting him to grow up a heathen.'

Willa said she must go out and get some messages in. They were needing a few things from the grocer. 'I'll take Malcolm. He could do with some air.'

She held out her hands to him but he didn't want to leave the comfortable knee he was settled on.

'He's not wanting to go out,' said his granny, holding him tight. 'He's wanting to stay.'

'He loves his gran, so he does,' said Elma. She loved to say that and Willa was convinced she did it to annoy her.

She reached over, and forcibly lifted up the baby, who squawked loudly and trod air with furious feet. She put him under her arm and carried him out of the room and down the stairs to the bottom lobby. She strapped him into his pram, still protesting, resisting with all the strength of his small body, clutching his rattle.

'There now, young man,' she said, fastening the buckle. 'You and I are going for a walk whether you like it or not.'

He tossed the rattle over the side and looked down to see where it had landed. She picked it up and handed it back to him. He threw it overboard again, with a grin that reminded her of his father.

'I'm not playing this game, my lad,' she told him and put the rattle at the end of the pram out of his reach. 'You'd like to lead me a dance, wouldn't you?' He roared. She released the brake and they set off.

She wheeled the pram along to Melville Drive and up Middle Meadow Walk and Malcolm decided to forget his gripes and enjoy the trees shimmering in the sunshine, making pretty patterns against the blue of the sky. Willa loved the month of May when everything was fresh and green and the whole of summer lay ahead. A number of students were on the path, on foot mostly, a few on bicycles, going to and fro between the university and their digs in Marchmont. Willa thought of Richard and wondered if he would be in the library, though, glancing at her watch and seeing that it was a quarter to four, she realised that he would have left by now to go and do his afternoon tutoring. She had not seen him since the day he had kissed her in the secret garden. When she thought of him she became confused.

They met near the top of the path. He had books under his arm.

'Willa!' he cried and for a moment they stood there like two people in a game of statues, gazing at each other and saying nothing. Then Willa had to move the pram to the side so that two ladies could pass and that broke the spell.

Richard looked into the pram. 'What's his name?'

'Malcolm.'

'Hello, Malcolm.'

Richard smiled uncertainly at him and the baby stared back with his wide-open dark eyes. Richard lifted the rattle and shook it and Malcolm stretched out his hand imploringly and Richard put the rattle into it. Malcolm crowed and bestowed a wide smile on his benefactor, making him smile in turn.

'He's a beautiful baby,' said Richard. He said it a little sadly, Willa thought.

He came round the side of the pram to join her and put his hand close to hers on the handle. Even that slight touch disturbed her.

'I've been dying to see you. I've been to the library every day. Willa, I must see you! Don't you want to see me?'

'I do but—'

'What about tomorrow afternoon?'

'I don't know.'

'*Please!*'

'I'll try. But we're beginning to be noticed in the library.'

'I'll be in our café from two onwards. I'll wait. Come when you can.'

He must go for he had a lesson with a boy at four o'clock in Grange Road. He had afternoon and early evening classes now every weekday and Saturday morning; he was trying to save money so that he could go back to university in the autumn to do his final year.

'You'd better go or you'll be late,' said Willa, glancing around, in case Mrs Cant or any others of her kind might be lurking.

His hand had crept over hers so that their fingers were interlinked. He wanted to kiss her and for a moment it looked as if he would, but they could not risk it, not here, out in this wide-open space, where half of Edinburgh might observe them.

'*Go!*' she told him.

She watched him as he hurried down the path. He turned back to wave halfway and then again as he reached the end of the Walk and prepared to cross Melville Drive. Four o'clock sounded from a nearby church clock. He was going to be late. She saw him break into a run and sprint across the road. He had an athletic frame and moved well.

Malcolm was ginning and rocking the pram. He did not like to be ignored. Willa looked down and saw the rattle on the ground. When he saw her looking he put on his grin again. He was a wee devil; he knew how to twist her round his little finger. She shook her head at him and smiled and, picking up the rattle, she presented it to him, telling him not to dare to throw it out again.

On her way back, loath to return so soon to the flat and Tommy's mother, she called in at Bunty's. She found her in the back shop with Mrs Mooney.

Mrs Mooney was wearing a lime-green cloche hat and she was smoking. She held a lime-green cigarette holder to carmine lips, inhaled deeply, sucking in her rouged cheeks, and blew out a stream of smoke. She was smoking Sobranie cigarettes, favoured by Bunty when she wanted a change from Craven A. Willa recognised the smell.

'Willa,' said Bunty, 'this is my friend Mrs Mooney. Maureen, this is my nephew Tommy's wife.'

'Nice to meet you, Willa. I've heard a lot about you. And is this your wee boy? Isn't he just gorgeous?'

Malcolm, in his mother's arms, eyed the woman uncertainly, but seemed bemused by the lime-green cigarette holder. He put out his hand for it but its owner wagged her finger at him and said, 'That's not for you, not till you're a big boy, like your daddy. I hear he's gorgeous too.'

Willa shifted Malcolm onto her other arm. Mrs Mooney seemed to have heard a great deal and was obviously more than an occasional visitor to Bunty's inner sanctum.

'Have a seat, hen,' said Bunty, shifting over to make room. 'There's still some tea in the pot.' She took another cup and saucer from the cupboard.

Willa sat down on the opposite side of the table to Mrs

Mooney and Bunty, anxious to keep Malcolm out of the line of their cigarette smoke.

'I'm just on my way actually.' Mrs Mooney released the cigarette end from its holder and stubbed it out on an ashtray on the table. They'd had a few cigarettes, to judge from the number of butts. Malcolm was watching every move the woman made. 'I want to catch the greengrocer before he closes. I've got a nice juicy pork chop for my tea so I thought I'd get some mushrooms to go with it. Nice meeting you, Willa.'

'You, too, Mrs Mooney.'

'Call me Maureen. Everybody does. I'll see you, Bunty.'

Mrs Mooney clicked out on high green heels. Now that she was on her feet Willa could see that she was wearing a cream silk dress with a low-slung waist and knee-length hemline. Around her neck was slung a rope of lime-green beads.

'Don't forget your *Evening News*,' Bunty shouted after her.

They heard the shop door ping as Mrs Mooney closed it behind her.

'Classy dresser, isn't she?' said Bunty. 'She's quite a girl. She was doing the cancan in here one afternoon.'

Mrs Mooney must be well over forty, thought Willa, but Bunty referred to everyone of her own age, and even older, as a girl.

'She's a good laugh,' added Bunty. 'And we can all do with a laugh now and then.'

Willa drank her tea and Bunty gave Malcolm a biscuit to keep him happy.

'She's got a nice juicy chop for her tea. Did you catch that?'

'Is Gerry still seeing her?'

Bunty shrugged. 'How should I know?' But she obviously did.

'I thought Elma was going to explode this afternoon.'

'Maureen's not doing her any harm. She's not going to take Gerry away from her. She wouldn't want him full-time. She likes her independence. You get used to it, you know.'

'I suppose you do.'

'You've not got much, have you?'

Willa shrugged.

'That's what having a baby does to you.'

'I wouldn't be without him.'

'I'm sure you wouldn't now that he's here.'

Malcolm was doing a good job at mangling the biscuit with his three front teeth. Bits of soggy biscuit had spilled down his front which Willa wiped away. She had written to tell Tommy about the teeth but he had never referred to them when he'd written back.

'Maureen's been on her own for ten years. Her man died of a burst ulcer. He was in the spirits trade so he left her well provided for. She's got a comfortable flat, very smart it is, with two bedrooms, a big sitting room, kitchen, bathroom, in Tarvit Street.'

'We'll have to hope Mrs Cant doesn't find out where she lives then.'

'They were a bit careless, the two of them, going walking in the Hermitage in broad daylight. If they'd gone down to Portobello or somewhere on the other side of town they'd have got away with it. Something to keep in mind.'

'What do you mean?' asked Willa sharply.

'Nothing,' said Bunty, trying to look innocent. 'Another wee drop of tea?'

'No thanks. I'd better be getting back.' Willa stood up and stretched herself. She had half intended to confide in Bunty about Richard but had changed her mind, after having met Mrs Mooney.

~ 13 ~

Sydney again!

Dear Willa,
  *Here we are back in Sydney for a couple of days
– no complaints about that! – before sailing on to
New Zealand.*

This time Tommy had sent a picture postcard, of Sydney
harbour, with just a couple of lines written on the back of it.
If he'd picked up a girl first time round in Sydney he'd be able
to take up with her again on his second visit.

'That's two days in a row you've heard from him,' said the
postie. 'He must be missing you.'

'He told me the post could be a bit topsy-turvy.' Willa
closed the door.

She stood with her back to it, thinking about Richard,
trying to decide should she or should she not go to the café
this afternoon at two o'clock. She had wakened early and
lain in bed turning it over and over in her head. If she did it
would be the first time they would meet by appointment. All
the other times had been casual, a case of bumping into each
other. At least that was how she liked to think of it. This
would seem to shift their relationship onto a different
footing.

'Was that the postie?' called Ina from the kitchen.

'Card from Tommy.' Willa took it in to her.

Ina was still eating her porridge and hadn't taken her stays down yet from the pulley. Malcolm, seated in his high chair, liked to watch the suspenders swaying in the draught from the fire. The coals were banked high in the range.

'It's awful hot in here,' said Ina.

It was smelly too. It was time she washed her stays again. Trouble was they took ages to dry because you couldn't put them through the mangle and she refused to peg them out in the back green on public view.

Willa went over to the window and pushed the bottom half up a few inches. In a minute or two Ina would be complaining about the draught.

'Tommy never forgets us, does he?' said his mother, gazing at Sydney harbour. 'So he's going on to New Zealand? Show us where that is, Willa. I get lost trying to think where he is.'

Willa lifted the globe down from the shelf and spun it until she found New Zealand. Another pink country.

'Lord help us, he is at the end of the world. He couldn't be much further away, could he?'

'He could if he went a bit further on, down to the South Pole.'

'They're not going there, are they?'

'No, they're not.'

'That's good then.'

The bell went.

'I hope that's not Elma again,' said Ina. 'I had enough of her yesterday. I feel real sorry for her but she raved on for about three hours. After all, it's over now, Gerry and that woman, so why can't she let it be? Anyway, it seems the only thing they did was go for a walk.'

The bell sounded again, and again. Willa hastened to answer it.

'I'm coming,' she shouted.

Pauline stood on the mat. She was carrying a small cardboard suitcase and she'd been crying.

'I need to talk to you, Willa.'

'You'd better come in.'

'Who's that?' called Ina from the kitchen.

'Pauline. We're going into my room for a minute.'

Willa took her into the room and closed the door. Pauline sat down on the bed and resumed crying.

'What's happened? Has Ernest dumped you?'

'No.' Pauline retrieved a handkerchief from the leg of her knickers and blew her nose loudly. 'But I've lost my job and my mum's thrown me out.'

Willa sat down beside her. 'Because you lost your job?'

'And other things.'

'Better tell me what.'

Between sobs Pauline related the course of events that had led up to her dismissal from work and eviction from home. She'd gone to Pitlochry with Ernest on Friday.

'I thought you would.'

'Willa, I'm in love with him! And we had a wonderful time. He's ever such a gentleman, he squired me round the town, had me on his arm, like he was proud of me. We stayed in a lovely hotel.'

'And then?'

'On Saturday morning I telephoned in to the office and told them I was sick.'

'What excuse did you give?'

'Diarrhoea.'

Willa wanted to laugh but did not.

All appeared to have been going well in Pitlochry. Ernest had done his orders around the shops and had bought Pauline a thistle brooch which she was wearing now on her lapel (a bit tinny looking, Willa thought) and then they'd gone strolling along the river and had lunch. And after that they had come home.

'Trouble was, Saturday morning, my mum ran into my boss, old Frosty – he'd gone out to the chemist for his digestive tablets – and she said to him that it was nice he'd given me the morning off to go and visit my cousin Madge in Aberdeen.'

'And he said no, he hadn't?'

'So when I went to work yesterday morning he gave me my books.'

'But your mother didn't throw you out then?'

'No, she still thought I'd been to Aberdeen. And then, would you believe it – talk about my rotten luck! – we got a letter by the late afternoon post—'

'Don't tell me it was from cousin Madge!'

Pauline nodded. 'She'd written it Saturday morning and said she hadn't seen or heard from us for ages and could she come down for a visit?'

Willa agreed that that was bad luck. 'So your mother would want to know where you had been?'

'She dragged it out of me. Then she started screaming, calling me all sorts of names. Old Mrs Blaney came in from next door to see what was up and my mum told her I was a hoor!' Pauline was crying again. Willa moved over on the bed and put an arm round her. 'She told me I'd let her down and I was to get out of her house. She said I could stay till morning but that was it.'

'And she didn't change her mind after she'd slept on it?'

Pauline shook her head.

'And your dad?'

'You know him! He sat behind his racing paper pretending it wasn't happening.'

'What about Ernest? Have you told him?'

'I haven't seen him. I don't know where he lives.'

'Pauline, I don't know how you can stay here. We haven't the room. You can hardly swing a cat in here as it is.' Nor did they have any spare money to feed an extra mouth and Pauline, Willa presumed, would have none. She gave her pay packet to her mother every week and her mother doled out pocket money.

'Just for a night or two, Willa, till I find something. You've got a double bed.'

'I'll go and talk to Tommy's mother. It's her house.'

'Don't tell her about Ernest!'

'What am I to tell her?'

'Anything!'

That was all very well, thought Willa, as she returned to the kitchen where her mother-in-law was cuddling her grandchild, but what was she to actually say? Fortunately Ina liked Pauline and didn't like Mrs Cant. Who did?

'Pauline wants to stay for a couple of nights. Would that be all right? She's had a row with her mother.'

'That woman.' Ina sniffed. 'She's a troublemaker if ever there was one.'

'Well, what do you think? She could sleep with me.'

'I suppose she'll be out all day at her work, for I couldn't abide her hanging about in my kitchen. Why is she not there now?'

'She wasn't very well this morning.'

'Oh, all right, if you're willing to give up half your bed. But only for a couple of nights, mind.'

Willa returned to Pauline and gave her the news.

'You'll have to go out in the morning, though, as if you were going to work. I didn't tell her you'd been sacked.'

'I will, I'll be out at half-eight every morning. Don't worry about that! Thanks a million, Willa, I knew you'd come up trumps. You're my best pal after all.'

Pauline then revealed that she had left another suitcase outside the door, a larger one. She dragged it in and unpacked its contents, cramming the wardrobe so full that each garment, her own and Willa's, had to be squeezed into the smallest space possible. Everything would be bound to come out crushed when it emerged. Pauline's shoes overflowed on the shoe rack underneath and some had to be placed on the floor alongside.

'If you want to borrow any of my shoes feel free!' she said. Her feet were a full size bigger than Willa's.

Amongst her clothing were six pairs of brand-new, flesh-coloured, rayon stockings, two of which she gave to Willa. 'For having me. Presents from Ernest. He also gave me a suspender belt.' She held the black lacy belt against herself before tossing it onto the bed.

She then proceeded to lay out on the walnut-veneered dressing table numerous cosmetics in the shape of jars, bottles and tins, until there was not an inch left uncovered.

'It's only for a couple of nights. I knew you wouldn't let me down, Willa.'

When the cases were empty she heaved them up on top of the wardrobe.

'You couldn't lend us five bob, could you? Or half a crown? I've nothing on me. Well, maybe sixpence.'

Willa gave her two shillings, which was all she could afford.

'I'll pay you back, Willa, I promise. When I see Ernest he'll give me something, I know he will.'

'How are you going to find him?'

'He usually waits for me outside work. I'll go along and hang around at coming-out time.'

'Better start looking for a job,' said Willa.

She set off up the hill at ten minutes to two, having finally made up her mind to go only at half-past one. She'd kept thinking she should, she shouldn't, she would, she wouldn't, and back round again. But now, as she was hurrying up Lauriston Place, she admitted to herself that, deep down, she had intended to go all along. Thinking about Pauline's predicament was making her feel a little queasy. She had no intention, however, of going off for the night anywhere with Richard. She just wanted to see him and talk.

She slowed when she saw Richard's mother emerging from a stair doorway. She wore a different hat today, a black one that looked rather like a large plate, with a pink rose on one side that bobbed as she walked. Willa followed in her wake, studying her dignified back.

Moving at a measured pace, Richard's mother turned along

Forrest Road and Willa became anxious in case she might continue along George IV Bridge, but she turned off down Chambers Street.

She arrived at the café at quarter-past two. Richard was there with a teapot in front of him.

'Sorry I'm a little late,' she said, unable to tell him that she had been walking in the footsteps of his mother and that this had delayed her.

'That's all right. I'm just relieved to see you. The tea's probably a bit cold. I had to order.'

'I don't mind.'

He poured her a cup. He was right; the tea was barely tepid. He must have been there a while.

'I must go to the library afterwards,' she said. 'I've got my books with me. I finished *Northanger Abbey*. It's amazing how all those people at that time didn't seem to have to do any work.'

'Only certain people.'

She nodded.

'I've got a new author for you. Another American lady. Edith Wharton. My mother loves her books.'

Willa resolved not to let that put her off.

'If you can't find any of her books in the library I'll borrow a couple of my mother's for you. She's a great book-buyer. She's never away from Thin's bookshop.'

Willa drank her cold tea and Richard paid.

'Shall we go for a walk?' he said.

They headed down the hill. He took her hand.

'Better not,' she said, disengaging it.

They crossed North Bridge and entering the Canongate

made their way to Dunbar's Close. Someone had been sick halfway down the entry, a drunk, probably. They stepped over it. There were many pubs in the Royal Mile and, consequently, at night, drunkards frequented the closes, relieving themselves, one way and another, making it an area to be avoided. So Tommy had told Willa. She had never been here after dark herself.

They had the garden to themselves again. When Richard took her into his arms she realised she had been longing for this moment since morning. Their kiss lasted longer and was not as gentle as before, nor was her response.

'I love you, Willa,' he said into her hair.

'You just can't,' she said.

'But I just do.'

He kissed her again, running his hands down her back and letting them rest on her hips. He pulled her in even closer to him. 'I love you, love you, love you!' he whispered. 'Believe me! Do you love me?'

She nodded. A refrain was running through her head. *You made me love you, I didn't wanna do it...*Tommy had sung it to her. *I didn't wanna do it...*

They were interrupted by a long wolf whistle from overhead. Looking up they saw two children hanging out of the upstairs' window of one of the tenements that overlooked the garden. Nothing, it seemed, could ever be completely secret.

They retraced their steps back up the close and the street.

'When can I see you again?' he asked.

'Depends on when I can manage to get away.'

'I'll go to our café every day at two in case you can come.

Otherwise I'll be in the library until half-past three every afternoon.'

'Don't come in with me today.'

'I'll go into the art department.'

She walked in ahead of him through the main door, conscious of his eyes on her back.

The librarian, the nice one, said, 'Your friend's not in today.'

Willa said, 'Do you know a writer called Edith Wharton?'

'I've never read her but I think I've seen some of her books on the shelf.'

Willa found *The Age of Innocence* straightaway and went to see if there was anything of Willa Cather's in. There was. *A Lost Lady.* She took it down at once.

After she'd had the books stamped she went down to the ladies' toilet to tidy her hair which she feared might be all over the place, which it proved to be. And the skin round her mouth and chin was bright red, as if someone had been kissing her passionately. She'd thought the librarian had been giving her a funny look. She splashed her face with cool water until the colour started to fade, then she set off homeward where, awaiting her return were her child, her mother-in-law, and her best friend.

~ 14 ~

Auckland,
New Zealand
16th May, 1924

Dear Willa,
We spent a week on the South Island before
coming up here. While there we were invited to
afternoon tea in a house outside Christchurch which
was decorated with sayings from Dickens. It was
amazing, everywhere you looked, even in the
bathroom. Things like 'Barkis is willin' (to do what?)
and 'Umps,' said Mr Grewgious.' (Hope I've spelled
that right). All that would have appealed to you! I told
the lady of the house you were a fan of Mr Dickens.

'Are you?' asked Bunty.

'We had to read *David Copperfield* at school,' said Pauline
before Willa could answer. 'Do you remember, Willa? I was
bored stiff.'

'I enjoyed it,' said Willa. 'But there are other writers I prefer.'

None of them would be interested to hear about Jane Austen,
Katherine Mansfield, Edith Wharton or Willa Cather. She
seemed to be hung up on women writers at present. Pauline was
reading *The Sheik* by Ethel M Dell and kept reading out bits in
bed when Willa was trying to concentrate on *A Lost Lady*. She
was enjoying it, in spite of the fact that Richard's mother was a

fan of Willa Cather, and felt for Marian Forrester living in the little backwoods town of Sweet Water (though that was a nice name, a bit like the ones in LM Montgomery's books), married to a much older man, and tempted by another.

She'd also been deeply involved in *The Age of Innocence*. Phrases from it had stuck in her mind, as when Newland Archer, contemplating his young innocent bride-to-be, felt thrilled that he was going to possess this girl as well as 'a tender reverence for her abysmal purity'. Was that how Tommy had looked at her? He'd known she was a virgin; that had pleased him. But *abysmal* purity? Later, Newland Archer found marriage not to be 'the safe anchorage' he had expected but rather 'a voyage on uncharted seas'. She could identify with that. At times she felt she was being tossed around on the high seas, a long way from dry land.

'They wouldn't all go to tea at that house, would they?' said Ina.

Willa glanced up. She'd been miles away, often seemed to be these days.

'Hardly,' said Bunty. 'How many men are there on Tommy's ship, Willa?'

'Four hundred and seventy.' She had told them more than once but they loved to go over things.

'Must be kind of cosy on board.' Bunty laughed but Ina did not.

There was also a fine picture of the Bull Inn, Rochester, on the wall. Made my mate Bill (he comes from down there) feel homesick. Said he was dying for a pint of bitter in a good old English pub.

But as the rest of us pointed out, there was no lack of liquid refreshment here. Beer was flowing like water.

'Where on earth is Rochester?' asked Ina.

'Somewhere in England,' said Willa. 'Yorkshire, maybe.' Or was she thinking about *Jane Eyre* and Mr Rochester? So many things she had in her head had come out of books.

'The folk must have come from there originally,' said Bunty. 'Homesick themselves, I wouldn't be surprised.'

'Who wouldn't be, living down there near the South Pole?' demanded Ina.

A Navy team played the New Zealanders at rugby, their national game, and were soundly beaten. It was only to be expected so were we downhearted? No, we were not! Some of my mates and me had a good game of footie in the park, cheered on by the local lasses. I managed to score a goal!

'Bravo, our Tommy!' said Bunty. 'Expect he got an extra cheer from the lasses for that.'

'He was good at football when he was at the school,' said his mother.

'Seems he was good at everything,' said Pauline.

Willa wondered if Richard had played football at school. Rugby, more likely, in that kind of school. She wondered if it would be his kind of game.

'What's that Malcolm's got in his mouth?' asked Bunty.

Willa started and came back to reality. She must stop letting her mind wander. Her child was crawling round the floor between their chair legs with something in his mouth that he could potentially choke on and kill himself. She reached down and took a tube of lipstick out of his mouth. He immediately began to roar. Willa picked him up and comforted him, and herself, saying, 'There, there, it's all right, love.'

Pauline claimed the lipstick.

'You should be more careful about leaving things lying around,' said Ina. 'The wee one's at the stage of wanting to eat everything he can get his hands on. He might have choked.'

'Sorry,' said Pauline meekly, slipping the lipstick into her pocket.

They had ceased to keep up the pretence that she was going to work every day at the Co-op. It had proved to be too big a strain for her, putting in the days, hanging around. Ina had had a few things to say about St Cuthbert's Co-operative Society when she'd been told that Pauline had been paid off; they had not disclosed the reason. Pauline was looking for other work but so far without success. The problem was that she had no references. She'd only ever worked at the Co-op and she couldn't very well ask them for one there. Her father was slipping her a few shillings now and then, usually when he'd had a win on the horses. She saw him down at the betting shop. Her mother was showing no signs of relenting and Pauline said that even if she did now she wouldn't want to go back. She couldn't stick her mother. Willa had told her that she couldn't stay here when Tommy came home and Pauline had said she'd find something else long before that. Tommy wasn't due back till October, was he? It was only June.

As for Ernest, she hadn't seen him again, although she had

gone along to the Co-op several afternoons when the workers were coming out. One of her former colleagues thought she'd seen him hanging around looking as if he was waiting for somebody so Pauline was convinced that it must have been him. She was still looking for him. The trouble was that he was away a lot, travelling all over the country selling ladies' hosiery, so it wasn't as if he was in Edinburgh every day. Sometimes she cried about him before she went to sleep at night.

'Read a bit more, Willa,' urged Ina.

> *The Maoris gave us a right royal time, executing various dances in their native costumes. They are a fine race of hardy sea men, hospitable, brave and chivalrous, and the most intelligent natives in the world, so we were told. They are also very patriotic and took their place in the last war, proving their worth. Queen Victoria is held in very high esteem by them.*

'Fancy,' said Pauline.

'Why shouldn't she be held in high esteem by them?' demanded Ina.

'That old dumpling,' said Pauline.

'*Pauline!*'

> *The modern Maori lives now in peace in his tribal village with his wife and picaninnies, for the most part in primitive style, a simple-hearted child of nature, possessing a humour and shrewdness entirely his own.*

'No jigs?' asked Bunty.

'There's bound to be some,' said Willa, letting her eye travel on down the page over a description of Auckland. Fine parks, fine buildings, a hospital with pretty grounds, more about the Maoris and their customs – a lot about them; he seemed to have been very impressed by them – hot springs, mud volcanoes, yachting, sugar refining. He wrote that this was a wonderful country with wonderful people but they wouldn't want to hear that yet again. Nearly everywhere he'd been, maybe with Sierra Leone as an exception, left Scotland in the shade.

'Oh yes, here we are!'

> *Numerous entertainments, parties and dances, were organised for us and places were lit up at night, including the Town Hall, with banners welcoming the squadron.*

There was a bit more about the young ladies of Auckland and their bobbed hair but Willa didn't bother to read that out. As she was putting the letter back in its envelope she realised that there was a postcard inside. A picture postcard of a bare-footed, large black woman with fizzy hair and a headband, with her tongue sticking out. On the back Tommy had written: *A Maori welcome.*

Bunty and Pauline were much amused.

'Isn't that a scream?' said Bunty.

Ina frowned at the picture, not knowing what to make of it. 'It's rather rude, if you ask me.'

'Wouldn't it be a laugh if we were all to go round Edinburgh sticking our tongues out at each other?' said Bunty.

Pauline tried it but Ina was not amused.

'I expect they'd find some of our customs funny too,' said Willa.

'Such as?' demanded Bunty.

'Winking.'

She put the postcard and letter in her handbag. Richard would be interested to hear about New Zealand. He was interested in the world outside Edinburgh. As for these three here, they thought anything they weren't familiar with was a joke. At times they got on her nerves, Pauline especially. Willa would never put her out unless she had somewhere to go to but she resented losing the time and space she had had alone with Malcolm. The only time she had him to herself now was when she took him for a walk in his pram and even then Pauline often tagged along, preferring to do that than sit with Ina in the kitchen.

Willa picked up Malcolm, removed a piece of paper from his mouth, which caused him to yell in protest, and took him to the sink to wipe his mouth and hands.

'He's tired. I'm going to put him down for a sleep.'

'I'll keep an eye on him if you want to go to the library,' said Ina.

'I'm sure Willa won't pass up that offer,' said Bunty, turning her head to give Willa a wink.

Willa had told Richard not to go into Bunty's shop as she would just wangle things out of him. She was a dab hand at it. Not that there was a great deal to wangle. When they did manage to meet they just went down to the secret garden and had a kiss and a cuddle. They only ever had about an hour together and part of that was spent drinking tea and talking about books and Tommy's travels. Still, even that would be more than enough to light a fuse in Ina's kitchen. Walking up the hill to meet Richard, Willa would be troubled by stirrings of guilt but when she opened the café door and saw his face the flutters in her stomach subsided and she went forward to meet him on a surge of happiness.

'I've a wee job for you, Pauline, if you'd like it,' said Bunty. 'I'll pay you. Not a fortune, mind, but something. Delivering the *Evening News*. My paper boy's sick.'

'Delivering papers?' said Pauline and seeing Ina's disapproving stare, added, 'Oh, all right, Bunty.'

'A friend of mine needs some cleaning done,' Bunty went on. 'There's just herself in the house so it wouldn't be a heavy job.'

'Cleaning?' said Pauline.

'Beggars can't be choosers,' said Ina.

'You can come along with me now, Pauline,' said Bunty. 'The papers'll be coming in soon and you can sort them.'

They were getting ready to go when the bell went.

'Who in the name can that be?' said Ina.

'Might be Rudolph Valentino,' said Bunty.

Pauline pretended to swoon.

The caller was Gerry, who had come with a parcel of meat.

'I was right after all!' declared Bunty.

'Right about what?'

'I said you were Valentino.'

He gave her an uneasy look.

'But of course you're not, are you?' said Bunty with a smile.

'I've brought you a steak and kidney, Ina. And some tripe and sausages.'

'Thanks, Gerry.' Ina took it from him. 'That's good of you. You never forget us. We haven't seen you for a bit?'

'Business is busy.'

'Seems to be,' said Bunty.

'How's Elma?' asked Ina. 'I thought she was looking rather peely-wally last time she was in.'

'She had a wee stomach upset there for a bit but she seems to have got over it now. She's going to a church social this afternoon, some sort of women's do.'

'That's nice for her,' said Bunty.

'Anyone wanting a lift?' asked Gerry.

'I expect you could give Willa a hurl up to the library,' said Bunty. 'Save her a hike.'

Willa accepted since it would save her ten minutes at least, extra time that she could spend with Richard, but when they arrived at the library Gerry parked and switched off the engine. He was in a mood to talk.

'How's life treating you these days, Willa?'

She shrugged. 'All right, on the whole. Malcolm's doing well. That's the most important thing.'

'You must get fed up living with Ina though?'

'I do at times, of course. But I've no choice.'

He sighed. 'Aye, we don't seem to have that much choice in life. Well, not after you get yourself set on a certain path. When you look back you can't help asking yourself how you got into some things.'

She wondered if he was inviting her to ask questions which would then lead to him unburdening himself but she didn't feel she could cope with his confidences on top of everything else.

'You know, Willa, I've always felt you understood me more than anyone else in the family.'

She liked him and she wished for his sake that he could run off with Mrs Mooney and live happily ever after but then, even if he were free, Mrs Mooney wouldn't want it. Bunty had said so.

'Maybe we just have to enjoy what we can while we can,' said Willa.

'You're right, love.'

It was easy to say these things, thought Willa, as she stepped out of the van, but less easy to carry them through.

She went into the library for two or three minutes to give Gerry time to drive away, then she came back out and hurried up to the High Street.

As she pushed open the café door her heart began to thump. A smile spread across his face as soon as he saw her. She felt such a rush of happiness that she wanted to laugh aloud. He came forward to take her hands and lead her to the table in the corner. Their table. Their café.

While they drank their tea she read Tommy's letter to Richard. She sometimes wondered why she did this and had thought it was due partly to his being so interested in foreign parts, and partly because it kept Tommy's name alive between them so that their relationship wouldn't get too out of hand, for it should not, could not, must not.

'I wouldn't mind going to Australia and New Zealand,' said Richard. 'Wouldn't you?'

Willa nodded.

'I'd like to go to Australia and New Zealand with you,' said Richard. 'Make a new start. Away from everyone.'

From his mother and Tommy's mother.

'That can never be,' said Willa sadly.

'My mother says never say never. She says life is unpredictable.'

Perhaps he was hoping that Tommy would fall overboard and get eaten by a shark. Willa's mouth twitched at the thought. Not that she would want that to happen. Of course not!

'What are you smiling at?' he asked.

'I just like being here with you.'

'Let's go for a walk.'

Today, they did not go as far as Dunbar's Close. He pulled her into Advocate's Close, opposite St Giles Cathedral, unable to wait, and pressed her up against the wall.

'Richard, Richard,' she murmured when he lifted his mouth from hers. Tommy was no longer a presence between them. They were conscious only of each other and did not notice the occasional person passing up and down between the High Street and Cockburn Street. This was not a cul-de-sac like Dunbar's Close and therefore less private.

Richard said he couldn't bear being parted from her. 'It's driving me crazy. I want to be with you all the time.'

She wanted that too but did not dare say so. She had a child to think of.

They stayed so long in the close that when they went back to the library Willa did not have time to change her books. She ran downstairs to the ladies' toilet to sluice her face with cold water while Richard waited upstairs, determined to walk her most of the way home. They walked closer than usual, their hands brushing from time to time, and then they would turn to each other and smile, like conspirators, and lovers.

Coming down Lauriston Place they met Richard's mother emerging from her door.

Willa's step faltered. Today, Mrs Fitzwilliam wore a different hat, a black straw with a white rose.

Richard took Willa's arm and led her forward. 'Mother,' he said, 'I'd like you to meet my friend. This is Willa whom I've told you about. Willa, this is my mother.'

His mother hesitated a moment, then she gave Willa a smile and extended her gloved hand. 'I'm pleased to meet you. Is this the friend who has been reading Willa Cather, Richard?'

He said that it was. Willa put her naked hand into the white kid-gloved one. The leather felt smooth in her palm but there was no warmth in the grasp. Her hand was soon dropped.

'How very nice. You like her books then, do you, dear?'

'Yes,' said Willa, wishing she could think of an intelligent remark to make to Richard's mother about *A Lost Lady,* but could not. Her tongue felt as if it were stuck to the roof of her mouth. The smile the woman had given her had been polite, but, like the handshake, not friendly.

'I'm on my way to Thin's to buy one or two books,' said Mrs Fitzwilliam. 'Would you care to accompany me, Richard?'

Richard looked from his mother to Willa and back again.

'I must be going,' said Willa hurriedly. 'Nice to meet you,' she added to Richard's mother, and walked off down the hill, trying to keep her head up and shoulders back, trying to look dignified.

~ 15 ~

Suva, Fiji,
South Pacific
25th May, 1924

Dear Willa,
Fiji consists of 844 islands and islets though only about 100 are inhabited. It became a British possession in 1874.

'Is there any country that doesn't belong to us?' asked Ina.

'Italy doesn't,' said Elma, sounding a bit snarky. Willa wondered if it was meant to be a dig at Ina's late husband. She'd never liked him apparently. 'It might be better for it if it did. Mrs Jolly who lives in the next stair to us was telling me it's quite a backward country.'

'Read on, Willa,' said Ina.

'You might be interested in our address of welcome which reads as follows (in translation): It is a precious thing to the chiefs and people of Fiji that Vice Admiral Sir Frederick Field and those under his command have arrived at Fiji in the great fleet which has anchored in the harbour of Suva. Today the natives give thanks to God for being permitted to see with their own eyes the great chief who has come from England on a world cruise to visit these islands that shelter under the

protection of the British Flag. They are the shield and
buckler that ensure freedom and the right to live in
peace for those who inhabit the British possessions.'

'Isn't that nice?' said Ina.

'Nice to know they're grateful,' said Elma. 'And that they're giving thanks to God. We've been collecting clothes for African babies at church.'

'I don't think Fiji's anywhere near Africa, is it, Willa?' said Ina, with an element of snideness creeping into her voice now. 'Show Elma on the globe.'

Elma gave the world a scant look and spoke to Willa. 'So if you've anything of Malcolm's going begging?'

'By the time he's done with his clothes they're only fit for the rag-and-bone man, isn't that right, Malkie?' said his grandmother, beaming down upon him.

Hearing his name, he looked up. He was busy building and knocking down bricks with the alphabet printed in bright colours on their sides. Bricks were quieter than the pots and pans that he liked to haul out of the cupboard.

'It's no wonder, the way he gets to crawl all over the place,' said Elma. 'Would he not be better in a playpen?'

'He likes being in amongst us,' said Ina. 'Don't you, Malkie?'

'He likes being the centre of attention, if you ask me.'

Like his father. Tommy had always had the family's attention focused on him, being his mother's only son and his aunts' only nephew. Willa suspected he'd liked being the only child. But he could be kind, she would say that for him. She'd seen him helping an old lady up the step of the tram and he often carried up Mrs Begg's messages. And, yes, he was good to his mother.

'Nobody was asking you, Elma,' said Ina.

Elma gave one of her sniffs for which she was famous, within the family, that was. 'What's that smell?'

'It'll be the nappy pail likely,' said Ina cheerfully. 'Malkie did a big one this morning, didn't you, Malkie?'

> *The population is a mixture of Chinese, Indian, European and Fijian. The Fijian is a different type of native from any other in the world. His hair is thick and stands upright, about 7 inches deep, and is roundly and evenly trimmed in the way a garden hedge might be.*

'Wouldn't fancy that,' said Elma, patting the back of her hair, neatly ridged as usual. 'By the way, a Chink came into the shop yesterday. He told Gerald he was doing something at the university.' She didn't sound convinced.

'No reason why he shouldn't,' said Willa.

'Well, I don't know. They wouldn't be able to read our writing, would they? Theirs is all funny squiggles.'

> *The Fijians are of fine physique, the women particularly. They dress in semi-European style but with no footgear or headgear. Their thin dresses are brilliant in colour.*

Elma sniffed again, possibly at the mention of thin dresses. Thin, revealing dresses. Elma wore heavy corsets even in the month of June; you could see the whalebones lying underneath her blouse and skirt. She creaked when she leant to the side. Willa supposed that the Fijian women might not wear anything underneath their dresses, not when they lived in such a hot climate. It must be pleasant to wear light clothes and go bare-legged all year round. It would give you a feeling of lightness and freedom. Willa had given up wearing stockings for the summer months, though Ina did not approve. She thought married women should keep themselves covered from head to foot. She herself would never consider crossing the doorstep without her hat on, even in summer. One day they'd gone to Portobello on the tram and she'd sat on the beach crowned with her old brown felt hat, a feather sticking out the side.

> *The highlight of our stay was the native dancing. There was no music but a party sat on the grass chanting low monotonous songs. The attitudes in some of the dances seemed very comical to us but they might have been meant to be tragic for all we knew. Their brown bodies were blackened with some substance and dabbed spotted fashion with red which made them look like black- and redcurrant pudding.*

'Must look as if they've got the measles,' said Ina. 'I hope they didn't.' She cocked her head. 'Is that the door?'

'It'll be Pauline,' said Willa. She'd been given her own key.

'Is she still living with you?' asked Elma.

'She's got nowhere else to go,' said Ina. 'Her mother put her out because she lost her job.'

'I heard different,' said Elma in a low voice, but was

interrupted by the arrival of Pauline into the kitchen.

'Oh, hello there, Mrs McGill,' she said to Elma. 'How're you doing?'

'Very well, thank you,' said Elma in her best pan-drop voice, primping her mouth. 'Have you managed to find yourself other employment yet, Pauline?'

'I'm helping Bunty out in the shop.'

'And she's doing some cleaning for a friend of Bunty's,' put in Ina.

'A Mrs Mooney,' said Pauline.

'A Mrs *Who*?' Elma's eyes bulged.

'Mooney,' repeated Pauline. 'She's great to work for. She's a good laugh.'

'I'm sure she is!' Elma rose up from the chair, her back as stiff as a poker. 'I've always known I couldn't trust Bunty.'

She picked up her message bag and left without another word.

'What did I say wrong?' asked Pauline.

'Well, you see,' said Willa, 'Gerry was kind of friendly with Mrs Mooney.'

'You don't mean she was his fancy woman?'

'Maybe she still is,' said Ina, looking at Willa, who shrugged.

'Mrs Mooney's in and out the shop a lot, mind,' said Pauline. 'She comes in for her *Evening News* and usually twenty Craven A. Sometimes Sobranie. But she says Craven A are good for her throat. Come to think of it, Mr McGill often seems to pop in at the same time.'

'Pauline,' said Ina, 'not a word of this to anyone else!'

'Of course not,' said Pauline. 'You can rely on me.'

'I hope so. This is a family matter, you understand.'

'Mrs Costello, I was wondering if you'd look after Malcolm while I take Willa out for a wee while this evening? I thought I'd like to treat her. Mrs Mooney's just paid me.'

'The two of you were out at the pictures a couple of nights ago.'

They'd had a great night out, of the kind they used to have before Willa married and Pauline had forgotten about Ernest for a few hours. They'd gone to a double bill at the St Andrew's Square cinema to see Rudolph Valentino and Mae Murray in *The Cabaret Girl* and Pola Negri and Jack Holt in *The Cheat*. Coming out Pauline had said she could sit right through it all again. They'd walked home talking non-stop about Valentino.

'So where are you thinking of going the night?' asked Ina suspiciously.

'Nowhere special. Just to a café for an ice cream, something like that.'

'Oh well, all right then. You might bring me back a slider. And mind you're not too late.'

It was a fine June evening, ideal for strolling along Princes Street and through the gardens.

'Put on your glad rags and a bit of make-up,' said Pauline. 'I thought we'd go to a cocktail bar first.'

'Whereabouts?'

'What about the Caley?'

'Would that not be too dear?' Willa had never been in the Caledonian Hotel at the west end of Princes Street.

'Mrs Mooney paid me well. She's rolling. She said to me,

"Take Willa out and give her a good time. She needs it with
that husband of hers philandering his way round the world!"'
Pauline giggled. 'Maureen's got a good way with words.
Maybe it's with her being Irish.'

'Pauline, Tommy is not philandering. He's working.'

'You can't call that work, can you? Come on! Picnics,
parties, dances, runs in motor cars, afternoon tea.'

'But in between they have to work. When they're at sea.'

'They spend an awful long time on shore. And what about
those dances and parties? The hospitality that he's always on
about? Everybody loves the boys in blue, can't do enough for
them. You don't think he's staying faithful to you for a whole
year, do you? Maureen says it'd be too much to expect of a
lusty young man. And Tommy's lusty. So get dressed!'

'I don't know what to wear.'

'Put on your mauve chiffon dress.'

That was one Willa used to go dancing in. She hadn't worn
it since before she'd fallen pregnant with Malcolm.

'We're not going dancing and that's definite!'

'Put it on! It'll make you feel good.'

Willa was surprised that the dress still fitted her.

'You've got your figure back,' said Pauline. She herself had
put on a little weight though Willa did not say so. 'Do you
want to borrow my new lipstick? It'd go nicely with your
dress.'

This was like told times, the two of them together, getting
dressed, making up, for a night out.

'Pity we can't go to the Palais,' said Pauline.

'I couldn't,' said Willa.

'Oh, all right!'

'Don't be late,' Ina repeated, when she saw them setting out. A frown creased her forehead. Willa realised she didn't like her going out all dressed up with Pauline. She was uneasy. Willa was a little herself.

Once out in the balmy summer evening, she felt liberated. She could have danced her way down Lothian Road, letting the gauzy chiffon swirl around her bare legs. The feel of it made her feel carefree again. Pauline linked arms with her. She was wearing a scarlet silk dress with black fringes bordering the knee-length hemline and round her head she sported a scarlet band that looked dramatic against her glossy dark hair, neatly clipped just below the ears. She'd spent some of her wages at the hairdresser's. A few men turned their heads to look at them and one or two called out.

'We could get off with anybody we want,' said Pauline. 'And why the hell shouldn't we?' She sounded reckless, more reckless than Willa had ever known her.

'I don't intend to get off with anybody!'

'All right, keep your hair on!'

Pauline began to sing. '*Ma, he's making eyes at me, Ma, he's awful nice to me*...I could do with somebody to be awful nice to me.'

They sailed past the uniformed commissionaire into the formal splendour of the Caledonian Hotel.

'Can I help you ladies?' Another uniformed employee was at their elbow.

'Could you please direct us to the cocktail bar?' said Pauline.

Once ensconced in comfortable chairs, they proceeded to study the menu.

'I'm going to have a Singapore Sling,' announced Willa. 'Tommy went to Singapore. It was wonderful! Well, of course it was. What else could it be?'

'Expect he drank a bucketload of slings while he was there. Two Singapore Slings, if you please,' Pauline said to the waiter.

Rather good, they decided, after the first few sips. Nice fruity taste, not too strong on the rum. The first drinks slid down easily and Pauline ordered another.

'Maureen gave me a fiver to take you out.'

'A fiver,' echoed Willa. 'She *must* be rolling.'

Halfway through their second drinks, they were approached by a couple of men who had been eyeing them and whom Pauline had been giving the eye in return, even though Willa had tried to discourage her. They looked like business men in their dark suits, well-laundered white shirts and silk ties and gold signet rings on their pinkies.

'Well heeled,' whispered Pauline, when she saw them getting up to come across. 'They won't be selling stockings and suspender belts like Ernest.'

'Pauline, leave me out of this,' said Willa in an even lower voice, for the men were upon them, commenting that it seemed a shame that two such lovely ladies should be sitting on their own. Would they mind if they joined them?

So they did, and immediately ordered another drink each for the two ladies and double brandies for themselves. As Willa's third drink was set in front of her she began to wonder if Singapore Slings were not stronger than she'd thought to begin with. She was going to sip this one slowly.

'What brings you gentlemen to Edinburgh?' asked Pauline.

'Business, business!'

'That's what we thought!' laughed Pauline, who had moved into high flirtatious mode.

'And you ladies?'

Pauline informed the men that they lived in Edinburgh and worked as stenographers.

'I'll know where to come then if I want any dictation taken down.'

There was more laughter.

When the men ordered another round Willa got up and went to enquire about the ladies' toilet. The ladies' powder room was on the first floor, she was informed. She felt slightly light-headed as she made her way up the grand staircase holding on to the banister rail. Pauline came tripping up behind her.

'What do you think then, Willa?'

'That you and I should go for a walk in the gardens. On our own. I'm beginning to feel drunk.'

'They're nice though, aren't they? I rather fancy Ralph, he's got such a lovely smooth English accent. Oxford, wouldn't you say?'

'He'll be off back to London tomorrow morning.'

'It's just a night out.'

'And you know what they'll be looking for.'

'I'm not going to give it to them, am I? It's just a laugh.'

They used the toilets and combed their hair and Pauline refreshed her lipstick, making a face at herself in the mirror. The powder-room attendant was watching them.

'Ralph's company imports shoes from Italy,' said Pauline. 'He's promised to bring me a couple of pairs next time he's up in Edinburgh. He says the leather's as soft as a baby's bottom.'

'Let's go,' said Willa. 'I need air.'

Pauline dropped a penny in the attendant's dish.

When they returned to their table in the cocktail bar, they found that Ralph had a proposal.

'Why don't we all go up to my room for some more drinks? It's quieter and there's a good view of the castle. We could have room service, a little smoked salmon, caviar, anything you ladies would fancy.'

'I'm sorry,' said Willa, who had remained standing, 'but I must go.' She looked at Pauline.

'We thought we might have a wee walk in the gardens. Take the air like.'

'Why don't we join you ladies for a stroll?' suggested Ralph. 'You might fancy a little something to eat and drink later.'

They left the hotel, the men having paid for all their Singapore Slings, leaving Mrs Mooney's five pound note intact. Willa and Pauline walked in the middle, with their escorts on the outside.

They crossed the road and took the nearest entrance down into Princes Street gardens. Willa was relieved to see that they were well thronged and an orchestra was playing on the bandstand. Ralph took Pauline's hand almost immediately and swung it playfully to and fro between them. Willa avoided the other man, whose name was Neville, taking hers. She kept both hands clasped firmly behind her back.

'Lot of people about,' commented Neville.

'Yes,' she said.

'Edinburgh always this busy?' he asked.

'No,' she said.

Willa turned her head as Pauline erupted into giggles. Ralph had moved from holding her hand to sliding his arm around her waist. Now he was tickling her ribs and she was saying, 'You're terrible, so you are. Stop it, stop it!' But Ralph knew that she didn't really want him to stop it.

Neville, feeling perhaps that he was being shown up, tried to move closer to Willa and take hold of her arm, but she side-stepped and allowed a man coming in the opposite direction to pass between them. If it were not for Pauline she would have wheeled sharply to the right and made off.

'Not very friendly, are you?' said Neville, when they had reformed into a group of four.

'No, not very. I'm married, you see. I expect you are too?'

'You're very direct.'

'No point in being anything else.'

'I like girls with a bit of spirit.'

'What's your wife like?'

'No need to bring her into it.'

He was probably right about that. She wouldn't wish to bring Tommy in either, whichever ocean he was in. Pauline and Ralph now had their arms entwined around each other.

Willa sighed and looked away and then stood stock-still. Coming down the bank below the castle ramparts was a figure that she recognised.

'Richard!' she shouted and began to run up the hill towards him, Pauline forgotten.

He had heard her above the sound of the music and came running to meet her. They collided and fell to the ground where they rolled over on the grass together, oblivious of the people in the gardens below them. They lay face to face, feeling the flow of the other's breath.

'What have you been doing?'

'Drinking Singapore Slings.'

'Did I ever tell you you were beautiful?'

She had no time to answer for his mouth had found hers.

They lay until the band had ceased to play and the light had waned. People were starting to move out of the garden. The attendants would soon lock the gates.

'Come on,' said Richard, lifting Willa onto her feet. 'Let's go up higher.'

It was darker higher up, out of reach of the street lights. There was only a small slice of moon. They heard the attendants' distant voices calling closing time. In a little while it became very quiet inside the gardens except for the swish of traffic moving along Princes Street.

'What are you wearing?' Richard ran his hands down her body.

'Chiffon.'

'It feels like a spider's web. Oh, Willa, I love you so much I want to shout it out all over Edinburgh.'

He kissed her again and then, what she had vowed should never happen, happened. Now that it had, their coming together seemed to be so easy, so inevitable, like something that they had been gradually moving towards and which nothing could prevent for, at that moment, the world beyond did not exist. There was no question of resisting.

Suva, Fiji

Dear Willa,
    Thought you'd like to see what a Fijian man looks like. It'll give you a laugh.
    Tommy xxx

'Gey funny-looking hair,' said the postman who, as a matter of course, examined all postcards before delivering them.

'Seven inches deep, so I believe,' said Willa, making to close the door.

'Could nest a couple of birds in there.'

'Cheerio now, Sandy!'

Ina and Malcolm were still sleeping, thank God for that at least. Willa had been at the window watching for Pauline when she'd seen the postie cross the road. She'd opened the door before he could ring the bell and wake the sleepers.

She'd risen early, having gone to bed late, very late. Two o'clock had been striking when Richard had finally kissed her goodbye at the bottom door. She'd crept up the stairs in her stained, ragged chiffon dress and prayed that Tommy's mother would be asleep. She had been, deep asleep, in bed, lying on her back snoring, with Malcolm curled up against her side, breathing softly. Willa had wanted to lean over and kiss his flushed cheek but had dared not. She had closed the door on the sleepers and crawled into her own bed where she'd dozed restlessly.

The first thing she had done on rising was fetch some vinegar from the kitchen and go into the bathroom where she'd mixed it with warm water and used her douche. She had then buried her dress in the bucket, under a pile of vegetable peelings.

With the postcard in her hand, she went back to the window to look down on the street. There was still no sign of Pauline. It was nearly eight o'clock and Malcolm would be sure to wake soon. The St Cuthbert milk cart was parked at the kerb below while the milkman moved from door to door with his crates of bottles. Willa ran down the stairs.

'We could do with a couple of pints,' she said.

'I was coming up.'

'Thought I'd just come down. It's a nice morning.' Willa stroked the horse's nose. Sometimes she brought him a carrot but not this morning.

When she glanced up she saw a cab coming round the clock. It pulled neatly into the space behind the milk cart.

'Somebody's in the money,' said the milkman.

The taxi door opened, and out stepped Pauline. The black fringe round her red hemline had become detached at one side and was hanging down. Her red headband was missing and her hair no longer looked sleek.

'Had a good night out, hen?' asked the milkman.

Pauline was not looking at them.

'Come on,' said Willa, taking her by the arm and managing to juggle the two milk bottles at the same time. 'Let's get you up the stairs before Ina wakes and all hell's let loose.'

She had just got Pauline into her room and shut the door when she heard Ina's voice.

'Willa, are you up?'

'I'm coming!'

Willa went out. Ina was standing in the lobby in her voluminous off-white interlock nightdress with her hair screwed into tight steel curlers. She had Malcolm in her arms. Willa took him from her and kissed the top of his head.

'He's dirty,' said his grandmother.

'I'll change him,' said Willa. 'And then I'll put the kettle on.'

She went into the bathroom and changed his nappy. It was heavily soiled and she wondered how long he'd lain in it. His bottom looked chapped.

'There you are, my little love,' she said, smiling down at him where he lay peaceably, face-up, on her knee. It was not often he was so docile, usually only first thing in the morning when he had not quite emerged from sleep. By the time she took him through to the kitchen he was struggling to be put down. She gave him a rusk to keep him going until he had his porridge. She had weaned him a couple of weeks ago after he'd decided he'd had enough breast milk. He was a child who was going to want to take his own decisions.

Ina was sitting at the kitchen table. 'The kettle's on.'

'I'll make the tea.'

'What time did you come in last night?'

'Didn't really notice. Will I put your porridge on?'

'It was gone eleven before Malkie and I went to our bed.'

'Must have been not long after that.'

'And what about Madam Pauline?'

'She's still in bed.'

'Shouldn't she have been out delivering the morning papers for Bunty?'

'She wasn't feeling too well first thing.'

'And what's Bunty meant to do? That girl's bone lazy, if you ask me.'

Willa poured the boiling water into the teapot and stirred it round with the tea leaves. The pot was a big Brown Betty that Ina had had since she got married. One day, thought Willa, she would have a nice new china teapot of her own with roses on it and cups and a milk jug to match. She had wanted to buy a set when Tommy had been home on leave the last time but he'd said, 'What's the point? Mother's cupboards are full of stuff.' So they were. *Her* stuff. All the good china stayed in the cupboard to be admired behind the glass and was brought out only on high days. About four times a year, such as when the minister called. The rest of the time they used the old chipped cups and cracked plates. Tommy couldn't understand why she was bothered. There was a lot about her that he didn't understand and he wouldn't ever try, she knew that.

'Where did you go, the two of you?' asked Ina.

'We had a walk in the gardens. It was a nice night and there were lots of people out. There was a band too.' Willa talked on.

'I used to enjoy a walk in the gardens on a warm evening.' Ina sounded wistful, which was not like her.

'Did you used to go there with Tommy's dad?'

Ina shrugged, her pensive mood quickly banished. 'I might have done. How's the porridge coming on?'

'Nearly done.' Willa gave it a stir. 'We could go down to the gardens one evening if you'd like and take Malcolm in his pram.'

'Depends on the weather.'

Willa lifted Malcolm into his high chair and tied a bib round his neck, ignoring his protests. She put out two platefuls of porridge, one for Baby Bear, the other for Grandma Bear.

'You not having any?' asked Ina.

'I'm not hungry this morning.'

'What's that in your hair?'

Willa put a hand to it.

'Lean over, let me see. Looks like a bit of stick.' Ina extracted a piece of twig from the back of Willa's hair. 'Where in the name did you get that?'

'I must have brushed up against something.'

Willa turned aside to shield her burning face. At that moment Malcolm created a diversion, for which she silently blessed him, by tipping the contents of his porridge bowl over the floor.

'Naughty boy!' she told him nevertheless, since she felt it incumbent upon her to try to teach him to recognise the difference between right and wrong, not that she was always sure of the distinction herself. It was wrong to throw food on the floor, especially when there were people in the world starving, like those African babies who kept Elma occupied knitting matinee coats and bootees. That, to Willa, was clear cut. She also believed it was wrong to be unfaithful to your husband. *Thou shalt not commit adultery.* It was one of the imperatives that had been burned into her brain early on, like *Thou shalt not steal. Not bear false witness.* And so forth. She'd gone to Sunday school every week as a child and had even won prizes for her knowledge of biblical stories and sometimes she and Ina went to church, though less than they used to, with Malcolm being unwilling to sit quietly on a knee and listen to a man in black droning on. But what if your husband was unfaithful to you? Willa was well acquainted with the saying that two wrongs don't make a right but might they not sometime? Or was she just trying to quell her feelings of guilt? These thoughts running and rerunning through her mind were giving her a headache, on top of too little sleep, and a hangover, the first she'd ever had.

Malcolm, being accustomed to getting his own way on most occasions, began to cry.

'Och, don't scold the wee soul,' said his grandmother. 'He didn't know what he was doing. Did you Malkie, pet?' She lifted him up from the chair and he rewarded her with an enormous smile. 'Come and sit on Granny's knee and have some of Granny's porridge.'

After Willa had cleaned up the mess she went into the bathroom to cool down. There were times when she wanted to hit Tommy's mother with the poker.

LOCAL WOMAN BATTERS MOTHER-IN-LAW TO PULP.

She could see the headline on the *Evening News* billboard outside Bunty's shop.

Thou shalt not kill.

Someone was tapping on the door. 'It's me, Pauline. Can I get in? I'm going to be sick.'

Willa vacated the bathroom and went into her bedroom. Pauline returned ashen-faced and sat down on the bed beside her.

'Too many slings,' she said.

'Did you spend the night in the Caley? With Ralph?'

Pauline sighed.

'Maybe you should use my douche?'

'No point.'

'How do you mean *no point*?'

'I'm expecting already. At least I'm pretty sure I am.'

'Oh God!' said Willa.

'That's why last night I thought, "What the hell?"'

'Whose is it?'

'Ernest's.'

'Are you sure?'

'Of course I'm sure! I'm not a hoor.'

Pauline began to cry. Willa looked longingly at Willa Cather's *O Pioneers!* lying on her bedside table and wished she could pick it up and lose herself in its world. To be a Swedish immigrant in Nebraska might be hard going but it seemed more straightforward than living with your mother-in-law in a small Edinburgh flat. Right now she would love to go to Nebraska. The other advantage of a novel was that it usually offered some kind of reasonable resolution in the end, whereas here, sitting beside a sobbing Pauline, she could not foresee one, not a satisfactory one, anyway.

She comforted Pauline as best she could. 'I'll help you in any way I can.' But in what way? Tommy's pay didn't allow much for extras and Ina couldn't be expected to give shelter to Pauline *and* a baby in this already overcrowded flat.

'What am I to do?'

'I think Ernest should be made to do something. Why should he get off? Perhaps we should try to find him.'

Pauline cheered up a little at that. She sniffled and blew her nose. 'I do love him, you know. And he loved me. But it was difficult for him. He was torn.'

He might well have been, thought Willa, for all she knew. She understood what it was to be torn: it was like being ripped apart in the middle.

'What about you?' asked Pauline. 'Where did you run off to last night? Who is Richard when he's at home? Your man from the library?'

And so Willa told her. She had been needing to tell someone; the secret had become too big to hold.

'I thought something was going on with you,' said Pauline. 'You were going about with a kind of faraway look in your eyes. Have you fallen for him? Really fallen?'

Willa nodded.

'So now what?'

'Now nothing. There's no future for us. There can't be. I'm married.'

'People get divorced.'

They didn't know anyone who had.

'I've got a child. I could never give up Malcolm.'

'Take him with you.'

'Tommy might try to get custody if I was the guilty party.'

'Come on, Willa, he's guilty too, I'll bet you anything on that! How many girls will he have had?'

'I've no proof.'

'But you *know*. There's no way he wouldn't, not *Tommy*.'

'Yes, I know. There's other things besides.'

'Such as?'

'Richard's mother.'

'Not another mother,' groaned Pauline. 'You know how to pick them.'

'This one wouldn't take me in, I can tell you that.'

'Maybe she wouldn't need to.'

'There's no chance of Richard being able to support a wife and child. He's hoping to go back to university in the autumn. But if it weren't for all of that, all—' Willa stopped. If it were not for all those difficult, impossible, insurmountable things she could live happily ever after with Richard. She felt convinced that she could. 'We get on so well together, we understand each other, we can talk for hours about books, the world, all sorts of things. I know I'll never have that with Tommy. Richard's like a pool of calm, clear water, open and honest. He would be lovely to live with, I can tell.'

'Oh, Willa!' said Pauline and they cried together.

When they'd dried their eyes, Pauline made them laugh saying, 'Mind you, you can't beat your Tommy on the dance floor.'

'Trouble is you can't spend your whole life dancing.'

'Pity,' said Pauline.

The doorbell rang and Willa said, 'Who in the name can that be?' using Ina's well-worn phrase, which gave them another laugh.

The caller was Bunty and, as she herself might have said, she was on her high horse, and snorting. She was looking for Pauline.

'I'm sorry, Bunty,' said Pauline, 'Honest I am. I had an awful bad stomach this morning. I must have eaten something last night.'

'You'd better be there for the evening papers!'

'I will, I promise I will. I won't let you down.'

Bunty went in to the kitchen and Willa fetched Malcolm

from his granny's knee, saying that she and Pauline were taking him out for a walk, it was far too nice a day for him to be inside a hot kitchen. He fought as usual, but she prevailed.

'Go and wash your face,' she told Pauline. 'We're going out to look for Ernest.'

~ 17 ~

Honolulu, Hawaii,
The Sandwich Islands
10th June, 1924

Dear Willa,
   We are now on United States territory. No need
to tell you, that being so, the Yankee element
predominates, with dollars, autos, chewing gum,
horn-rimmed spectacles and ice cream everywhere.
Mother would love the ice cream. Any kind of
flavour you want.

'Tommy always brings me in a double-slider when he's home,'
said Ina.

'Is Hawaii not where the girls wear grass skirts?' said Bunty,
shoogling her hips. 'And flowers round their necks.'

'What about sharks?' asked Ina.

'You and your sharks!' said Bunty.

'Here's something about fish,' said Willa. 'He says they're
very pretty and their vivid colours are remarkable. He's
enclosed a cut-out of one.' She dug in the envelope and
brought out the shape which was passed from hand to hand
to be admired. The fish was green, blue, orange and black
and quite unlike anything to be seen on their fishmonger's
slab.

'That reminds me,' said Ina, 'if you're going out get us a

couple of smoked haddies for our tea. I fancy one with a poached egg on top.'

Pearl Harbor, about nine miles away, is an American naval base, where approx. 15,000 US sailors and airmen are stationed. Pretty nice posting for them! Wouldn't mind a few months out here myself. I love the heat of the tropics.

'That's with him being so dark,' said Bunty. 'He can take it. It wouldn't suit me.'

'He's not *dark*,' said his mother. 'He's just got black hair.'

'And olive skin, like most Ities,' said Bunty. 'Malkie is going to be the same.'

The American authorities have been doing everything they can to make our stay enjoyable and interesting. Entertainments of various kinds have been arranged for us at the Moana Hotel. The Hawaiians put on a Hula Hula dance, which is a kind of love dance.

'Love dance,' said Bunty, clicking her tongue and annoying Ina again. 'Hear that, Pauline?' she added, as Pauline came into the room. 'Fancy going to Hawaii and getting yourself a grass skirt? A bit itchy when you sit down.' She laughed but Pauline was not in the mood for laughing.

In Waikiki Park there is a dance pavilion, with a jazz band at one end and, at the other, a Hawaiian band which plays dreamy waltzes, while the Hawaiians in

the audience sing along in harmony. The nights are
balmy and mild and the moon seems bigger than it
is in Edinburgh.

'Dreamy waltzes, eh,' said Bunty. 'In the moonlight. *Oh shine*
on, shine on harvest moon up in the sky, I ain't had no lovin'
since January, February, June or July.'

Pauline joined in and Ina tetched and plucked at the top of
her corsets where the bones were sticking into her bosom.

Willa hoped Tommy was dancing dreamily with any girl he
fancied. She wasn't getting the chance to dance with Richard
though at nights she dreamt about it. They'd only managed to
meet two or three times since the night in Princes Street
gardens; they'd had cups of tea in their café and frustrating,
dangerous embraces in Dunbar's Close and each time they had
met she had told him that this would have to be the last time
and he had told her that he couldn't live without her.

As for their search for Ernest, she and Pauline had not had
any luck so far but they weren't ready yet to give up. Willa
reasoned that he must be somewhere in Edinburgh and
someone must know him. They'd tried the hosiery department
in Patrick Thomson's and then gone down to Princes Street to
work their way along, calling at Forsyths, Jenners and
Darlings, by which time their legs were tired and Malcolm
was grumpy so they'd gone into Crawford's tea room and had
a pot of tea and cream cakes.

They had avoided their own area since they were known to
the shopkeepers but Willa had decided they would have to
start asking them too. And after that, they'd have to go
further a field. There were dozens of shops, if not hundreds,

in Edinburgh, selling stockings. Meanwhile, the search was helping to keep Pauline from sliding right down into the dumps.

Honolulu is very modern and well ahead of any other island in the South Seas. I guess they've got the Yanks to thank for that. All kind of coloured races are to be found here, Japs predominating.

'They're off up to Canada next,' said Willa, deciding to cut the reading short as Malcolm was getting restless. She folded the letter and put it away, to finish reading it with Richard when she got the chance. 'Pauline and I are going to take Malcolm out.'

'You look as if you could do with some air right enough,' said Bunty to Pauline, who gave her a somewhat sickly grin. She was sick only first thing in the morning now, usually before Ina wakened. 'You're a bit wan looking.'

Pauline fetched her handbag and Willa carried Malcolm down the stairs, but before strapping him into his pram she took him into the shop next door, the Scotch Wool and Hosiery Stores, which, until now, they had avoided. Pauline followed. Mrs Andrews was behind the counter having a chat with Mrs Begg. She broke off to address them.

'Well, girls, what can I do for the two of youse today?'

'A friend of ours was asking us to make enquiries about a Mr Ernest Smith,' said Willa. 'He's a commercial traveller for a hosiery firm. We were wondering if you'd ever come across him?'

'A Mr Smith?' Mrs Andrews frowned. 'Can't say I have. No, sorry.'

'Thanks, anyway.'

'You might try Miss Piper,' offered Mrs Begg. 'She kens everybody. Oh, just a minute there, Willa. Could I have a word with you?'

She came out onto the pavement with them and she and Willa stood a little apart from Pauline.

'I was wondering if you'd like a wee job? Working in the shop Wednesday afternoons – that's my half day – and all day Saturday?'

'Well, I'm not sure...'

'The pay wouldn't be much but it would give you a bit of pin money. I thought maybe Mrs Costello could look after your wean. She seems right fond of him?'

'I'll need to think about it. Thanks for asking me, Mrs Andrews.'

She told Pauline about the offer as they set off up the hill towards Bruntsfield and Morningside.

'Are you going to do it?' asked Pauline.

'I'd like to but I wouldn't want to leave Malcolm with Tommy's mother all that time.'

'I could look after him.'

'She'd take him from you. I'll see. Today we're looking for Ernest!'

'Where can we start?

'We'll ask at every shop,' said Willa. 'It's the only way.'

It was a nice day for a walk; warm, but not hot, the way it would be in the tropics. Malcolm, once he'd accepted his confinement, was enjoying the outing. His bright eyes were alert, noticing everything that was going on around him, and he rewarded everyone who stopped to smile at him with a large grin. Pauline observed that he could charm the birds out of the trees, like someone else they knew. As well as being handsome, Willa was sure that Malcolm would be good at his lessons when he went to school. Perhaps, one day, he might be able to go university like Richard. She might have gone herself had it not been necessary for her to leave school at fourteen and earn a wage to help her mother. There were scholarships for clever children whose parents were not well off.

As they passed the greengrocer's they saw one of the MacNab boys snaffling an apple from an outside box. It made a bulge in his trouser pocket. He gave them a quick startled look, aware that he'd been seen, and ran off.

'Good luck to him,' said Pauline.

Willa nodded in agreement, deciding that sometimes the sixth commandment should be overlooked. Whenever she saw the MacNab children out on their own she slipped a sweet or a small bar of chocolate into their hands. She knew they wouldn't tell their father. They'd have it eaten before they got home. She hadn't seen their mother for a week or two.

The greengrocer came out of the shop, wiping his hands on his apron. 'Did you see that boy taking anything?'

'What boy?' asked Pauline.

'That one running. Him and his brother are aye hanging about. Quick-fingered, they are. I'll skin them alive if I get my hands on them.'

Pauline shrugged and the man went back inside, muttering to himself.

They carried on to Miss Piper's. She sold everything from pins and needles, reels of thread of all the colours of the rainbow and others besides, skeins of wool and needles to knit with, hair nets for every shade of hair, cards of knicker elastic and babies' rompers to hat pins and father boas. This was a shop that Willa loved. She'd come here with her mother since she was a small child. The counter was cluttered and boxes were stacked on shelves from floor to ceiling. Miss Piper looked as if she'd been left over from the last century.

Willa put her question again.

'So is this gentleman someone your friend is *particularly* anxious to track down?' enquired Miss Piper, leaning over the counter, on the small space that remained clear. Behind her round glasses her watery blue eyes had an amazingly innocent look. 'Would it be an affair of the heart?' Her voice had a catch in it. She was a great reader of romances.

'She didn't really tell us much,' said Willa. 'But thanks anyway, Miss Piper.'

'If I do come across him I'll be sure to let you know. Ernest Smith, did you say?' She was reluctant to let them go. 'I'll write it down so that I'll remember. Call in again when you're passing in case I hear anything. And how is Mrs Costello, Willa? Well, I hope?'

'Very well.'

'And Tommy? Such a charming young man. I wasn't surprised when he captured your heart. When will he be coming home?'

'October or so.'

'Not till then? Dear me. His mother must miss him. He was always the apple— Is that you off now? Remember me...'

After another two shops they decided they were in need of refreshment. Willa unstrapped a joyful baby and they went into a café and sat at the window licking ice-cream sliders.

Willa bought a small cone for Malcolm and tied on the bib which she kept at the bottom of the pram. There was no danger of his throwing the cone on the floor. Porridge, yes; ice cream, no. He knew what he was about, that boy.

Willa blinked as a man went past the window.

'Richard!' she cried, dumping Malcolm on Pauline's knee and rushing out of the café. She called his name again and he turned and, without thinking, they went into each other's arms, in plain daylight, for all who were passing up and down Morningside Road to see. Realising this, Willa drew back and glanced around but saw no one in the immediate vicinity that she recognised.

Pauline had come to the door of the café with Malcolm in her arms. 'He was crying for you. He wants his mammy.'

Willa took him. 'You're all right, baby. I'm not going anywhere.' He was eyeing Richard.

'Aren't you going to introduce us?' said Pauline.

'Let's go inside,' said Willa.

They moved to a table at the back and Richard treated them to a milkshake. Halfway through hers, Pauline excused herself to go to the ladies. 'I've got a bit of a cramp in my belly. Maybe I shouldn't be eating cold things.'

'She's pregnant,' said Willa after she'd gone.

'Oh,' said Richard uncomfortably.

He tried to take her hand but Malcolm didn't like it. He glowered at Richard and his face turned brick red. Willa was glad that he had not yet learnt to speak: he would not be able to go home and tell Granny about the nasty man his mummy had been with in the café.

'When can I see you?' asked Richard urgently. 'Properly, I mean.'

'I don't know,' said Willa helplessly.

'Come to the library at least!'

'I might be able to after lunch. About two o'clock. While Malcolm has his nap.'

'Try, please, Willa love!'

'I will, I promise!'

Pauline came back. Willa wondered if she had been sick but didn't ask. She wasn't looking too good. Malcolm was getting restless, having finished his ice-cream cone; he would have liked to get down to do some exploring, but the floor was not overly clean. Willa's arms ached from trying to restrain him.

'We'd better go,' she said.

They parted outside the café and Richard walked on ahead of them.

'He's nice,' said Pauline. 'I can see what you see in him. Pity Tommy wouldn't run off with some hula-hula girl in Hawaii.'

'He can't run off while he's in the Navy. He'd be court-martialled.' Unfortunately for me, thought Willa.

Coming down the hill from Bruntsfield they saw that Miss Piper was at her door. She signalled to them and they stopped when they reached her.

'I might have some news for you!' She sounded excited.

Willa put the brake on the pram and left it at the open door where she could watch Malcolm. He was busy tearing a pom-pom to bits.

'Did you hear anything about Mr Smith?' asked Pauline who, Willa thought, was looking more peely-wally by the minute. Perhaps ice cream had been a bad idea.

'Well, I'm not sure.' Miss Piper liked to draw out her stories. 'But, strangely enough, after you left one of my ladies came in and she was telling me about Ernie Stapleton who calls on me – he carries a nice line of hosiery – and I wondered if by any chance you'd got the name wrong? It didn't occur to me earlier.'

Willa thought it very possible that Pauline had been given the wrong name. When Pauline had said his surname was Smith, Willa had said, 'Are you sure?' and Pauline had said that loads of people were called Smith. 'Exactly,' had been Willa's response.

'What does he look like?' asked Willa.

'Gingery sort of hair, a small moustache, middling height for a man, I would say. Probably in his mid-forties.'

Willa looked at Pauline, who nodded.

'Sounds like he might be the one our friend was asking about,' said Willa. 'So what did you hear, Miss Piper?'

'That he'd been in a bad car accident a few weeks ago. At the junction of Queensferry Road and Princes Street. It wasn't his fault – the other car was over the speed limit. I believe it's only four miles an hour at that point and he was doing twenty!'

'I knew he wouldn't have dumped me,' cried Pauline and then she doubled over, in evident pain. She screamed and a spate of blood gushed from between her legs.

'Oh, my goodness!' cried Miss Piper.

'We'll need to get an ambulance,' said Willa.

'The chemist two doors up has a telephone.'

'Keep an eye on the baby for me, will you, Miss Piper?' To Pauline, Willa said, 'Hang on now. I'll get help as quick as I can.'

The chemist offered to phone the Infirmary himself,

allowing Willa to return to the haberdasher's straightaway. Elma was there. She had noticed Malcolm sitting outside in his pram.

'What's going on?' She was gazing at the blood on the floor.

'Can't you see?' snapped Willa. 'Pauline's haemorrhaging.'

The chemist arrived to say that the ambulance was on its way and could he help?

'Maybe you should sit down,' he said to Pauline, who was standing in the middle of the floor trembling. There was an upright chair beside the counter for customers who were waiting to be served or had stories to tell.

'I'm all bloody,' said Pauline.

Miss Piper gave her chair a horrified look.

Willa put her arm round Pauline and gave her a hug. 'It won't be long coming.'

As she spoke they heard the wail of the siren.

By the time the ambulance pulled in to the kerb, a small crowd had gathered and was able to witness Pauline being borne out of Miss Piper's shop on a stretcher.

'Come with me, please, Willa,' she begged, holding out her hand.

'You can't bring the baby,' said one of the ambulance men. 'Maybe one of these ladies wouldn't mind looking after him?'

Willa appealed to Elma. 'Could you wheel him down the road to Ina's please?'

Malcolm would not like that but she had no other choice. Whenever Elma came into the house he turned his face away from her. As Willa climbed into the ambulance she saw that he was doing it now and preparing to let out a scream of annoyance. As the ambulance bore them down the hill to

Tollcross and up Lauriston Place, its blue light winking and its siren bleating, she held tightly on to Pauline's hand and prayed that Elma would cross the road carefully with the pram and manage to carry Malcolm up the stairs without his throwing himself out of her arms onto the stone steps. It was one of the things that she liked least about being a mother: being constantly jabbed by little shards of anxiety. She saw him now, arching his back, falling backwards, his head meeting the stone...*Stop it*! she told herself. *This is ridiculous.*

Pauline was whisked away on the stretcher as soon as they arrived at the hospital and Willa was asked to take a seat in the corridor. Sitting stiffly there on a hard chair, she thought of Richard waiting for her in the library, glancing up from his book whenever the door opened and each time feeling let down. She couldn't bear the thought of his disappointment. She kept looking at her watch, the one that Tommy had given her as a wedding present. Time trickled slowly past and she wished she had something to read. After a while she began to think they'd forgotten about her and when she sought out a nurse she found that they had. Pauline had been in theatre and had had a D&C and was now back in the ward asleep.

Willa raced round to the library but Richard was not there. She couldn't have expected him to have waited this long. It was four o'clock. She then went home to find that her imagination had not been so wildly off the mark with regards to Elma and Malcolm. He was fine now but he had led Elma a dance, said Ina, not sounding totally disapproving; she'd heard him screaming and had rushed down the stairs in time to catch him before he'd toppled out of his great-aunt's arms onto the pavement.

'Elma's gey cack-handed when it comes to handling bairns, isn't she, Malkie? You're all right now though. Your granny saved you. So what was up with Pauline? Was it a miss?'

Willa nodded.

'That lassie! Whose was it?'

'Some man called Ernest. A commercial traveller. She met him at the Palais.'

Ina shook her head. 'She's got nae sense, that one.'

'I find it kind of funny to think of her lying up there in the hospital and nobody in her family knowing.'

'You're not proposing to go round and tell Mrs Cant, are you?'

'Certainly not!'

Malcolm was in a wild mood for the rest of the afternoon and Willa was glad when it came to bath- and bedtime. She'd started reading him stories which he listened to quietly, trying to grab the book out of her hand only from time to time. Ina swore he was too young at nine months to understand what she was reading, but Willa knew he was not. Tonight it was the story of the three bears. He laughed when the baby bear found his porridge had been eaten all up.

'You're a scoundrel, aren't you?' said Willa, picking him up and giving him a cuddle. He felt soft and smelt of soap and baby powder.

He tumbled into sleep at once, which left the evening free for Willa, in the sense that she had no chores to do, but not to go and walk in Princes Street gardens and enjoy the air. They were having a run of good June weather. She felt too restless even to read. She picked up O Pioneers! but could not concentrate. She moved over to the window.

He was standing down there, on the opposite side of the street, staring up at their windows. She waved and he waved back. He motioned to her to come down.

She went through to the kitchen where Ina was reading the paper. She had taken off her stockings and stays; they were suspended from the pulley.

'I was thinking I might go out for a wee breath of air. Would you keep an ear open for Malcolm for me? He's sound asleep.'

'On you go,' said Ina, settling her bare feet comfortably on another chair. She needed to pare her corns. 'Just leave the door ajar.'

Willa lifted her jacket from the hook in the hall and ran down the stairs, almost bumping into Mr MacNab in the hazy light. The stair lights came on later now that it was summer. He went on up without a word. He'd smelt of drink.

'Don't come close,' said Willa, when Richard came dashing across the road to join her. 'Everybody knows me round here.'

They turned along Brougham Place towards the Meadows and Willa told him why she had not been able to come to the library in the afternoon.

'Poor Pauline,' he said.

'Yes, but maybe it's just as well. She'd probably have had to give the baby up for adoption. She couldn't have kept it.'

'I suppose not.'

'She's got no money.'

There were a lot of people out on the wide green swards of grass, kids playing football and tag, men and women strolling, some lying on the grass. Richard said he wished they could lie on the grass; Willa said it was not possible.

'Not much is for us, Richard.'

'Don't keep saying that! My mother says that if you want something badly enough you can usually find a way to get it.'

'She wouldn't have had you and me in mind, though.'

He had no response to that.

'Let's pretend we have all the time in the world,' he said, taking her hand and leading her round by a side path which was less frequented. They had gone only a few steps before he stopped to kiss her. She had no chance, nor any desire, to protest.

As they broke apart, Willa heard a woman say, 'Evening, Willa. It's a nice evening, isn't it?'

Startled, Willa turned to see a woman in a cream-coloured dress with lime-green trimmings. She was walking a tiny Pekinese.

'How d'you like my new dog?' asked Mrs Mooney. 'A present. I'm calling him Geraldo.' She gave Willa a wink. 'Aren't you going to introduce us?' She looked at Richard.

'This is Richard,' said Willa awkwardly. 'Richard, Mrs Mooney.'

'Call me Maureen, Richard. Everybody does.'

'Pleased to meet you,' said Richard.

'Who was that?' he asked after Maureen had tripped off on her three-inch heels, tugging Geraldo behind her.

'I suppose you could say she's about the only person in Edinburgh I don't mind seeing us together!' said Willa.

Back in her room, after her stolen hour with Richard, she felt uneasy, about the encounter with Mrs Mooney. She did not think the woman would tell on her, it wasn't that, but it was as if she and Mrs Mooney were now in some way linked together. *Birds of a feather*. Mrs Mooney would be regarded by a lot of people as *fast*. *A fancy woman*. *A bit of fluff*. Willa didn't see herself in the same light, nor did she want anyone else to see her in that way either. She was not having a good time *on the side*. She was in love with Richard.

But then, trying to be fair, which she had always been encouraged to do by her mother, a woman of principle, she had to admit the possibility that Mrs Mooney and Gerry might also be in love.

~ 18 ~

Esquimault and Victoria,
Vancouver Island,
British Columbia,
Canada
1st July, 1924

Dear Willa,
     About a day and a half out at sea crossing from
Honolulu we had a little bit of excitement when the
Repulse reported that she had found a stowaway. It is
seldom a stowaway is found aboard a man-of-war as
he is almost certain to be discovered. He was a private
in the American Army with a Hawaiian name. A
murder had been committed just before we arrived in
Honolulu, so we think he may have been the culprit.

'Ina, aren't you glad the murderer wasn't on Tommy's ship?'
said Bunty.
     Ina ignored that. 'Is Canada ours?' she asked Willa.
     'Yes.'
     'Everybody knows that,' said Bunty.
     Willa resumed reading.

     During the trip we carried out gunnery and torpedo
exercises, the weather remaining good the whole
time. We are now berthed at Esquimault, the

*headquarters of the Royal Canadian Navy, a seaport
nine miles from Victoria, the capital of BC. The
harbour is circular in shape and one of the safest and
best defended harbours on the Canadian coast.
Lumbering is a big industry in BC and logs make
huge rafts floating on the surface of the water. Quite
a sight.*

'I've always fancied going to Canada,' said Pauline. 'My Uncle
Billy went. I think he got a job as a lumberjack, funnily
enough. He's never come back.'

After a week in hospital, Pauline had returned to them. As
Willa had said to Ina, where else was she to go? Willa had
enjoyed having her room back to herself and Malcolm for that
week. Since her return Pauline had been getting on her nerves
more than before, spilling talcum powder over the dressing
table, leaving dirty clothes lying on the floor. As Ina said, she
was a right slitter. And she wanted to talk, endlessly, about
Ernest. She kept badgering Willa to go back and ask Miss
Piper if she'd heard anything more about him, since she
couldn't go herself, not after the mess she'd made on the
haberdashery floor. Willa had gone once but there had been
no further news.

'That's a long one he's written,' said Ina, indicating the letter.

Tommy seemed impressed by Canada. New country, new
opportunities, he wrote. You could have a good life here
though the climate in South Africa was better so, given the
choice, he'd probably opt for the latter. Willa skimmed the
next two pages, which related facts mostly about buildings
and the population.

Victoria, pop. around 50,000, the capital of BC, and a port of call for Trans-Pacific liners, is a modern city with many fine buildings, the Hudson Bay Company's being a miniature skyscraper. The Gorge – a large stretch of water with delightfully wooded and shady banks – is its pleasure ground.

That perked the interest up.

'How do all those places come to have pleasure grounds?' asked Pauline. 'Everywhere he goes. We don't have any in Edinburgh.'

'We've got Portobello,' said Bunty, pronouncing it Porty-belly, knowing it would annoy Ina.

'Portobello!' said Pauline. 'Water's always freezing there.'

A regatta was held and taking part in the races were three boats from the squadron. Two races were won by the Danae, *which shows what a great racing ship she is! We were delighted with her performance.*

'Good for Tommy,' said his mother.

'I don't suppose he was sailing the boat single-handed,' said Bunty. 'But never mind boat races. What about the dancing?'

'There must be some,' said Willa. 'After all, it's part of Navy life. Yes, here we are!'

The drill hall of the Armouries is being used for dancing. It has a very large floor with a bandstand in the centre, with a balcony running round the entire hall. Beside the dancing there were other entertainments—

'I'll bet!' said Bunty.

'I wish you wouldn't keep interrupting,' said Ina, who was good at it herself. 'I can't concentrate. Any road, should you not be getting back to the shop? There might be a queue outside. You never know your luck.' Bunty had a number of cards that she put on the door when she felt like going out for a bit. *Back in ten minutes. Fifteen.* 'Read on, Willa. Don't pay any attention to Bunty.'

—entertainments such as racing with cardboard horses stretched on lines across the hall with young and old of both sexes gambling eagerly with imitation dollar notes. The more one won the more chance one had when the draw took place before the last dance and then the lucky ticket holders won real money.

'Some gey funny places in the world,' remarked Ina.

'I don't think Canada's too odd,' said Willa. 'I believe it's full of Scots.'

'Mr Parkin's going to take me to the races at Musselburgh,' said Bunty. 'But they'll be real horses, none of your cardboard cut-outs.'

'I had a friend who used to go,' said Pauline.

Willa felt sure that would be Ernest.

The Canadian people are very open and friendly.
They have been extremely generous to us, couldn't
ask for more. A small trace of the American element
is displayed in their ways and they have a bit of the
Yankee twang. Autos, as in the US, are cheaper here
than in the UK.

'Wouldn't mind a car,' said Ina.

Apart from Gerry with his butcher's van, the only person they knew with a motorised vehicle was Bunty's Mr Parkin who had a Baby Austin. Not that any of them had ever met him, except for Bunty, of course. They had seen him in the distance, with Bunty on his arm. He walked with a straight back and appeared to wear a dark trilby and spats even on warm days.

'We could go runs down the coast,' Ina went on. 'You'd like that, wouldn't you, Malkie?' He looked up from the brick tower he'd been building. In a moment he would knock it down, gleefully. 'You could make sandcastles. Granny would help you.'

Bunty rolled her eyes. 'Maybe it is time I was getting along. Anything else of interest?'

Willa shook her head. 'They're to be there for fourteen days, the longest stay of the cruise.'

Plenty of time to go dancing with a Canadian girl in a smart frock several times over and wander hand-in-hand at night through the dark streets. Willa felt an ache, an overwhelming desire to see and touch Richard, to smell his scent, feel the shape of his body against hers. She and Pauline had talked about going to the pictures that evening but if they did she didn't see how she could abandon Pauline to go off with him. It was all right for Tommy wandering freely through the pleasure grounds of the world, far away from wife, mother and child. He usually ended his letters saying that he hoped Malcolm was getting on fine and he was looking forward to seeing his big boy in October. They'd have fun together! They'd play footer on the Meadows. He seemed to be unaware that Malcolm couldn't walk yet.

And then, well, naturally, he would send Mother his love.

'He says next stop is Frisco!' said Willa.

We expect to have a whale of a time in that fair city! The boys have been looking forward to this for weeks. Just wait till we go through those Golden Gates! Wow-wee!

'Frisco?' said Ina.

'San Fran,' said Bunty, shaking her head at her sister's ignorance.

Ina was frowning. 'I thought you went through the golden gates to heaven?'

'Pearly, Ina.'

With that, Bunty left them and Willa and Pauline took Malcolm out in his pram. This had become their routine in the mornings, once the cleaning or washing and ironing was done. Since her miscarriage Pauline hadn't been delivering Bunty's papers or cleaning Mrs Mooney's flat and she seemed in no hurry to resume. Her National Insurance money had run out but her dad had had a big win on the horses and given her ten pounds. She'd become even more addicted to the cinema, going three or four times a week, often to the same film, and sometimes she took Willa with her, to the decent sixpenny seats, not to the fleapit where you could get in for tuppence. They'd rather stay at home than go there. Fleas might be the least of what you would pick up. Ten pounds would buy a lot of ice creams and visits to the cinema. That was all Pauline seemed interested in now, apart from Ernest. She was worried about him and sure that if it had not been for his accident he would have been in touch.

They went to their usual café on the Morningside Road and sat in the window so that Willa could watch for Richard should he come by. He often did, knowing they would be there.

Pauline had an ice-cream sundae with tinned peaches and raspberry sauce, which Malcolm eyed covetously. He was having to make do with his usual cone.

'You'll be putting on weight,' Willa told Pauline. She already was. Her skirts wouldn't fasten.

She shrugged and dug her spoon down deep to reach the peaches.

Richard didn't come. Well, sometimes he couldn't, Willa understood that. His mother might want him to do something for her, such as accompany her to a bookshop and carry her heavy parcel of books home. She might find all manner of excuses to keep her son tethered to her side. Willa wondered how she managed to buy so many books when her husband wasn't earning much. But perhaps 'much' meant something different to them.

On their way back down the hill Miss Piper popped out of her shop. 'I thought it was you! I recognised the pram.' She turned to Pauline, who was looking embarrassed. 'How are you, dear?' Willa thought it possible that Miss Piper would not have realised what had happened to Pauline. 'I'm so pleased to see you out and about again.'

'I don't suppose you've heard anything more about the commercial traveller? Ernest Stapleton?'

'As a matter of fact, I have! My customer was in again yesterday and she said he was improving.'

'That's wonderful!'

'Is he a friend of yours too then?'

'I just know him a bit,' said Pauline hurriedly. 'Is he in hospital still?'

'Apparently. That must be quite a few weeks he's been there now.'

'Did your customer say which hospital?'

'The Infirmary, as far as I know. It probably would be, wouldn't it, after such a bad smash?'

Continuing on down the hill Willa said, 'I don't think it would be a good idea to try and see him in hospital. You might run into his wife.' And four children, she wanted to add, but that would be cruel. But sometimes she thought Pauline might need a jolt to make her face up to reality and not think she was living inside a movie where, in the end, the lovers would come together and live happily ever after.

As they neared their door they saw Richard rounding the clock. He came running to meet them. Willa glanced up at the windows of their flat but Ina would doubtless be in the kitchen at the back.

'Don't worry,' said Pauline. 'Folk'll think he's with me. After all, I'm free. Ha, ha.'

'I'm glad I caught you!' Richard was out of breath. 'Can I speak to you for a minute, Willa?'

'Don't mind me,' said Pauline. 'I'll walk on with Malcolm.'

She took hold of the pram. Malcolm was well used to her by now and raised no protest. Willa and Richard went round the corner.

'Could you get away this evening?' he asked urgently.

'I said I'd go to the pictures with Pauline. You could come and sit beside us, I suppose.' They could hold hands. It would be better than nothing. Many things were, but they were not enough.

'I've got something better to propose! My parents have gone on holiday, to Arran. They went this morning. I've just seen them off at Waverley. They're to be away for a week, a whole week. Willa, we could have the place to ourselves! Wouldn't you like us to spend a whole evening together, *inside,* where nobody could see us?'

'Of course I would.' She trembled at the thought.

'Well then?'

'I'll talk to Pauline.'

'She owes you a few favours, doesn't she?'

He waited while Willa went back to Pauline, who straightaway said, 'That's fine by me. We'll just tell Ina we're off to the flicks and we can come back in together. She'll never know the difference.'

Unless some busybody should happen to be there too. But Elma didn't often go to the pictures, not to ones featuring glamorous men like Valentino or Fairbanks. She found most films distasteful. The cinema, as she saw it, was a place of temptation, a way of putting ideas into young girls' heads.

Some of the love scenes went too far, showing a man and a woman glued together on a sofa kissing passionately. They should fade long before they did.

Willa walked down Lothian Road to the Caley Cinema with Pauline, then she quickly crossed the road and took a detour round the back streets to emerge onto Lauriston Place.

As soon as she pulled the bell Richard came cascading down the stairs. He seized her hand and they ran up to the first floor together. He took her inside, closed the door and kissed her. And then they went into his room. She felt suddenly shy. All their courtship, for that was how she saw it, had taken place out of doors, with both of them half dressed. Now, suddenly, she was in a room with him, bounded by four walls, without the need for secrecy. No one could spy on them here. It was as if they were alone together for the first time.

She wandered round the room studying the books on his shelves and the pictures on his walls. He came up behind her and enfolded her in his arms.

'I love you,' he whispered into her ear.

'I love you too,' she said, turning to look him full in the face. It is true, she thought; I know it now for sure.

He had only a single bed but she was glad he did not try to take her to his parent's bigger, matrimonial one. This bed was wide enough for them and Arabella Fitzwilliam would never have lain here. He pulled her down onto it.

The telephone rang somewhere in the nether regions of the flat. Hearing it, she smiled, thinking it might be Richard's mother who, for once, could not come between them. Nothing could. Their lovemaking was feverish to begin with but as the evening light began to dwindle they realised that it need not be, for they had all the time in the world. Or so it seemed. From time to time the telephone rang but they heard it as if it were ringing in some far-off place on the other side of the world.

~ 19 ~

San Francisco, California
11th July, 1924

Dear Willa,
Frisco, at last! Whoopee! You'd absolutely love it.
We all do. We could stay here for ever. An aeroplane
dropped a beautiful floral lley on the Hood on the
opening of the Golden Gate, along with the
following message:
'This floral lley is a symbol of welcome to the
Special Service Squadron and the city is at the
disposal of the British Fleet.'

'The whole city?' said Ina. 'At their disposal?'
'Jings,' said Bunty.
'He sounds awfy excited,' said Ina.
'I hope it's all it's cried up to be,' said Bunty. '*San Francisco*
here I come...'

And so we passed through the Golden Gate and
anchored in a large bay. There were a number of
US ships already berthed there, among them the
USS Mississippi, *which 17 days earlier had had a*
big gun accident on board, with two men being
killed. We sent a wreath and a message of
condolence.

'That was nice of them,' said Ina. 'But a big gun accident?'

'I'm sure they're more careful on Tommy's ship,' said Willa.

'They seem to be doing all right,' put in Bunty. 'They haven't had anybody eaten by a shark either, not so far.'

Tommy had written pages about San Francisco and Willa began to think that he might have made a career as a journalist after all. Sometimes she thought he was writing as if he had the *Evening News* in mind.

> *Ocean Beach, with three miles of sandy beach, is very fine, rivalling the Golden Gate Park in its popularity with Franciscans and visitors. High above the northern end is Cliff House where millionaires of mining days, kings and lords have wined and dined and watched the sea lions at play.*

How was it that everywhere else in the world, Willa wondered, seemed to be built around leisure and pleasure? How would one *not* want to go and live in America or Canada or Australia? Why would anyone want to stay in a place where the streets were grey and the tenements were grey and even the sky was grey a lot of the time?

> *Golden Gate Park itself is truly wonderful, with seventeen miles of driveways bordered by flowers and shady trees. Lake Stow, which circles around Strawberry Hill, is spanned by picturesque stone bridges and studded with small islands. The park also embraces the Japanese Tea Gardens where one*

can have tea amongst surroundings of dense greenery and lily ponds containing fat goldfish accompanied by the haunting odours of flowers of Japan: climbing wisteria, petalled iris and pink and white cherry blossoms. We drank tea under shady trees served by dainty Nippon maidens attired in satin kimonos patterned with brighter flowers than grow in any garden.

Surely some of that had come out of a book, thought Willa. *Haunting odours of flowers...*

'It would be a real treat to get your tea served like that,' said Ina wistfully.

'By a dainty Nippon lady?' said Bunty.

'Who are they anyway?' asked Ina.

'Japanese,' said Willa.

The bell rang and Pauline got up to go and let the caller in.

'If it's Mrs Begg tell her we're busy,' Ina called after her.

'That wouldn't stop her,' said Bunty. 'Say we've got the plague.'

Pauline came back with Elma.

'Sit yourself down, Elma,' said Ina. 'Willa's reading to us about Frisco.'

'Frisco?'

'Tommy's been having tea with dainty Nippon maidens,' said Bunty.

'What on earth...?

'Shush,' said Ina.

On Wednesday, July 9th, a dance and reception was held at the very fine Civic Auditorium for about 10,000 people, 6,000 of whom were seated in the gallery and the remaining 4,000 on the floor, with 3 bands in attendance, so that there was continuous dancing.

'You can be sure Tommy was on the flair all evening,' said Bunty.

'I don't know why you should say that,' said his mother.

'Can you see him sitting in the gallery?'

'You must be joking,' said Pauline, which earned her a frosty look from Ina, in spite of which she went on to say, 'No show without Punch.'

On Thursday, July 10th, 1,200 petty officers (myself among them) and men were entertained in Oakland across the Bay. After crossing by ferry we were met by a cavalcade of 500 motor cars waiting to drive us around. The streets were lined with people, everyone in great spirits and wishing us well. We were lustily cheered, which was very nice, considering the US does not belong to us.

'More's the pity,' said Bunty.

'Who does it belong to?' asked Elma.

'Themselves,' said Willa.

'Fancy, lusty cheers,' said Bunty. 'Tommy'll be coming back thinking he's the next best thing to Valentino,'

'What's it all about anyway?' asked Elma. 'What are the people cheering for?'

'They're welcoming the British Special Service Squadron,' said Ina scornfully. 'You ken fine Tommy's serving with it. You seem to have left your brains in bed this morning, Elma.'

> *We visited Berkeley University, one of the largest in the world, so we were told, occupying a site which slopes gradually down towards the high hills and commands an excellent view of the Golden Gates. An hour and a half's drive brought us to the house of our hosts where an excellent dinner was served and after that we went to a dance in a civic hall which had an excellent floor and could accommodate 2,000 dancers.*

'They seem to do everything in large numbers,' observed Bunty.

'It's a big country,' said Willa, thinking of the hard lives lived on the plains of Nebraska, so different from this west coast playground or sophisticated downtown New York that she'd encountered in Edith Wharton's novels. How could it be that this was one country?

> *It has been truly wonderful to spend time, however short, in the beautiful state of California.*

'Oh, well,' said Bunty. 'It's all right for some.'

Willa sensed, like herself, that the others felt deflated after hearing one of Tommy's letters read out. They seemed to say who *would* want to live in a dump like Edinburgh when you could enjoy such pleasures in better climes?

'It seems a nice place, California,' remarked Elma.

No one responded.

Willa folded up the letter, Bunty rose from her chair and Ina turned her attention back to her grandson who was amusing himself perfectly well without her. He had found a clothes peg to chew on.

Willa went through to her room and stared at the wedding photograph on the dresser showing herself and Tommy standing side by side, awkwardly posed, she in a navy-blue costume with a little navy hat with a half-veil, he rigid in his naval uniform holding his cap, po-faced, quite unlike the Tommy she'd met in the Palace ballroom. There was no life in that face. Or in hers, either. Willa thought that he looked bleak, as if he had been dragooned, dragged into this against his will, yet he had wanted to marry her. Or so he'd said. But had he?

She turned as Pauline came in.

'Will you chum me up to the Infirmary this afternoon, Willa? I'm feart to go alone.'

Willa was about to ask if this was wise but desisted. She feared it would be a mistake but recognised that Pauline would have to go.

They told Ina they were going to see a friend of Pauline's in the Infirmary at the afternoon visiting hour. Ina was not particularly interested. She was absorbed by her grandson.

'She's fair gone on that child,' said Pauline, as they set forth. 'She dotes on him.'

'I know,' said Willa gloomily.

'I don't know how you stand it.'

'Neither do I.'

Approaching Richard's door Willa felt a quickening of excitement, but there was no sign of him. They had had a wonderful week, a week to remember, while his parents were away. She had gone there every day at some time or other and they had shut the rest of the world out. What they had together was too much to lose, Richard had said.

'Will you see him today?' asked Pauline.

'Probably later.'

If they didn't meet during the day he would come and stand on the pavement across the street in the evening and she would find an excuse to go out so that they could at least spend a few minutes together. He said that he couldn't sleep at night unless he had seen her.

A swarm of people was moving through the Infirmary gates, anxious to arrive for the start of visiting hour. They joined it and went first to Reception where Pauline, after clearing her throat a couple of times, managed to ask which ward Mr Ernest Stapleton was in.

'Are you relatives?'

'No, just friends. Close friends.'

'You'll need to speak to Sister.' She told them the number of the ward.

They made their way up the stairs and Willa said it might be better not to speak to Sister. They found a nurse instead. She was coming out of the ward carrying a covered bedpan.

'We were hoping to see Mr Stapleton,' said Pauline.

'He's got someone in with him.'

'Is it his wife?' asked Willa.

'Oh, no, I don't think he's married. I'm pretty sure he's not.'

'He's not?' cried Pauline.

Willa saw that Pauline was about to jump for joy and put a hand on her arm, fearing her exhilaration might be misplaced.

'No, he's got a lady friend in with him.'

'Maybe it's his sister?' said Willa.

The nurse smiled. 'I wouldn't think so. Well, you can always tell, can't you?' She lowered her voice 'There have been a few. Seems he's quite a ladies' man. Do you want me to tell him you're here?'

'No, it's all right,' said Pauline, her voice dulled, then she rallied to ask if they might take a peep round the door in case they knew the person.

'Don't see why not. He's in the sixth bed up the left-hand side.'

They peeped round the door into the long ward. Ernest was propped up against a bank of pillows and his visitor was sitting on the bed as close to him as it was possible to get, which would certainly be frowned upon by the ward sister should she come by. There was no question from what they could see that the person was a lady friend and not a relative. She had her hand on his heart, inside his pyjama jacket. He had his hand on her thigh. The man in the next bed looked in danger of falling out so keen was he to get a good view.

Willa took Pauline's arm and led her out of the hospital. She came with dragging footsteps. They went to a café and had a cup of tea.

'The solution for all ills,' said Willa.

'What is?'

'Nothing.'

Pauline stirred her tea madly, round and round, until it threatened to slop over into the saucer. 'So he was a rotter after all.'

'I'm afraid so. Best to forget him.'

'Easier said than done. I really liked him, Willa. I thought for once this could be it! But it wasn't.' The saucer was swimming with orangey-brown liquid now.

Pauline needed a break, said Willa, away from Edinburgh. What about going to visit her cousin Madge in Aberdeen for a while?

Pauline wrote a letter that evening and Willa went out to post it, rendezvousing with Richard on the way, and two days later a reply came back from Aberdeen saying that Pauline would be welcome to come any time.

Willa saw her off at the bus station.

'Thank the Lord for that,' said Ina. 'She was beginning to get on my nerves, mooning about the house like a sick cat. That girl needs to pull herself together. Matter of fact, I was thinking of having a wee change myself.'

'You were?' cried Willa.

'Just for a couple of nights. You mind my old friend Minnie?'

'She was your bridesmaid, wasn't she?'

'Aye, we were great pals when we were young.'

'Didn't you get a letter from her this morning?'

Minnie, who was a widow and lived in Grangemouth, had written to suggest Ina come for a visit. Willa could scarcely believe it. Two nights free from Ina!

'It's not much of a place of course, Grangemouth,' said Ina.

'That doesn't matter. The main thing is to visit your friend.'

Then came the snag. She might have known there would be

one. Ina wanted to take Malcolm with her. She said Minnie was dying to see him though Willa doubted that. If she were that keen she could have come through on the bus long before this. It couldn't be more than twenty miles or so.

'I don't know,' said Willa. 'He's never been away from me.'

'It's only a couple of nights, for goodness' sake! You'd think I was taking him away for a fortnight. He'd enjoy a ride on the bus, wouldn't you, Malkie? Of course you would.'

'Maybe one night. Not two.'

Ina was in the huff for the rest of the day. She wrote a reply to Minnie and after it had been posted she told Willa that she'd said she was coming for two nights. It wasn't worth going all that way for one night.

On the morning of her departure she said to Willa, 'Well, am I taking him or am I not? You can't keep him tied to your apron strings for ever. After all, he's weaned so he's no needin' your milk now.'

'He's not a year old yet.'

'He'll not fret. You ken your old granny too well, don't you, Malkie?'

He laughed and his mother gave in, saying wearily, 'Oh, all right.'

She accompanied them to the bus station and stood waving them off while Malcolm batted both hands against the window at her in return. She was standing so close she could see the little circles in his plump wrists that looked like bracelets. The very chubbiness of him made her want to snatch him out of Ina's arms and hug him tight. But there was glass between them. And he was laughing.

As she watched the bus drive off she wanted to howl.

Instead she went into a corner and quietly shed a few tears. Telling herself that it was not for ever, only two days, she walked home cutting across Princes Street and up the Mound to George IV Bridge and the library. Richard was not there. This was not going to be her lucky day, that seemed plain. She sat at his usual table and read for an hour, or tried to, but she kept looking up to see who was coming and going. She took Virginia Woolf's *Jacob's Room* back to the shelf and replaced it in its slot. She couldn't seem to engage with it. She then went to their café. It was empty.

'He's not been in,' said the waitress.

On the way back down to Tollcross Willa had no luck either. Here she was with a totally free day – for once, for the first time since Malcolm was born – and she was alone. The irony of it made her want to choke. She went to see Bunty who took her through to the back for a cup of tea.

'So she got her way,' said Bunty. 'I thought she would. She was determined to take the boy with her.'

'It's only for two days,' said Willa, feeling suddenly alarmed at the prospect that Tommy's mother might not return Malcolm to her. But she couldn't stay at Minnie's for long and she'd have nowhere else to go.

'Ina was aye good at getting her own way. You have to stand up to her.'

'I do! As best I can. But I have to live with her and it's her house. When Tommy comes back I'm going to tell him I can't go on like this.'

'Where's he going to get the money for another place?' Tommy paid the rent of his mother's flat.

'I'm trying to put a wee bit by each week,' said Willa. A

sixpence or a shilling here and there. Once Malcolm went to school she would get a job, maybe in the library, if she was lucky, but that would not be for a while of course. Four years. God save her, four more years with Tommy's mother! But if she were to go out working now she'd have no choice but to leave him with Ina all day.

'Ina couldn't manage on her own, paying the rates and that. Tommy feels he has to look after her, with her having to bring him up on his own and no father. She had to go out scrubbing stairs. She gave him everything he wanted.' Bunty lit a cigarette and blew out a stream of smoke. 'What are you going to do when Tommy comes home?'

'You mean—?'

'Richard. Aye, Richard.'

'It's impossible.'

Bunty sighed. 'I can't see a way out for you, I have to admit. You're in love with him, aren't you?'

'He's in love with me too.'

'I ken. He comes in here quite often, nearly ever day, in fact, to talk to me about you.'

'Bunty, I want to see him. *Now*! This very minute! I've been looking for him all over.'

'You have got it bad, haven't you? Why don't you phone him? They'll likely have a telephone?'

As Willa was leaving Mrs Mooney arrived with her dog.

'How are you then, love?'

'Fine, thanks.'

'You must come and visit me one day. You can bring that nice young man with you if you like.' Mrs Mooney clicked her tongue.

Her attention was diverted by the dog which, small as it was, had jerked its lead out of her slack hand and made off up the street. Mrs Mooney yelled after him. Willa escaped.

She had to stand in a queue outside the telephone box at Tollcross while three men in front of her made lengthy calls. One had been smoking a cigarillo, a cheap one, from the smell of it, and now the cabin was full of acrid smoke. She rifled through the directory and found Fitzwilliam. And there was Edward John, Lauriston Place. That must be his father. Bracing herself she lifted the receiver and when the operator answered she gave him the number and on being put through she inserted the money in the slot with fumbling fingers.

'Arabella Fitzwilliam,' said the smooth voice at the other end. Polished, thought Willa, like a piece of hard, cold stone.

'Could I speak to Richard please?'

'I'm sorry, he's not in. Who would this be speaking?'

'Willa.'

'Willa?'

'Willa Costello,' she said awkwardly.

'Costello? I'm sorry...'

'I met you with Richard.' Now she was mumbling. 'You lent me a book. By Willa Cather.'

'Ah yes, I think I do recall you now. Richard has so many friends one cannot keep up.'

The smoke caught Willa's throat and she began to cough. She coughed and spluttered and her eyes smarted. When she tried to speak only a hoarse sound emerged.

'Are you still there? Do you have a message you would like to leave for Richard?'

'If you'd just tell him I phoned.'

She won't, thought Willa, as she hung up the receiver.

As she pushed open the door she almost knocked Richard over. She fell on top of him, oblivious of the passers-by, among whom happened to be Pauline's mother, Mrs Cant. Willa dragged him to one side.

'I'm on my own in the house,' she told him. 'I'll go on up and you come five minutes later.'

~ 20 ~

SAN FRANCISCO WELCOMES THE WORLD
Conservatory, Golden Gate Park

'Looks all right,' said the postie, nodding at the picture postcard. 'Ever been in the conservatory in the Botanics?'

Willa nodded, whilst clutching the card in one hand and the edges of her dressing gown together with the other. She had nothing on under the gown. The postie had wakened them and when no one had answered he'd pulled on the bell for a second and third time, knowing that there should be somebody in. They were always in.

'Is he liking it?'

'Who? Oh, Tommy? San Francisco?'

'Aye.'

'Very much. Seems it's a great place. Thanks, Sandy.'

She closed the door and went back to the bedroom.

'Was it all right?' asked Richard, who by now was up and pulling on his shirt. 'I'd better go.'

'What will you tell your mother?'

They hadn't planned on him staying the night but they had fallen asleep and slept soundly for eight hours in each other's arms. Willa's left arm was numb from lying under him.

'I'll think of something.'

'She'll probably have been worrying.'

'I'm twenty-two!'

'That won't make any difference to her. Have you ever stayed out all night before?'

'No!'

They smiled at each other, like conspirators.

He kissed her goodbye, went as far as the door, came back and kissed her again and said, 'Love you, love you,' and left for his mother's house. They had arranged to meet later in the library.

Willa sat daydreaming over her breakfast and was still at the table in her dressing gown when the doorbell rang again. She went to answer it wondering if he might have come back again.

'Are you not dressed yet?' said Elma with her characteristic sniff as she stepped over the threshold. Not to have your clothes on at this time of the morning would be a sin in her eyes.

Willa led the way into the kitchen.

'Don't tell me Ina's not up!'

'She's gone to visit her friend Minnie in Grangemouth for a couple of days.'

'She didn't tell me she was going.'

'She just decided on the spur of the moment.' Willa lifted the teapot. 'Would you like a cup?'

'I had my breakfast some time ago, thank you very much.' Nevertheless, Elma seated herself at the table. 'It was actually about you that I've come, Willa.'

'Oh?'

'I was talking to Mrs Cant yesterday.'

'That old bitch.' Willa felt reckless this morning.

'Willa! I never thought I'd hear such foul words coming from your mouth.'

'Well, she is. Anyone who can put their daughter out in the street must be.'

'Depends on what she's done, doesn't it? She's a Christian woman, Mrs Cant. She has her standards.'

Willa couldn't be bothered arguing. She poured herself another cup of tea.

Elma straightened herself up. 'She told me she'd seen you embracing a young man in the street yesterday!'

Willa drank her tea. It was cold.

'Did she tell a lie?' asked Elma.

'No,' said Willa.

Elma drew in her breath as if in shock, having expected, it would seem, to have had her allegation denied.

'I almost knocked him down when I came out of the telephone box.'

'But that didn't mean you had to *embrace* him.'

'I had to stop him from falling over.' Willa got up and threw the rest of the tea down the sink.

'Do you know this young man?'

'I've seen him in the library. If you'll excuse me, Elma, I must go and get myself dressed.'

She took her time and while she was still in the bedroom she heard the front door closing behind Elma. Poor Elma, she said to herself, though she did not feel in the least bit sorry for her.

They met in the library an hour later and he said, 'Why don't we go down the coast since you're free?'

'Why don't we?' she cried gaily.

They rode on the top of the bus, going as far as Gullane, at

Willa's suggestion. She had no wish to continue on to North Berwick where she had spent her honeymoon, though she did not mention that to Richard.

The day was mild and there was little breeze. They paddled in the edge of the sea, running in and out of the waves like a couple of children and laughed when she got her skirt soaked and he the bottoms of his rolled-up trousers. Afterwards they lay together in the sand dunes, in a private place away from the main paths. She asked him what he had told his mother.

'I didn't tell her anything.'

'She must have asked.'

'She did. I said it was my own business.'

'And she accepted that?'

'Not really. We had a bit of a row.'

Willa suspected they seldom did.

'Did she mention my name?'

'She asked if I'd been with you and I refused to answer.'

In that case, his mother would know that he had been. Richard seemed to be like George Washington, unable to tell a lie. Washington had been held up as an example to them at school. Willa knew herself not to be so virtuous; she was capable of telling a lie if the need arose and sometimes she felt that it did, in order to avoid bringing on a disaster. She preferred not to have to resort to untruths but thought it was not the worst sin you could commit. Perhaps it suited her to think this, to appease her conscience; she was not sure.

Richard's mother seemed unimportant and faraway as they lay in the hollow of the dune listening to the murmur of the waves. Such a pleasing, rhythmic, relaxing sound that eventually they fell contentedly asleep and woke to find that the sun had moved round, as had the hands of Richard's watch, which stood at ten minutes to eight.

'This is bliss,' he said, 'being like this together.'

He had missed his afternoon tutoring classes but he didn't care, he said. 'Why don't we run away together, Willa?'

'I can't,' she said sadly.

'If you want to enough, you can.'

'Sounds easy.' She sighed.

When they took the bus back into town they got off at Leith on the north side of the town where nobody of their acquaintance lived. Tommy's family, like Richard's, were south-siders, having always lived on that side of the Princes Street divide.

They were ravenous by now. They bought fish and chips and ate them walking along the waterfront as the sun flared and slowly sank behind the cranes and ships' masts. It was the most perfect day that Willa could ever remember, one that she wished could go on for ever.

They walked all the way home, arms around each other. Coming up Leith Walk, she stopped at some hopscotch marks on the pavement left by children earlier. The yellow chalked lines were just visible in the lamplight.

'Did you ever play at hopscotch?' she asked.

Richard shook his head. 'I didn't play in the street. Only the back garden behind a big stone wall so that I couldn't see out and nobody could see in.'

'Poor you,' said Willa. She took his hand. 'Come on!'

They jumped the squares together with Willa leading the way and ended up laughing and collapsing onto each other's shoulders. A policeman on the beat had stopped to look at them.

'What's up with the two of you?'

'Nothing,' said Willa. 'We're happy, that's all. That's enough.'

'Been drinking, have you?'

'Not a drop. Only water.'

The constable went on his way and so did they, arriving back at a deserted Tollcross well after midnight.

'I suppose I should go home tonight,' said Richard. 'But I'm not going to!'

~ 21 ~

San Francisco and Bay as seen from Twin Peaks –
550 feet above the city

'That's the second card you've had from there,' said the postie, as he handed the postcard to her. It was in wishy-washy colour, like the last one. 'It seems to have made a big impression on him.'

'It does, doesn't it?' said Willa, fully dressed this morning. She'd been up for two hours after a restless night of little sleep. She turned the card over.

> *Remember to keep all postcards and letters safe. I am thinking of making a book out of them for my son to read when he is older.*
> *Tommy xxx*

'Is he going to Hollywood?' asked the postie.

'I expect he will, if he can.'

'Who wouldn't?'

'Thanks, Sandy.' Willa closed the door.

She tossed the card onto the kitchen table, then she went round to Bunty's. The shop was busy at this hour with men buying cigarettes and newspapers on their way to work. Bunty raised an eyebrow at her from behind the counter. When the queue abated she came round to join her.

'What are you doing in here at this time of day?'

'Ina didn't bring Malcolm back yesterday.'

'Are you wanting a cup of tea?'

'I'm drowning in tea. I've been up since six.'

They went through the back.

'They were supposed to have come home yesterday. That's *three* nights they've been gone!'

'Calm down now, hen. She'll not have run off with him.'

'She wouldn't dare!'

'Where would they go?'

'If they're not back by teatime I'm going out to Grangemouth to get him.'

'Do you ken where Minnie lives, for I haven't the faintest? Now listen, I expect they'll be back sometime the day.'

The shop door jingled and Bunty went to serve her customer. Another came in after that, and another. This was her busy time. Willa left.

When she reached the stair door, she paused, undecided. If she were to go down to the bus station she might cross with them on the tram on their way up. If she strayed far away from home at all she could easily miss them.

She paced up and down the street, going as far as the King's Theatre up the way and the beginning of Lauriston Place down the way. The street bustled with shoppers and milkmen and bakers delivering from their carts. Some small girls were skipping with a piece of old clothes line. The rope whirled and the girls' feet stamped and the chanting went on. *One, two, three a-leerie, four, five six...*She saw wee Mary MacNab watching from behind a lamppost. Her nose was snotty and her dress torn. The kids in the street didn't play with the MacNabs. Willa went over and slid a penny into her hand.

'Go and get yourself a sweetie,' she said.

The girl ran. Willa watching her go hoped the shopkeeper wouldn't think she'd stolen the penny. She must remember to ask Bunty for some cigarette cards to give to the boys.

She resumed walking.

A few yards up the street, she met Mrs Cant, who gave her a sniff and glanced away.

Further on, she met Richard's mother, who gave her a look of cool disdain and passed on by.

Then she met Elma, who stopped to speak.

'What are you doing hanging about in the street?'

'Waiting for them to come back from Grangemouth.'

'I thought they were due yesterday?'

'They were.'

'Ina will always do what she wants, Willa, you can take my word for that.'

For once they were in sympathy, Willa and Elma. Willa was even quite pleased to stand chatting to Elma for a few minutes since it helped to pass the time. Elma was having trouble with a neighbour who encroached on her washing line in the back green. This had led to a few angry exchanges.

'She's got four children and that makes for a lot of washing, she told me. I told her that wasn't my fault. It was up to her how many children she had.'

Willa sympathised, though whether it was with the woman who had four children and a lot of washing or Elma herself, she didn't make clear.

Elma was off to the fishmonger's. 'You get fed up with too much butcher meat at times. Gerry doesn't seem to but I do.'

Richard's mother came back down the street and this time, she, too, stopped.

'If you're waiting for Richard, I wouldn't, if I were you. He has gone to visit his grandfather in Perthshire.' She moved in closer to Willa and lowered her voice. 'I would strongly advise you to stay away from my son.'

'Perhaps you should tell him that,' said Willa boldly, looking the woman in the eye.

'Men are easy prey – especially young, inexperienced men – for women with loose morals.'

Willa wanted to slap her and almost did but held herself back. Richard's mother would be the type to lay charges. She would consider it her duty.

LOCAL WOMAN CHARGED WITH ASSAULT OF LOVER'S MOTHER.

'He loves me,' she said.

The woman's eyes blinked. She knows it, thought Willa, and that is why she is so disturbed.

Richard's mother drew herself up to attain her full height and carried on up the street, her shelf-like bosom going ahead of her, making her look like a galleon in full sail. Ina might have a similarly large bosom but her overall shape and mode of walking made her look more like a rolling barrel than a stately ship.

Willa decided she would go mad if she hung around any longer. She would go away for half an hour and by the time she came back the travellers might have returned. She went again to see Bunty, who was ensconced in the back-shop smoking with Mrs Mooney. Willa heard their laughter as she came into the shop.

'No sign of them?' asked Bunty.

Willa shook her head.

'You're having your troubles, aren't you, love?' said Mrs Mooney. 'Bunty was telling me. I don't know how you put up with a harridan like that. If you're ever needing a place to stay you can come to me, dear. I've a spare room.'

'Maureen's got a lovely flat,' said Bunty.

'So you've told me,' said Willa. 'Bunty, I'm wondering if something's happened to them. I mean, they could have got run over or the bus might have had an accident.'

'You'd have heard.'

'But how?'

'The police would have come. Look, why don't you sit down? I'm sure they'll turn up right as rain.'

'Funny that,' commented Mrs Mooney. 'Why do we say rain is right?'

'Willa will know,' said Bunty.

Willa did not.

She forced herself to stay for an hour before returning home. Opening the door she knew at once that they were not there; the flat had an empty, silent feel to it.

'Hello,' she called out. There was no answer.

The wanderers returned late in the afternoon.

'Where have you been?' cried Willa, seizing her child from his grandmother's arms.

'What do you mean, where have we been? You ken fine. We were at my friend Minnie's in Grangemouth.'

'You were to come back yesterday.'

'It was only an extra day. What in the name are you making

such a fuss for? For crying out loud! You'd think we'd been gone a month. Did you expect me to send you a telegram? Malkie was enjoying himself, weren't you, Malkie?'

'I agreed to two nights only.'

Malcolm began to cry.

'Now look what you're doing to him!' His granny tried to take him from Willa's arms. Willa stepped back.

'Leave him alone!' she shouted. 'He's my child.'

'You are in a right stushie! It doesn't do a bairn any good to see his mother all worked up in a lather like that. You want to come to Granny, don't you, Malkie?' He was holding out his arms to her.

'Stay away from him!'

'He wants me, you can see he does.'

His cries were turning to sobs and tears were rolling down his face.

'It's a crime to put a bairn into a state like that,' said his granny. 'Give him to me this minute, Willa! It's me he wants, not you.'

The women faced each other.

'I'm leaving,' said Willa. 'And I'm taking Malcolm with me.'

'You can't!'

'Oh yes, I can! Watch me!'

Carrying her sobbing child, Willa stormed out of the kitchen and went into her own room, powered by fury such as she had never known before. She closed the door and dragged over a chair to put in front of it. There was no key for the lock. Then she dumped Malcolm in his cot and yanked the bigger of the two suitcases from the top of the wardrobe to add to her barricade. No sooner was it done than Ina was at the back of the door trying to push it open and demanding to be let in. Malcolm cried the louder. Willa ignored him and set to work.

She packed first Malcolm's clothes, taking her time, making sure that she left out nothing vital. Her possessions went into the space that remained.

Having closed the suitcase, she hoisted Malcolm up from his cot, tucked him struggling and wriggling under her arm and opened the door with her free hand. She then swiftly bent down and picked up the case.

Ina was standing in the hall in front of the entrance door. She was trembling.

'You can't take him away. Tommy'll be angry.'

'Well, he's not here, is he? He's dancing his way round the Pacific. Twinkletoes himself. Now, if you will excuse me.'

Ina did not move.

LOCAL WOMAN KNOCKS DOWN MOTHER-IN-LAW.

'Open the door!' said Willa, controlling her voice.

Still Ina did not move.

Willa put down the suitcase and nudged – not pushed, not too much, at least – her mother-in-law to the side making her stagger, just a little. While she was regaining her balance Willa opened the door, lifted the suitcase again, and was gone.

'You just walked out?' said Bunty. 'Here, give the bairn a chocolate bar, for God's sake. Anything to shut him up.'

He was screaming. Bunty unwrapped a bar of white chocolate and stuck it in his hand. He gulped a couple of times then took the bar to his mouth and silence descended.

'Thank the Lord for that,' said Bunty, lighting a cigarette from the stub of the old one. 'He's got some pair of lungs on him.'

Willa dried his face and neck which were wet with tears, then she hugged him close to her. She would never let him go, no matter what.

'You can't stay here, you know, Willa. I haven't the room.'

'Mrs Mooney said if I was ever needing a place to come to her.'

'Aye I ken, but I don't know if she'd mean with a baby. She's not used to bairns. Her flat's as neat as a new pin.'

'Even for a night or two till I find something? I should have enough money to rent a room.'

'Maureen will be in soon for her *Evening News*. You go on through the back with Malcolm and I'll ask her when she comes in. Save you having to.'

When they went into the back room Malcolm wanted to get down and investigate the various boxes lying about. Willa set him on his feet, which made him chuckle. The sound warmed her heart after all that screaming. He could walk now, holding on to things as he travelled round the room.

Before Mrs Mooney came for her newspaper, Ina turned up. They'd been expecting that. On hearing her voice, Willa closed the connecting door and leant against it, staying there until Bunty tapped and said, 'It's all right, hen. She's gone.'

Willa heard Mrs Mooney arriving too. Her laugh was unmistakable. It faded and then a conversation commenced in quiet voices, too quiet for Willa to make out what was being said, after which Mrs Mooney came breezing into the room to say, 'I hear you're homeless. Of course you can come home with me! I wouldn't see the two of youse out in the street. I love babies, so I do. And he looks a darling boy.'

~ 22 ~

Colloa, Lima, Peru,
S. America
1st August, 1924

Dear Willa,
  We arrived here, in Colloa, the chief seaport of
Peru, after 14 days at sea, the longest stretch of the
cruise, but it passed quickly as we had exercises and
sports and concerts, as well as pictures and a band,
also a song competition.

'Has Tommy much of a singing voice?' asked Mrs Mooney.

'Not bad at all,' said Bunty. 'His mother thinks he could have gone on the stage. He's especially good at love songs. *I'll be your sweetheart*...He knows how to put it over, doesn't he, Willa?'

Willa made no reply.

They were sitting in Mrs Mooney's living room with Gerry, who had dropped by with some liver, and Bunty, who had brought the letter round. Willa had waylaid the postman and asked him for any letters addressed to her to be delivered to Bunty's shop. Sandy was an obliging man. He'd asked no questions. As for Gerry, who was also obliging, he had come to accept that they all knew about his friendship with Mrs Mooney and was no longer embarrassed.

'Here's the first verse of the winning song,' said Willa. 'To be sung to the tune of "The Mountains of Mourne".'

'*Sweep down to the sea,*' sang Mrs Mooney in a quavering voice. 'I know it like the back of my hand.'

> *Have you heard of Sir Harry, a benevolent old gent*
> *Who followed the Danae wherever she went?*
> *Without him, without him, oh what should we do?*
> *To pay for a tram ride would give us the blues.*
> *So while we're about it our caps we will doff*
> *To good old Sir Harry, a genuine old toff.*

'Who's Sir Harry?' asked Gerry.

'Tommy says Sir Harry Freeman is a term the sailors use for free entertainments,' said Willa.

'They've had plenty of those,' said Bunty.

'Nothing but,' said Gerry, 'from what I've heard.'

'Pity Sir Harry doesne live in Edinburgh,' said Bunty.

> *Lima has one of the biggest bullrings in the world.*
> *The Fiestas de Toros are said to be more amusing*
> *than bloodthirsty these days because the matadors*
> *deliver their death thrust with nothing more harmful*
> *than sharp sticks.*

'That's nasty enough,' said Mrs Mooney with a shudder. 'I wouldn't find it much of a laugh.'

'Folk in those countries see things differently,' said Gerry.

'I expect they're heathens and don't know any better,' said Mrs Mooney.

'They're mostly Roman Catholic in Peru,' said Willa.

'Tommy says there are sixty-seven churches in Lima, all RC.'

'Fancy that,' said Mrs Mooney, who wore a cross at her throat and had religious pictures on every wall in her house. To begin with, Willa had found them a bit creepy, especially ones with Jesus on the cross with blood dripping from his hands and feet. Having been brought up in the Church of Scotland she wasn't used to such scenes. Mrs Mooney went to mass regularly and Willa wondered if she also went to confession. She supposed she might for then each week her sins would be forgiven and then she could start all over again. Willa had been told that when they confessed they were supposed to be giving up the sin for good but she didn't think that Mrs Mooney would let a detail like that worry her. She was a practical woman.

> *The squadron was treated to a special performance of a bull fight, attended by the President of the Peruvian Republic. Six bulls were killed and each time the crowd went wild with excitement. We ourselves did not care for the ghastly sight though there were plenty of women present who seemed unconcerned and cheered loudly at the kill. I suppose they grow up with it.*

'Thank God your Tommy didn't take to it, Willa,' said Mrs Mooney. 'I wouldn't like to think you were married to a man who'd enjoy that sort of thing.'

There was a slight pause while they all wondered, silently, Willa included, if she was going to stay married to him, before Bunty said, 'I wonder if they eat the bulls afterwards.'

'It'd be an awful waste of good meat if they didn't,' said Gerry.

'Wouldn't catch me eating it,' said Mrs Mooney, breaking off to say, 'I don't think you should be in there, son,' to Malcolm, who had opened a cupboard and was busy hauling out china dishes.

Willa jumped up to take him away from it and then of course he roared. She was trying to teach him that he couldn't have everything he saw but she wasn't making too much progress. He was as stubborn as his grandmother! Though she preferred not to connect the two in her mind. They'd managed to avoid seeing Ina in the two weeks they'd been here; Bunty had steadfastly refused to tell her where they were living.

'Will he not sit in his chair?' asked Mrs Mooney who, while being good-natured, was sometimes finding her patience tested. Willa was aware of this and knew that if they stayed much longer they might outstay their welcome. Mrs Mooney – or Maureen, as she now called her – liked her place to be neat and tidy and free of finger-marks, especially on her cream and pale-green wallpaper.

'I could try,' said Willa.

After a struggle she squeezed Malcolm into the high chair which Bunty had borrowed from a customer – her customers were many and varied and obliging too – and he then proceeded to throw out every toy Willa gave him.

'Come and sit on your Uncle Gerry's knee,' said Gerry and he lifted the baby out of the chair. He gave him his watch and chain to play with and that appeased him.

'I was aye telling Ina she'd have him spoiled rotten,' said

Bunty. 'Poor soul. She's as miserable as sin.'

'It's funny they should call sin miserable,' said Mrs Mooney. 'There's times when it's not, eh, Gerry?'

He blushed and bent his head to swing his watch to and fro in front of Malcolm's eyes.

Willa took up the letter again.

It was a long letter from Peru, much of it about the history of the Incas and other civilisations, which she did not read out as they would be questioning her about every sentence.

> *The people of Peru today are a mixture of Spanish and Indian, with some Negro blood mixed in. Only 15% are reputed to be white and this class dominates, filling the official and professional ranks.*

'That's the same everywhere he's been, isn't it?' said Gerry. 'The whites rule the roost.'

'Stands to reason,' said Bunty.

'Why?' asked Willa.

'Well, the darkies wouldn't be much good at running things, would they? What would they know?'

'Maybe more than we think,' said Willa. 'Anyway, I don't know that you should be calling them "darkies".' Richard had told her that his mother objected strongly to the use of words such as 'darkie' and 'nigger', that were common curency with some people. She said they robbed people of their dignity, and Willa understood what she meant, in spite of the fact that the woman was her enemy. The way Tommy wrote about some of the natives made her uncomfortable.

'Don't see why not,' said Bunty. 'They're dark, aren't they?

I wouldn't mind if somebody called me a whitey. What's wrong with that?'

Willa was not going to take this argument on so she went back to the letter.

> *Each day a military band plays soothing airs during the sticky afternoon heat until the sun sets and Pacific breezes stir the city to life. Illuminated arches and buildings, music, gaudy uniforms, dark-eyed señoritas and crowded restaurants are all part of the pulsating night life of this tropical capital.*

'It's a different life,' sighed Mrs Mooney. 'Sometimes you wonder if you shouldn't just pick up sticks and go. What about it, Gerry?'

'I couldn't stick the heat,' said Gerry. 'It'd bring me out in a rash.'

'It's the ginger hair,' said Bunty.

> *One day we were taken by train into the mountains. The scenery en route was a grand sight, the rugged mountains looking insurmountable but made possible by many switchback and V-shaped shuntings. Some parts of the journey were rather thrilling as when the train would shoot out of a tunnel straight onto a narrow bridge spanning a valley hundreds of feet below. Our destination, Rio Blanco, is 12,000 feet above sea level and a number of the men suffered from altitude sickness, though not myself.*

'I'd have given that a miss,' said Bunty. 'It's quite a nice run though on the train to North Berwick.'

None of the family, except, of course, for the world traveller, had been on any other train line. Willa didn't know about Mrs Mooney.

'It goes on for two or three pages about the mountains,' she said, leafing through them.

The doorbell rang and she got up to answer it. Richard stood on the landing.

'Hello there!' he said and they kissed. Since Willa had left Ina's house it had been easier for them to see each other though they were still careful, or relatively so, not to be seen out and about in the area too much.

The assembled company greeted him warmly, apart from Malcolm, who looked up from Gerry's shiny, ticking watch to scowl.

'I'll make you a nice cup of tea, love,' said Mrs Mooney, getting up. When Richard was around she put on what she considered to be a posh accent. They all thought him terribly polite. 'I'm sure Gerry could do with one too. Or maybe we should all have a wee drinkie instead?'

'I ought to be going,' said Gerry, without making a move. Mrs Mooney's house seemed to have that affect on people; once they settled in they were reluctant to stir. Her chairs were comfortable and her hospitality generous.

'Have you shut the shop, Bunty?' asked Willa.

'Aye, I closed a wee bit early. All my papers had gone and most of the regulars had been in for their smokes.'

'What'll it be?' asked Mrs Mooney. 'G and T?'

'Suits me,' said Gerry.

'All round,' said Bunty.

Willa helped Mrs Mooney by slicing the lemons. Maureen liked to do things nicely. She set the drinks out on little lace doilies that had been crocheted by her old grandmother in County Clare. Malcolm was given a mug of orange juice and a digestive biscuit and put back in his high chair. When he was allowed to roam free he pestered Maureen's wee Pekinese, Daffy, making him yelp.

'Well,' said Gerry, raising his glass, 'here's tae us, wha's like us, damn few, and they're a' deid!'

'Nary a one,' said Bunty.

They drank.

Richard sat beside Willa on the settee holding her hand, but unobtrusively, so that Malcolm would not notice. They made no effort to conceal their attachment for each other to the adults. 'I don't suppose I should approve,' Bunty had said to Willa, 'but to be honest, I don't blame you. Life's too short to pass up a bit of happiness. And I can see the two of you are happy together.'

It was warm in the room even with the window open so they were not long in finishing their drinks. August, so far, had been a kind month.

'A little more?' asked Mrs Mooney, coming round with the gin bottle. She was not known for pouring small drinks.

The doorbell rang and Gerry looked startled.

'Dinne fash yersel!' said Bunty. 'She doesne know you're here. This is Maureen's secret hideaway!'

The householder herself went to the door. The caller was only a neighbour wanting to borrow a bowl of sugar which Maureen supplied.

'She's always borrowing, that one, never returning.'

'Ina's got one of them too,' said Bunty.

They settled down again.

Malcolm's head gradually began to droop and he dozed off. Willa lifted him out and took him through to the bedroom and laid him down in the cot, on loan from yet another of Bunty's customers.

After their third drink Bunty declared herself to be 'well away'. She was needing food to sober her up. Richard and Willa's offer to go out and buy fish and chips was accepted. Gerry supplied the money.

Outside the flat door, on the landing, they stopped to kiss before going down the stair and out into the bright street, hand-in-hand. A secret romance in summertime was so much more difficult than in winter when the dark came early.

As they approached the chip shop Willa dropped Richard's hand.

'Don't stand too close to me in the shop. Just in case. Anyway, they know me in there.'

She pulled back from the door just in time. Ina was at the counter. Her back was unmistakable. She had on her old fawn felt slippers with the pompons which wobbled when she walked. Willa heard her ask for a black pudding and a small bag of chips, saying, 'It's just for me, I'm on my own,' and for the first time since leaving her Willa felt a stab of guilt. Then she told herself that Tommy's mother wasn't her responsibility and she owed her nothing, especially when she'd all but stolen her child from her. She pulled Richard round the corner and they waited until Ina came rolling out of the shop carrying her supper wrapped in newspaper. She was walking badly, listing to one side like a ship off its keel. Her legs must be troubling her. The sight touched Willa and a wave of guilt swept over her again.

'What's wrong?' asked Richard. He was aware of every change in her mood, unlike Tommy, who wouldn't notice even if she was right down in the dumps.

'Nothing.' She shrugged it off.

When Ina had limped out of sight, they went inside.

'Five fish suppers,' said Willa, laying the money on the counter. 'And plenty of salt and sauce.'

'You must be having a party,' said Lorenzo as he dug his shovel into the vat of hot, golden, tantalising chips.

'Every day's a party,' said Richard, who had forgotten that he was not supposed to come too close to Willa. He had slipped his arm round her waist and his hand was resting on her hip.

'Lucky you!' said Lorenzo.

'Yes, lucky me,' said Richard with a smile.

~ 23 ~

Valparaiso, Chile
South America
11th August, 1924

Dear Willa,
    As we steamed into harbour the Delhi *saluted the country with a 21-gun salute, which was returned by the shore battery. The Chilean man-of-war* Esmeralda *then saluted Rear-Admiral Brand with an 18-gun salute, which was returned by the* Delhi.

'They could go on all day at that rate,' said Bunty. 'They like playing themselves, don't they?'

This may not be British territory but we have been made very welcome even if not so boisterously perhaps as in places like Melbourne and Adelaide. But then they are our colonies.

'At least we got free,' said Mrs Mooney.
    'How do you mean?' asked Bunty.
    'Ireland. We're the Irish Free State now! You must have read about it in the papers? Back in 1921.'
    'Aye, of course. I was forgetting. The bit in the north doesn't belong to you though, does it?'
    'Not yet,' said Mrs Mooney.

Vicuna rugs (made from the fur of the S. American wild deer) can be purchased for little money, also brightly coloured wool rugs woven by the Indians which looked as if they would wear well. I considered buying one but decided the colours would be too vivid for our flat.

'For his mother's flat,' said Willa, speaking her thoughts aloud. She wondered what Tommy would think if he knew she had left it. It was all right for him: the flat was only a port of call, amongst many others.

'I saw Ina yesterday,' said Bunty. 'She's missing you and the wee one.'

'It's not me she misses.'

'She's gone downhill since you left.'

'Don't be making Willa feel guilty,' said Mrs Mooney. 'It's not her fault.'

'No, I ken.' Bunty sighed. 'Ina's her own worst enemy. She'd drive anyone up the wall. I couldne live with her if you paid me.'

Willa went back to the letter. 'He says Chile has had a violent history and a number of bad earthquakes, the last one apparently in 1906 when Valparaiso was almost completely destroyed. That's not that long ago.'

'Just as well Ina didn't hear any of that! She'd be up the wall in case Tommy got caught in one. She's been worrying herself sick because the letters had stopped so I let her know they were coming to the shop.'

'They are addressed to me,' Willa pointed out, 'not her.'

'I ken. She asked if there were any messages for her in them so I told her Tommy always sends her his love.'

*Yesterday, Sunday, we had the ordinary church
service in the forenoon and during the last dog
watch a memorial service to keep our memories
green of the sinking of HMS* Good Hope *and HMS*
Monmouth *by the Germans on 1st November 1914
when Sir Christopher Craddock and many officers
and men lost their lives in doing their duty. We
practically passed the spot, off Coronel, where the
ships went down. It was a sobering moment. I trust
that the widows and children of these brave men are
not in need today.*

Bunty snorted. 'You must be jokin'. One of my customers, a
Mrs Jackson – her husband died in France – has four bairns
and is hard pushed to feed them.'

Then there was Mr MacNab, thought Willa.

'It's all very well,' said Bunty, 'doing their duty, but who
cares afterwards? Not the damned politicians. Thank God
we're done with the war now.'

'Sounds like Tommy might be getting interested in religion,'
said Mrs Mooney. 'Two services in a day. I didn't think he'd
be the religious type.'

'They've no option,' said Willa. 'They have to do their duty
to God as well as King and Country. Doesn't matter if they
believe in it or not.' Richard had told her that his mother was
an atheist. She belonged to the Humanist Society. Richard said
he was still trying to make up his mind.

There was a crash in the walk-in cupboard off the kitchen;
they'd forgotten that Malcolm was on the loose. Willa jumped
up and went to see what damage had been done. Malcolm

was holding up half of a blue and gold oval-shaped dish looking for approval.

'Naughty boy!' said Willa.

He began to cry.

She took the piece of china out of his hand and carried it as well as him back to the kitchen.

'I'm terribly sorry, Maureen.'

'Oh no!' cried Maureen. 'That belonged to my mother and my granny before her!'

'Maybe it could be mended,' suggested Bunty. 'Stuck together. I've a customer who's good at things like that.'

'It'd never be the same.'

There was no hope of sticking anything together, Willa saw, when she went back to the cupboard and found the other half of the dish lying in fragments on the floor. She apologised again to Maureen and took Malcolm out for a walk in his pram. She was also going to see if she could find a room to rent within her budget.

Crossing the Meadows she had the ill luck to meet Richard's mother, who raised an eyebrow at the pram and said, 'I didn't know you had a child as well!'

As well as what, Willa wondered. All her other drawbacks?

'Have you a husband?'

'I think that is my business.'

Richard's mother smiled. 'Well, I don't think you'll be seeing much of Richard after September.' The little smile still curling her lips, she sailed on past.

What had she meant by that? At the end of September the fleet would be due back in Chatham but Richard's mother couldn't have been referring to that, could she? Richard wouldn't have told her. No, of course he wouldn't. His mother hadn't even known if Willa was married or not. Willa had been trying not to think ahead, had been living a day at a time. The end of September had always seemed a long way away. But now it was almost the end of August.

She pushed the pram up Middle Meadow Walk and along Forrest Road to the library where she lifted Malcolm out and carried him inside. She did a tour of the building but saw no sign of Richard. She asked the nice librarian if she'd seen him but she shook her head, saying he hadn't been in for a day or two.

Willa pushed the pram back down the hill and went to see if Bunty had any cards on her window offering rooms to rent.

'There's a couple nearby,' said Bunty. 'But goodness knows what they're like. I'll keep the wee one if you want while you go and have a look. I realise you can't stay at Maureen's much longer.'

Malcolm liked Bunty so he made no protest when Willa left him sitting in his pram inside the shop. As soon as she was out of sight Bunty would give him a piece of chocolate.

The first room was in a flat in Fountainbridge and it was horrible; Willa could think of no other word to describe it. The wallpaper was peeling off the walls, a wide crack zigzagged across the ceiling, and there was a single gas ring for cooking. In addition, the place smelt of grease. Willa looked into the toilet of the shared bathroom and blenched.

'You can have a bath on Saturday nights,' said the landlady. 'That's when I put the boiler on.'

'I'll let you know,' said Willa.

The second room in Bread Street was no better. The

wallpaper was intact but the bed sagged as if it were filled with sand when Willa pressed her hand into it and the window looked down into what appeared to be a knacker's yard. This place smelt of mould. As for the bathroom! The smell alone would nearly knock you off your feet.

'I have three other lodgers at present,' said the landlady. 'They are all a nice class of person. Mr Jamieson, left front, is a legal clerk. In quite a big office in town.'

They couldn't be paying him much, thought Willa.

'I'll let you know,' she said.

She went back to Bunty.

'They were both dreadful,' she reported.

Bunty was not surprised. 'The landladies are pretty dreadful too. Trouble is, Willa, to get anything half decent you'd need more money.'

Willa already knew that. 'What am I to do?'

'You've got two options,' said Bunty, 'as I see it. One is to stay at Maureen's. The other is to go back to Ina's.'

'You've already said I can't stay on at Maureen's.'

Bunty was saying nothing now.

'How can I go back to Ina's?' demanded Willa. 'She was trying to take my child away!'

'I think she's learnt her lesson.'

'I wouldn't be so sure.'

'Och, I understand how she's come to be the way she is.'

Malcolm was happy; Bunty had given him a set of keys on a ring to play with. He liked things that jingled and could be tested for strength between his six teeth.

'Let's go through the back,' said Bunty. 'The shop's quiet at the moment.'

AFTER YOU'VE GONE   301

They went through, taking Malcolm with them.

'Ina's had a hard time in life,' said Bunty.

'Yes, I know all that. It wasn't easy for my mother when my father died either.'

'Aye, but with men. I'm going to tell you something, Willa. Roberto – Tommy's dad – didn't die.'

'But she always calls herself a widow.'

'He did a runner. Went without a word. Just didn't come home one night from the ice-cream shop.'

'He might have had an accident.'

'He'd taken all his clothes with him. No, it was planned. When Ina looked in the closet later she found it was bare. Old Mother Hubbard, eh? It was a bitter blow to her. So there she was left all on her own with a baby and no money. Roberto had emptied out their post office savings account and all.'

'Tommy's never said anything to me about it.'

'He doesn't know. She didn't want him to. She has her pride. And then, when Tommy was fourteen, what did he do? He upped and left her too, went away to sea. That was another blow. And now you've taken Malcolm.'

'I had to.'

'I ken. I'm not blaming you. You stuck it longer than I thought you would.'

'Where did Roberto go?'

'Back to Italy. Naples, as far as we know. Ina has never heard from him from that day to this. But a few years back I bumped into his uncle and he told me that Roberto had married a woman over there and had a couple of kids by her.'

'But that's bigamy.'

'Aye. But who's to know in Naples? I never let on to Ina.

She was crazy about Roberto. She's been crazy about all the men in her life. This wee one here included.'

'Poor Ina,' said Willa, never having thought she would ever speak the words. 'I do feel sorry for her, Bunty, but that doesn't mean I could go back and live with her.'

'Think about it,' said Bunty.

They heard the shop door opening and Bunty got up to see who it was. She came back with Richard.

'I've been looking for you,' he said to Willa.

'And I've been looking for you.'

'Why don't the two of you go and have yourselves a wee walk. I'll mind Malcolm. He behaves himself with me, don't you, lad?'

Willa and Richard walked across the Meadows and she told him how she'd met and exchanged a few words with his mother.

'I'm really sorry about that. Willa, I've been meaning to tell you – she wants me to go to London to finish my degree.'

'*London?*'

'She thinks it would broaden my sights,' he said awkwardly.

'But that would cost more.'

'An aunt of Mother's down in Devonshire has died and left her some money.'

'Oh I see.'

'But I don't want to leave Edinburgh, Willa. And you!'

'It would be a big opportunity for you, though.'

'Well, I suppose.'

'Could you get into university, just like that?'

'A cousin of Mother's is a history don in London.'

Of course, thought Willa, if you have the right connections then doors will open for you and there is always the chance, if you're hard up, that an ancient, unmarried relative whom you may seldom have seen and care little about will die and leave you her fortune and you won't even have to grieve as you scarcely knew her. They seemed to be women, these relatives, more often than men. Willa had gleaned her knowledge about such things from her reading of books. Books, especially novels, had taught her a great deal. They had taken her into many different worlds and into different levels of society.

'I haven't decided yet,' Richard stressed. 'I'd miss you! Terribly. But if I do go it would only be for a few weeks at a time. The terms are short. And I'd write to you every single night, I promise you I would.'

But what would she do in the meantime? Stay with Tommy's mother and collect Richard's letters at the post office, secretly, shoving them into her bag, glancing over her shoulder like a thief, hoping not to be seen by Mrs Cant or Elma, who might well be standing at the counter?

'You could come with me!'

'How?' She shook her head. 'Richard, you know it would all be too difficult.'

'No, I do not, Willa!' He stopped and turned her round to face him. 'I'm deadly serious about this. If we want to be together enough we can find a way. We *will* find a way. Believe me!'

~ 24 ~

Buenos Aires, Argentina
24th August, 1924

Dear Willa,
We have just docked after a very difficult 12-day voyage, the worst trip of the cruise. On Tuesday 12th at noon we were abreast of Huaflo Island and at 10.30 p.m. ran into a ferocious gale. The sea swamped the quarterdeck and our waist was awash no matter how we maintained our speed. On Thursday we were due at the Magellan Strait but we could not see the entrance so the admiral decided that we should sound the horn. Unfortunately we were unable to get into Puula Arenas for our two-day scheduled visit. We heard the people were extremely disappointed.

'What a shame,' said Elma. 'I suppose it'll be a while till they're back there again?'

'If ever,' said Willa. 'The fleet couldn't go on a junket like that very often.'

'It must be costing a pretty penny,' said Elma.

'Just as well Ina's not here,' said Bunty. 'She'd be imagining them all at the bottom of the ocean.'

They were sitting in Bunty's back room, the three of them, and Malcolm. It was not often that Elma called in at the shop. They thought she suspected that Gerry was still involved with

Mrs Mooney. She'd come in asking in an offhand way if they'd seen him recently and if they'd thought he was looking well. She was worried about him, was wondering if she should get the doctor to take a look at him. She'd hung around for an hour, which was not like her, and then Sandy had brought the post. Every time the shop door pinged open they were on edge in case Maureen would walk in.

When Willa finished reading the letter she was going to go round and talk to Ina. Things had come to a head at Maureen's. After Malcolm had broken a blue and white ashet and a prized Chinese vase that her brother had brought back from the Far East, she had said, very nicely, to Willa, 'I'm terribly sorry, dear, but I'm afraid I'm going to have to ask you to leave. Daffy's not too happy with the wee boy always after him. I hate doing this—'

Willa had interrupted her. 'No, I'm sorry, Maureen. We shouldn't have stayed so long, I know that. I'm really grateful to you. And I'm terribly sorry about the vase. And Daffy.'

She had made another attempt at finding a room but they were either in a deplorable state or landladies didn't want small children. She'd gone to one earlier that morning where a family had offered to take them in but it would have meant sharing a room with two of their children. They had eight in all and were obviously trying to rent out the space because they were so hard up.

Buenos Aires is a delightful city with fine avenues and boulevards. In the park are to be found a zoo, an aquarium, a motor track, flying grounds and boating lakes, in one of which black swans are to be seen swimming, and the other white. It's quite a sight. On weekends the park is thronged with fashionable people, of Spanish, Italian, British and American stock, with the original Indian element so small as to be scarcely noticeable.

'I don't suppose they walk in the park,' said Willa. 'The Indian element.'

'Why wouldn't they?' asked Elma.

'I think they might be living in the slums.'

'Tommy hasn't said anything about slums.'

He'd said nothing about slums in any of his letters but then they wouldn't have been taken on motor trips round those. Only the best for the boys in blue!

'Where is that place, Willa?' asked Elma. 'I'm a bit lost.'

'South America. The east coast. They've been down the west coast already and now they're coming up the other side.'

'They can't have many places left to go to,' said Elma.

'Not many,' agreed Willa.

It was nearing the middle of September.

'Look what he's doing!' cried Elma.

Willa jumped up to rescue Bunty's handbag from Malcolm, who was staggering around on two feet now, unaided. He was about to be one year old. 'Give that to Mummy! Oh heavens, Bunty, he's had your powder compact! What a mess.'

'My fault,' said Bunty, retrieving the bag. 'I should have known better. You have to stay a step ahead of this lad.'

Willa wiped the orange-coloured powder off Malcolm's face and gave him an old magazine as a diversion.

'Your daddy will be coming home soon,' Elma told him.

'He won't be wanting to see you covered in ladies' powder, no, he will not! He'd say you were a naughty boy.'

Malcolm was more interested in ripping apart the magazine than in listening to what his Great-aunt Elma had to say. Willa longed for the time when he might start to be creative, build things, draw pictures instead of scribbling on walls whenever he managed to pick up a pencil. She had to be extra careful about leaving books lying around. He had torn up one library book and been astounded when his mother had screamed at him. 'You're not allowed to destroy books!' His bottom lip had trembled and then a flood of tears had followed. She had comforted him, realising he was too young to understand and knowing that she had overreacted. She'd then had to go up to the library and pay for the replacement of the book.

> *Cafés are numerous and comfortable, tastefully decorated, many with excellent bands. We have frequented a fair number, passing delightful evenings in pleasant company. Life in Brazil is a lot more relaxed than in Scotland.*

'Isn't that where they're tango mad?' said Bunty, swaying her hips. 'And the men like to dance with a rose between their teeth.'

'That could be dangerous,' said Elma.

'Life's dangerous, Elma,' said Bunty, making her sister sniff. 'Safer being dead. I like South American dances myself. They're more fun than slow waltzes. More sexy.'

One night Willa, desperate to go dancing to the sound of a big band again, had asked Richard to take her. 'Let's risk it!'

she'd said. They'd gone to the Marine Gardens Ballroom in Portobello where they'd seen no one they knew and danced the night away while Bunty had looked after Malcolm.

We had an interesting visit to one of the largest beef factories in the world. Nothing is wasted. From the time the bullock is killed to its being canned only an hour has passed.

'Gerry would be interested in that,' said Elma. 'Did you say you had seen him yesterday?'

'He was in for a paper,' said Bunty.

'He didn't happen to mention where he was going, did he?'

'There was a queue in. I'd no time to talk.'

'The Crown Prince of Italy was visiting at the same time as Tommy,' said Willa, scanning the rest of the letter. 'They held a ball in his honour. The Crown Prince, that is.'

'Imagine our Tommy rubbing shoulders with royalty,' said Elma.

'I doubt he'd have been invited to the balls,' said Willa. 'The admirals maybe, but not a Yeoman of Signals. I expect he's been to plenty of other dances though, with raven-haired, black-eyed señoritas.' She no longer cared. She wished he would jump ship with one of them and run off into the jungle.

'I can see him with a rose between his teeth,' said Bunty. 'He'd look the part.'

'That's one thing about Gerald,' said Elma, 'he wouldn't go for that. He's got more common sense.'

The shop door pinged and they heard Richard's voice. 'Anybody in?'

Willa felt her face heating up. Bunty left the room at once, closing the door behind her. A murmur of voices ensued and then she came back, alone. She and Willa exchanged glances.

'A customer?' asked Elma.

'Aye,' said Bunty. 'He was wanting *The Scotsman*. Tommy got anything else to say, Willa?'

'They're off to Rio de Janeiro next,' said Willa, folding up the letter. 'Brazil.'

'It wasn't Gerald, was it?' asked Elma.

'Who?' said Bunty.

'The customer?'

'Of course not. If it was I'd have asked him in, wouldn't I, to join the party?'

Elma said she'd better be getting home to make his tea. 'He's going to some sort of event for master butchers this evening. It's not a do for wives.' She left.

'I daresay it's not,' said Bunty. 'Poor thing. Still, what she doesn't know doesne hurt her.' She took a piece of a paper out of her pocket and gave it to Willa.

Can I see you this evening? I'll come round to Mrs Mooney's about 8 o'clock. Love Richard xxx

Willa put it in her bag alongside Tommy's letter.

'Will you be all right with Malcolm for an hour, Bunty?'

'No bother. Good luck!'

Willa pulled the bell and immediately wondered if she should turn and run. Then the door opened and there stood Ina in her slippers, her body slack, which meant the stays would be up on the pulley.

'Hello,' said Willa.

'It's you.'

'Can I come in?'

Ina stood back and allowed her to enter. They went into the kitchen.

'Want a cup of tea?'

'All right. Thanks.' At least it was an offering.

The tea made, they sat down opposite each other

'How's the wee one?' asked Ina, a catch in her throat.

'He's fine.'

'He'll be walking?'

'He is. He's a menace on two legs!'

'I thought he'd walk early. Tommy did.' Another catch. 'How's Tommy?'

'He's well. Sends his love.'

'He never forgets his mother.'

They drank their tea and then Ina said, 'I've missed you and the bairn.' She took a deep breath. 'Willa, I'd like you to come back!'

Willa looked up from her cup.

'I'll not interfere any more, I promise I won't. I'm sorry if I butted in too much. It was only, well, it was only that I loved the wee boy so much, from the minute I set eyes on him.'

Willa had never imagined she would see Ina shed a tear. She got up and put an arm round her shoulder.

'I know you did.'

'But it was wrong of me to come between a bairn and his mother. By the way, the children have been taken away next door, into care. Poor wee souls.'

'Poor Mrs MacNab,' said Willa.

'Aye.' Ina sighed. 'She's no had much of a life. He was

knocking her about again and she just fell apart. She's in the hospital and he's in the jail.'

What a mess, thought Willa.

After another pot of tea it was agreed that she and Malcolm should return the next day. Going down the stairs on her way out she was not so foolish as to think that Ina would keep totally to her promise, but if she were to go too far on any occasion she might pull herself up and remember that she had made one.

Maureen was going out for the evening. The flat smelt of gardenia bath salts and perfume.

'Can you do me up the back of my dress, love?'

Willa obliged. The dress was a sheath of orange silk as far as the hips after which it flared out to allow the wearer's knees to move. Maureen was going dancing at the Palace Ballroom at the foot of Leith Walk. Willa was envious.

'Pity you can't come with us,' said Maureen.

Gerry called for her at a quarter to eight. He smelt of after-shave lotion and he had on his best suit and was carrying his trilby in his hand. In the daytime, for work, he wore a flat cap, which Elma hated. She considered it 'common'.

'Have a good time,' said Willa.

They departed, Maureen on Gerry's arm, as they went down the stairs.

Maureen had been talking about selling up and going to live in Dublin. Would Gerry go with her? Would she want him to?

At eight, Richard came.

'Baby sleeping?'

'Sound.' One good thing that resulted from Malcolm's

hectic daytime activity was that he slept well and long at night, which gave Willa time to herself, to read, or to be with Richard.

They sat close together on the settee, Richard's arm round her shoulders.

'Does your mother know you come to see me?' asked Willa.

'I expect so. Well, yes, she does. I don't lie to her. I don't see why I should.'

'She won't like that, you spending time with me?'

'It's my life. And she's got to get used to you being a part of it.'

'She won't.'

'We'll see about that!'

'And London?'

'I'm going down tomorrow. Just for a few days,' he added quickly. 'To meet my tutor, check out the lie of the land. And, Willa, I still mean it, about you coming with me. No, don't say anything, wait till I come back.'

'You going on your own?'

'No, Mother's coming with me.'

~ 25 ~

Rio de Janeiro, Brazil
South America
5th September, 1924

Dear Willa,
    We are glad to be in port for seven days after
another difficult voyage. As before we had to reduce
speed to avoid damage from heavy seas. It was also
bucketing rain with almost continuous electric
storms. We should have called at Santos but there
was a revolution taking place there. We saw pictures
of it at the cinema and judging from those it was
very violent, with many women and children killed
in street skirmishes. Thank God we are not prone to
revolutions in Scotland.

'Thank goodness they didn't go to yon place,' said Ina.
    'The British Special Service Squadron aren't stupid,' said
Bunty. 'They know what they're about. They're having too
good a time to want to get caught up in something nasty like
a revolution.'
    'Anyway, Brazil doesn't belong to us,' said Willa. 'So they
wouldn't have had any right to interfere.'

A Canon Brady, who has helped to arrange
entertainments for us in both BA and Rio, travelled

with the Danae *from BA and was very popular on the trip. Even during rough seas he helped scrub the decks and cooked in the galley along with the cooks, performing both duties very well indeed.*

'That was nice of him,' said Ina.

'A true man of God,' said Elma.

'Can't see your minister doing that,' said Bunty. 'I can't see him dirtying his hands.'

'Maybe not. But he speaks well and he's got a great singing voice. People serve the Lord in different ways.'

'Like knitting bootees for African babies?' said Bunty.

'What's wrong with that?'

'Nothing. Did I say there was anything wrong with it?'

We were escorted into the harbour by two Brazilian destroyers and about ten aeroplanes (we wondered if that might be all they had in their Air Force). The scenery was very picturesque, with islands at the entrance of the harbour and Sugar Loaf Mountain, 3000 feet, standing high above it.

'I wonder if it's anything like Arthur's Seat,' said Elma.

'It couldn't be,' said Willa. 'It must be shaped like a Sugar Loaf. Arthur's Seat looks like a lion. And it's nowhere near three thousand feet.'

She had gone up Arthur's Seat a few days ago with Richard and they had stood on the top in the sunshine looking down on the city spread out before them and over to the blue waters of the Firth of Forth and beyond that the ancient Kingdom of

Fife. Willa liked thinking of Fife as a kingdom. It seemed to suggest magical possibilities. Standing up there, hand in hand, they had felt as free as birds who could take off and fly to wherever they wished.

'How could a mountain be shaped like a loaf of sugar?' demanded Elma, holding her hands parallel to each other to indicate the shape. 'It'd have dead-straight sides. Nobody'd ever get up it.'

'That wouldn't stop a mountain being that shape,' said Bunty. 'It's not obliged to let folk climb it.'

'No need to be sarcastic,' said Elma.

'It must be shaped like a sugar loaf,' said Willa 'or it wouldn't be called that. Here we are! Tommy says that access up the mountain is by a cage suspended from a wire so that the passengers are suspended in mid-air and have a splendid view of the city.'

'You'd never get me in a thing like that,' said Elma.

'Me either,' said Pauline, who had returned the day before from Aberdeen. She had been homesick, had missed Edinburgh and seeing her dad and her best pal Willa. She was back in the double bed with her though it had been made clear that it would have to be for only a limited time for its rightful occupier would soon be on his way home. It was a fact which Willa was trying to keep to the back of her mind. Reading Tommy's letters she felt as if she were reading a piece of fiction related by a made-up character called Tommy.

Rio is an enchanting city, especially at night when it is brilliantly illuminated. 'Rio Nights' are famous. People are out and about in the streets until all

*hours. They love to dance the nights away, samba-
ing and tango-ing. Cafés stay open as long as there
are customers. We have frequented quite a few. Rum
is cheap! The locals are being friendly to us boys in
blue.*

'I bet they are!' said Bunty. 'Very friendly.'

'Do you have to keep making remarks like that?' said Ina.

'I thought rum was cheap for the Navy anyway,' said
Pauline. 'A sailor I met once at the Palais told me.'

Elma gave her a look of disapproval. Willa read on.

*We are making the most of our time here since once
we leave South America we shall be heading for
Cape St Vincent, which, sad to say, will hold none of
the delights of Rio or BA. And, after that, back to
dear Old Blighty!*

'What date was that written?' asked Elma.

'The fifth,' said Willa.

'It's the twenty-fourth today,' said Bunty.

'So where will he be now?' asked Ina.

'At sea, possibly,' said Willa.

'I can't believe he'll soon be home,' said Ina. She looked
down at Malcolm who was on the floor building a tower with
wooden blocks, putting one on top of the other with careful
precision. 'Your daddy's coming to see you, Malkie.'

She had been telling him that ever since they'd come back
to stay with his grandmother. For the first few days Malcolm
had been wary of his grandmother and wouldn't go near her

but gradually he'd got used to her again though he didn't cling to her as much as he had before, which gratified his mother. She had come to the conclusion that babies were infinitely adjustable and if she were to take him to London he would soon forget the life here in his granny's flat with his great-aunts coming and going. Was she really thinking of going to London or was it a fantasy that she allowed herself to entertain before drifting off to sleep, in the hope that she might be happy in her dreams? Richard talked about it as if it really were feasible. But how wonderful it would be to go and live with him in London – anywhere at all in the world away from Edinburgh!

Malcolm looked at the tower which he had so patiently built and with one swift movement of his chubby hand he demolished it and then crowed with delight. He looked up at his mother seeking her admiration.

'I see you,' she said. 'Now do it again.'

And he began to do so.

'Tommy's going to be over the moon about that boy.' Bunty stood up and stretched herself. 'I must be on my way.'

'Me too,' said Elma. "I'm going to get us some tripe for our tea and do it in milk. Gerald's got a bit of a dicky stomach at the moment. It comes and goes with him.'

After they had gone Willa asked Ina if she'd like to take Malcolm out for a stroll in his pram. She'd carry it down the stairs for her. Ina was pleased to be asked.

'I might walk him up to Bruntsfield and get us an ice cream. You'd like that, wouldn't you, Malkie? Your old granny knows what you like.'

He was more interested in his building blocks at the

moment. Sitting on people's knees had lost its appeal for him.

'I was thinking,' Ina began hesitantly, 'that I might call in on Miss McIndoe on the way, see about getting fitted for a new pair of stays. The old ones are not that comfy anymore.'

'That's a good idea. If you're needing some help with the money...'

'No, no, I've some put by.'

Willa carried Malcolm down the stairs and buckled him into his pram – he was becoming too strong for his grandmother to handle – and watched them setting off up the hill. She was going to the library, which had become the main meeting place again for herself and Richard now that she was no longer living in Mrs Mooney's flat. Maureen had decided to move back to Dublin. 'Well, there's nothing here for me, dear, is there?' she'd said to Willa.

'I'll chum you up the road, Willa,' said Pauline, who had come down the stairs behind her. 'I thought I'd pop into the Infirmary and see if they need any extra staff in the office. You never know.' She'd been attending some classes at McAdams Institute for shorthand and typing.

On their way up Lauriston Place they met Maureen. She'd been shopping. She was carrying bags from several stores and had Daffy on the lead trailing behind her.

'I've sold my flat,' she told them, 'so I'll be off in a couple of weeks.'

'Dublin sounds exciting,' said Pauline.

'It does and it doesn't. I like the place, don't get me wrong, but there's an awful lot of poverty and that can get you down if you let it.'

'There is in Edinburgh too,' said Willa.

'But more in Dublin, believe you me! Ireland's poor as dirt. Maybe we should have kept in with Britain! You should see the shawlies in Dublin – the women in their black shawls with their hordes of childer – begging in the streets and at the railway station. Smelling like all get out. I know it's the church that keeps them that way, breeding all those childer. Still, I'm going back. There's something about the oul' place that gets to me. And an old friend of mine, well, we've been in touch.'

'And Gerry?'

'He'd be like fish out of water over there. He'd never make the break, you know that. He belongs here.'

With Elma, thought Willa. Did she belong here, with Tommy? But, then, would Tommy ever belong anywhere?

'Will you be taking Daffy with you?' asked Pauline.

'Probably not. There could be a problem with quarantine. Would you fancy having him, Willa? They say dogs are good for children.'

'I'm sorry but we've no room.'

'I asked Gerry but he says his wife can't stick animals.'

'She can't stick much,' said Pauline.

'Oh well, I expect I'll find a good home for you somewhere, won't I, Daffy pet? Your mammy won't leave you in the street. One of Bunty's customers'll come up trumps.'

'Will we see you before you go?' asked Willa.

'You certainly will! I'm not going quietly. We'll have a good old knees-up.'

Willa left Pauline at the Infirmary gates and wished her luck.

Richard was at his old table in the library, writing in his exercise book. He closed it as she approached.

'How's it going?' she asked.

He made a face. 'So-so. I haven't been working at it consistently enough. Too many other distractions.'

They smiled at each other.

'Shall we go and have a cup of tea?' he said. 'I'll just pop down to the gents first.'

When he'd gone Willa took a peep inside the exercise book, something she had been longing to do for a while. He had said he would let her read it sometime. She opened it at a page and froze.

Trinconmali, Ceylon

Dear Margaret,

We arrived here in a very heavy rainstorm. You never see the likes of it in Edinburgh! It just buckets down for hours without stopping.

Her eye travelled on to the signature at the end. *Love, Danny.* She had never read out the ends of the letters to Richard so there was nothing about giving mother his love.

She did not notice him returning.

'You shouldn't have read that,' he said quietly, taking the book from her.

'You've been writing a novel about a sailor called Danny and his wife Margaret! You've filched it all from Tommy's letters and what I've told you!'

'Writers often do take things from life, you know that yourself.'

'But this is stealing, from *me*, in cold blood!'

'It's not, Willa, believe me.'

'You've betrayed me.' She was up on her feet now. They stood face to face. 'You've used me!'

'I haven't, I swear I haven't! Please let me talk to you about it.'

'Would you two go and continue your conversation elsewhere, please,' said the nasty librarian, coming across to them. 'You can be heard all over the library.'

Willa ran from the room, leaving the door swinging behind her. Richard stayed long enough to gather up his possessions and then he went after her. By the time he got outside she was half way along George IV Bridge. He didn't catch up with her until the top of Middle Meadow Walk. He caught hold of her and held her fast.

'I love you, don't you understand that? I do. For God's sake, listen to me!' He was shouting. A couple of women had stopped to stare at them.

Willa collapsed. 'Why then? Why then did you do it?'

'I started because I was interested in what you were telling me. It was such a different world to mine, yet here we were, Tommy and I, both born and raised in Edinburgh. And then, after a while, I carried on because I wanted to try to understand what was happening to me. To us, Willa. But I didn't intend to publish it and I won't, I promise you. Trust me, *please!* For I do love you. How many times do I have to tell you?'

She shook her head, bewildered.

'Let's go for a walk,' he said. 'Let's go up Arthur's Seat. It's far away from everybody.'

They stopped halfway up the hill and sat in a sheltered hollow out of the wind.

'Willa, I am prepared to give up university and take you away somewhere. We could still go to London. I've been thinking it out. I've a bit of money in the post office and I'd get a job. I'm certain I could, in some kind of office.'

'But your degree?'

'It's not the be-all and end-all of everything. Anyway, I want to be a novelist and you don't need one for that. But it would take time of course to earn a proper living.' He seized her shoulders. 'Look at me! Don't look away! I mean it.'

She looked at him and she believed him. He was one of the most truthful people she had ever known. She caught her breath. Could it be, *was* it, might it be *possible*? 'But Malcolm?'

'He can come, too. I know you'd never leave him and I wouldn't want you to.'

'I wish, Richard, you don't know how much I wish it!'

'For goodness sake then let your wish come true!'

'But I'm worried that Tommy might get custody of Malcolm. I'd be the guilty party if I left him.'

'He wouldn't get custody. He's away most of the time. How could he look after a child?'

'His mother could. Courts don't like women who walk out on their husbands. They seem to think it's the woman's duty to sacrifice everything for the sake of the family, never mind the price! And maybe it is,' she added.

'You can't believe that!'

'I don't know!'

'Now listen, they would not give custody to his mother. Why should they? She's too old and they couldn't make you out to be a bad mother.'

'Sometimes I wonder.'

'Because you leave him with his grandmother from time to time?'

'But I've committed adultery!'

'And what about Tommy?'

'Oh that doesn't count, does it? He's just having a wee fling while he's away from home doing his duty to king and country. That's understandable. And you know what sailors are! It's different for me. I would be considered to have "ruined my reputation".'

'Are you worried about that? What people would say?'

'I wouldn't if I were going away with you, far away from here.'

'That's what I'm asking you to do.'

'And I'm tempted, yes, I am! But Richard, you might come to resent it in time—'

'Never!'

'You might because you'd given up your chance of finishing your education.'

'I wouldn't. Not if I had you.'

'You sound so sure.' He is so wholehearted, she thought. She could not be; she was torn too many ways.

'That's because I am. Willa, you love me, don't you?'

'You know I do!'

'Well then!'

~ 26 ~

Rio de Janeiro
A view of Rio with Sugar Loaf Mountain in the
background. Thought you'd be interested to see it.
Tommy xxx

She was not. Not remotely. She gave the picture postcard a
scant look before laying it on the kitchen table beside her note
for his mother. Ina had gone to have her hair permed in
anticipation of her son's homecoming. She would be away for
at least a couple of hours, more likely three. They were slow
in that hairdresser's. Women went for an afternoon outing.

Malcolm was playing on the bedroom floor with his bricks.
He looked up as she came in and grinned and she dropped a
kiss on his head before going to the wardrobe. She took out
her best clothes and shoes, wanting to leave most of the space
in the bag for Malcolm's. She worked quickly and within
minutes she had packed. She could take only what she could
carry in one hand; she had to keep the other arm free for
Malcolm.

When the bag was closed and ready to be lifted, she put on
her own coat and then his.

'We're going on a journey, love, on a train,' she told him, as
she hoisted him up onto her hip, 'so you've got to be a very
good boy.'

He chortled and reached up to bat her face with the palm
of his hand.

She felt calm this morning after a turbulent night during which neither she nor Pauline had slept. Pauline had cried and said she would miss Willa and Willa had cried for a number of reasons. *Do you think you're doing the right thing?* Pauline had kept asking. *I don't know what the right thing is,* Willa had said in return. *I simply know that I am doing what my heart tells me to do. I will never love anyone again the way I love Richard.*

She took a quick look round the room, lifted the bag and walked out of the flat, pulling the door shut behind her. There, she'd done it!

Outside, on the landing, she paused. It was very still and quiet in the stairwell. Almost eerily so. Not even a cat seemed to be moving. Malcolm sat immobile on her hip, his eyes large and bright. She descended the stairs carefully and at the bottom took a cautious look into the street before venturing out. Seeing no one she recognised she crossed the road to the tram stop on the other side to wait for a tram going to Princes Street.

A dray rattled by, its barrels rolling a little. The driver was yawning. The horse looked tired, too, about ready for the knacker's yard. A sweep passed carrying his spiky black brushes over his shoulder, whistling softly. Mrs Begg came out of the wool shop opposite. Willa shrank back but she hadn't noticed them. Now she was going into the stair door. Willa leant out to get a better view of the street. She didn't normally have to wait so long for a tram. But this wasn't a normal day. What if there'd been an accident? A hold-up? What if Ina were to come out of the hairdresser's early and see them?

What a relief when she saw a tram loom into sight and come swinging down the hill towards them, its bell clanging.

She clambered aboard with Malcolm laughing and wriggling so that he could see what was going on around him. He'd come back to life. He loved riding on trams and crowed whenever the bell clanged. She sat at the window and he stood up on her knee to look out, putting his hands flat against the window pane. With a lurch, they were off.

As the tram took the bend into Lothian Road, swaying on its tracks, Willa began to feel sick. She swallowed, opened the top button of her blouse. The tram was packed. A woman in front of her began to cough, a worrying, racking sound. A man, who had come down from the top deck, was smoking a foul pipe. Outside in the street, women were going in and out of shops, unaware of Willa in the hot, crowded tram, struggling to control her nausea.

What was she doing? Could she go through with it? Take Malcolm away not only from his father but his grandmother and his aunts? His family. They formed a circle around him, a protective one. They loved him, even Elma, who would never say so in words. Bunty, she knew, would be sympathetic and not blame her. She would miss Bunty. She'd wanted to talk to her before leaving but had thought it might be too big a secret to ask Tommy's aunt to keep.

But she loved Richard, more than she'd ever loved Tommy, and she wanted to live with him: that was what she would have told Bunty. *That was all!* It sounded simple, but of course was not; there were too many people involved whose lives would be touched. In the end, though, did she not have a right to some happiness herself? Was it so very selfish to want that? Her thoughts ran on and turned back and reran.

The tram braked at traffic lights and the man with the pipe

took the chance to jump off, leaving a whiff of acrid smoke
behind him. The red light ahead of them, caught in a blaze of
sunshine, glistened like a sucked fruit lozenge. Willa, her eyes
transfixed by it, felt hypnotised. They seemed to sit there for
ever. Was the light never going to change? The woman in the
seat in front was still coughing. Malcolm, annoyed by the lack
of movement, began to bang on the window. A woman across
the aisle glared at him but Willa did not notice. She wiped the
sweat from her brow with the back of her hand.

And then the light changed from amber to green and they
were off again but only briefly for soon the bell was clanging
and the tram pulling into a stop.

A woman with a large shopping bag got on and sat down
beside Willa. 'I'm not squashing you, dear, am I?'

'No, no, I'm fine.' Willa moved over.

The woman eyed Malcolm. 'That's a great wee lad you've
got there. What bonny eyes you have, son! I see you there!'
She wriggled her fingers at him. 'He doesn't look like you at
all. He must take after his dad?'

Willa nodded.

'His dad must think the world of him.'

The tram, completing its run down Lothian Road, turned
into the west end of Princes Street. The woman got off,
waving goodbye to Malcolm, who returned the gesture by
flapping his wrist up and down.

Willa caught hold of his hand and kissed the palm, making
him giggle.

'We'll be all right, wee one, don't you worry. We'll be
together. And Richard will look after us. You'll love Richard.'

He would be waiting for them in Waverley Station; she did

not doubt that. She would never doubt Richard's word. He, too, would have left a note on the kitchen table. He'd said that he would have told his mother straight out but he feared she might come to the station and make a scene and upset Willa. Willa believed that she would, given the opportunity. Arabella Fitzwilliam would not let go of her son lightly. She would denounce Willa, tell her that she was ruining his life, denying him the right to finish his education, burdening him with a woman and a child to keep when he had not the means to do so. She would not help them: Willa foresaw that. She would hope that struggling to survive in a dismal flat in London might bring them to their senses. They'd be poor. The little bit of money Richard had would soon run out.

Willa had a vision of their life: the flat like those she'd seen for letting in Edinburgh, skimpy, evil-smelling, in a mean back street; Richard gone all day, labouring as a clerk, doing mindless work for a miserable salary, returning red-eyed and tired, to find a grumpy baby cutting teeth; herself frustrated from struggling to fill long empty hours, knowing that no one would ring the doorbell and come into the kitchen ready for a cup of tea and a chat and liven up the place with a burst of laughter. They would be isolated, the three of them. Short of money, doing their best to stay alive, with the odds stacked against them, pulled people down. She'd seen it at first hand. Richard had not. And then there would be Tommy. He wouldn't take it sitting down. He'd come after them. She'd be afraid to go out. He might get extra leave, for compassionate reasons. *Poor Tommy, imagine, him away at sea serving king and country and his wife does a runner taking his kid! She must be a bad lot.*

'Next stop Waverley!' called the conductor.

The tram came to a stop.

Willa got up, putting Malcolm back on her hip. She stepped down onto the island and the conductor passed the bag over to her, telling her to mind how she went.

While they were waiting for the road to clear Malcolm saw something on the ground that interested him and lurched suddenly to the side to try to reach for it, causing her to wrench her shoulder. She gasped with the sudden pain and dropped the bag. He was no lightweight. A handful, Elma called him. Willa could not argue with that. If only she could carry him in the palm of her hand!

She lifted the bag and dodging a bicycle crossed the road to the top of the Waverley steps. A snell wind came swirling up around her ankles. It was a windy place this, where the warm air from the station rose to meet the cold of the street. She shivered. She stood staring into space, undisturbed by Malcolm, who himself had become still.

She just could not do it.

It would be too difficult.

For everyone.

She put her back to the steps. A tram for Morningside Station was waiting at the stop. With her child bobbing on her hip and their bag of clothes clutched in her other hand, Willa ran for it, and managed to scramble aboard. Malcolm giggled with delight.

'You just made it,' said the conductor cheerfully before reaching up to pull the cord.

~ 27 ~

St Vincent, Cape Verde Islands,
West Africa
18th September, 1924

Dear Willa
 Our last port of call before England!

'Can that be right?' asked Pauline. 'The *last* port?'

'It must be,' said Willa, though to her, too, it seemed unreal.

Everything did since that terrible ride in the tram car back to Tollcross. Malcolm had stood up on her knee the whole time, laughing at a man in the seat behind who was making funny faces at him and she had wept, unnoticed. Fortunately they had got home before Ina and Willa had been able to screw up her note and put it in the fire.

'What are you going to do?' asked Pauline.

'Do?' repeated Willa.

They were in the bedroom. Malcolm was in the kitchen with his grandmother and aunts Bunty and Elma.

'Tommy's going to be home soon, isn't he? And then he'll be away again. I know Ina's not a bad old soul, taken in small doses, but you'll go nuts if you have to sit in the kitchen with her day in, day out, for the rest of your life. Well, *her* life, at any rate.'

'I don't intend to sit in the kitchen day in, day out. I went in to see Mrs Andrews in the wool shop yesterday. The job was still open. Day and a half a week. Better than nothing. She says I can have it.'

'But I thought you didn't want to leave Malcolm with Ina?'

'Oh, that doesn't bother me any longer. He's not going to stop loving me because he spends the day with her. He'll probably be glad to see me at the end of it!'

They laughed.

'The money will be useful. I'm going to put it by, for later.'

'For what?'

'Who knows? I'll see when the time comes. Meanwhile, I've signed on for evening classes. I'm going to do my matric.'

'And Richard?'

'He'll go back to university, I expect.'

Willa wondered if one day he might publish his book, about her, about them, not in the near future, but at a later date when time had passed. She had a strange sensation that she might go into the library, recognise his name on a spine, take down the book and see her words, and Tommy's words. Perhaps, by then, the pain would have dulled enough to allow her to read them.

The door opened, turning their heads.

'Was that the post?' Ina's eyes went to the letter in Willa's hand.

'I was just coming through,' said Willa.

They followed Ina into the kitchen.

'Where's the brave lad now?' asked Bunty.

'St Vincent, in the Cape Verde Islands. Off the coast of West Africa.'

They settled themselves for the reading.

St Vincent belongs to Portugal and I am glad that it does and not to Britain as it is a God-forsaken place, mountainous, desolate and uncultivated. Although it belongs to Portugal the natives speak English fluently. The Portuguese are welcome to it!

'That's blasphemy,' said Elma. 'No place on earth is God-forsaken. Tommy should know better. He went to Sunday school.'

'That was a while ago,' said Bunty. 'And he was never that keen, if I remember rightly. Ina used to have to bribe him.'

'I did not!' Ina was indignant.

'You used to say you'd get him an ice cream or a lolly if he behaved himself and sat quiet. Only time he went willingly was to the summer outing at the seaside.'

'You get up my wick at times, Bunty, so you do,' said Ina.

'I always liked the outings best myself,' said Pauline. 'Who wouldn't, compared to singing hymns?'

'Lots of children *enjoy* singing hymns, Pauline, *and* reading Bible stories,' said Elma.

Sharks are plentiful. One was hovering near two men in a boat who hit it with one of their paddles hoping to flatten it, but to no effect. They then became even more excited but, luckily for them, the shark lost interest and swam quietly away. The Delhi put out a line with meat hooked onto the end and, next morning, they pulled in a ten footer.

'They wouldn't eat it, would they?' asked Pauline.

No one knew. Elma certainly hoped not.

'It doesn't sound as if there'll be any picnics on the beach in the Cape Verde Islands,' said Willa.

'Or dancing either,' said Pauline.

'He's done enough of that to last a lifetime,' sniffed Elma.

Pauline made a face at Willa behind Elma's back.

She was in good spirits. She was to start work as a stenographer at the Infirmary the next day. Also, she had met a really nice, attractive, well-heeled, well-mannered, unmarried, genuine man at the Palace Ballroom last Saturday night and he'd already taken her to the cinema and the cocktail bar in the Caley Hotel and paid for everything. She was going out later to look for a room to rent.

'Read on, Willa,' urged Ina.

> *Rear-Admiral Brand came on board last night to say goodbye. He was too upset to say very much as he was sorry to be leaving the squadron so he wrote a letter thanking us all for our loyalty and support of his endeavours during the Imperial Cruise.*

'That was real nice of him,' said Elma. 'Obviously a well-mannered man.'

'Probably God-fearing too,' said Bunty.

'You can tell when someone's top drawer,' said Ina.

'This is what he wrote,' said Willa.

> *'On bidding farewell to you I take this opportunity of thanking all captains, officers and men for their*

loyalty and devotion to duty, which has made the squadron an honour and a pleasure to command which I leave with very real regret. To have steamed some 45,000 miles in 10 months with no serious defects is a matter for congratulation. The general bearing and the conduct of the men ashore has, throughout, been only what I expected of them, that is, in accordance with the highest traditions of the Service and by this exemplary conduct have upheld the finest traditions of the British Navy.'

Rear-Admiral Brand was lustily cheered on leaving the ship.

'Makes you feel proud,' said Ina, wiping a spot of moisture from her eye with the edge of her pinny.

'Maybe Tommy did the right thing after all by joining the Navy,' said Elma.

'I'm surprised they all behaved so well on shore,' said Pauline. 'See when some ships come in to Leith, half the sailors are the worse for drink. They're vomiting all over the place. The stink in the gutters is something terrible.'

'But those sailors who come in to Leith are not *special*,' said Ina. 'They're a different kettle of fish to Tommy's Special Service Squadron. They're probably foreign too.'

Rear-Admiral Brand is a true gentleman and we know that he meant every word he said. There are people of high rank in all stations of life who make speeches and do not mean them but when an admiral addresses a ship's company on the quarter

*deck of a man-of-war and feels the position so
keenly that he is lost for words then it speaks for
itself.*

'Well, I'm glad they were appreciated,' said Ina. 'What do you
say, Malkie? Hasn't your daddy done well?'

He was trying to climb up onto the dresser, which was
cluttered with all manner of things to interest him, such as a
basketful of his granny's curlers, a toby jug full of hat pins and
a china boot saying PRESENT FROM BLACKPOOL,
brought back by Bunty after her weekend there with Mr
Parkin. Bunty lifted him down and gave him one of the
custard slices she'd brought in from the baker's. His mother,
who didn't approve of him being given sweet cakes, was too
busy with the letter to notice. Her eyes were fixated on the
next sentence.

*Once we get to Chatham we will be coming home,
for a month's leave! Yippee!*

Willa's mind was racing. A whole month, she was thinking,
with this man called Tommy, the father of her child. He had
faded away into a sepia-tinted picture in her mind. But he
could well be in Chatham at this very moment, for all they
knew, or even in London, at King's Cross, getting ready to
board the Flying Scotsman. There was always a long gap
between the letters being posted and arriving.

'You'll need to get out the fatted calf,' said Bunty. 'Maybe
Gerry could come up with one?'

'I'm not sure that he sells fatted calves,' said Elma. 'He's not feeling too well at the moment, did I mention that? He's been a bit down in the dumps though he says there's nothing wrong with the business. That's something anyway.'

They all knew why, of course, but nobody was going to say. They'd had a farewell party at Maureen's two nights ago, just Bunty, Willa, Pauline and Gerry. Daffy the peke had gone to his new owner, an obliging customer of Bunty's. The evening had not been as lively as the usual 'dos' in her house and Gerry had looked as if he might start greeting at any moment. Willa had not felt too cheerful herself.

'Well, herrin' in oatmeal isne going to be good enough for our Tommy when he comes home,' said Bunty. 'He'll have got used to fancy fare. Chinese banquets and that. You'll need to give him a hero's welcome, Ina.'

'He's not been at war,' said Willa. 'I don't know that he'd be called a hero.'

'Not seeing he's spent so much time dancing,' agreed Pauline.

'Some of those seas they'd to cope with were rough, mind,' said Ina tartly. 'It wasn't all a picnic.'

'But the beaches were blessed with sunshine and the dancehalls fair glittered with lights!' said Bunty. 'And the girls—'

She paused, as did they all. They cocked their ears to listen. Somebody had put a key in the lock and was opening the front door. Now there were footsteps coming along the hall. Quiet, almost stealthy footsteps. They all stood up and Malcolm, sensing an important moment, removed the half-eaten custard slice from his mouth.

The kitchen door was flung open and there stood Tommy,

the sailor home from the sea, his cap on the back of his head, his kitbag slung over his shoulder, radiating energy, a wide smile on his bronzed, handsome face. Immediately the room came into life, as if a Hallowe'en sparkler had been tossed into its midst.

'Tommy!' they cried.

He dropped the kitbag and throwing his cap across the room, said, 'Yes, it's me! I'm home, folks.'

His mother gulped and put a hand over her heart.

And then he came towards Willa, with eyes only for her, bypassing his mother, his son, and his aunts, saying, 'How're you doin', darlin'? How's my great big beautiful doll?' and she went towards him, hands outstretched to meet his, remembering why she had come to marry him.